"I want you," Walk... ...Amy. More than I've ever wanted anything or anyone. So if your answer is 'go to hell,' say it now."

Amy's expression changed again. Became even softer somehow. And she reached out to cup his cheek.

"But you're already in hell," she said quietly, almost sadly.

What was this? She felt sorry for him? That was the last, the very last, thing he wanted from her. Especially now.

"Pity, Amy?"

"No. A hundred times no." She drew in a deep breath, then looked up at him steadily. "Just need. Want. And impatience."

She slid her hand down along his arm, took his hand. Her fingers, warm, slender and strong, curled around his. She turned, clearly headed for the bedroom. Fool that he was, he resisted.

"Be sure, Amy. Because I can't promise to be polite, or even gentle."

"I don't want polite, or need gentle. I want you," she said. "I've always, always wanted you, Walker Cole. Even when I thought I hated you."

* * *

Be sure to check out the rest of the books in this miniseries—Cutter's Code: A clever and mysterious canine helps a group of secret operatives crack the case.

* * *

Dear Reader,

If you've been reading the Cutter's Code series, and have perhaps also read these letters in previous books, you'll know I've mentioned my fascination with brothers, the brother bond and how it's different from others. In *Operation Reunion* I explored a brother/sister relationship, in *Operation Unleashed* it was brother/brother. So I thought I was done with that, at least for a while. Now it was a best friend that had me fascinated, an awkward, rather nerdy child who had bloomed into an amazing woman I was really starting to like. But I had to come up with a hero who deserved her. And then one day a reader wrote me a note saying in essence, "Hey, you forgot a brother!"

And indeed I had. Walker Cole had been mentioned in passing a couple of times as Hayley's "walkabout" brother, but I hadn't really delved into where he'd been or why. Because I had no idea. Well, now I do, and wow, what a time he's been through! He had to work very hard for his happy ending—and his heroine—but he's learned the hard way how to be tough enough.

It was a long journey for both characters in this story. Nearly a lifetime, in fact. I hope you enjoy their story.

Happy reading!

Justine

OPERATION
HOMECOMING

———

Justine Davis

HARLEQUIN® ROMANTIC SUSPENSE

Recycling programs
for this product may
not exist in your area.

ISBN-13: 978-0-373-27931-9

Operation Homecoming

Printed in U.S.A.

Justine Davis lives on Puget Sound in Washington State, watching big ships and the occasional submarine go by and sharing the neighborhood with assorted wildlife, including a pair of bald eagles, deer, a bear or two and a tailless raccoon. In the few hours when she's not planning, plotting or writing her next book, her favorite things are photography, knitting her way through a huge yarn stash and driving her restored 1967 Corvette roadster—top down, of course.

Connect with Justine at her website, justinedavis.com, at twitter.com/justine_d_davis, or on Facebook at facebook.com/justinedaredavis.

Books by Justine Davis

Harlequin Romantic Suspense

Cutter's Code

Operation Midnight
Operation Reunion
Operation Blind Date
Operation Unleashed
Operation Power Play
Operation Homecoming

Redstone, Incorporated

Just Another Day in Paradise
One of These Nights
In His Sights
Second-Chance Hero
Dark Reunion
Deadly Temptation
Her Best Friend's Husband
The Best Revenge
Redstone Ever After

Visit the Author Profile page at Harlequin.com,
or justinedavis.com, for more titles.

Lucky
August 2000–October 2011

Lucky was the first dog my kids picked out, a pound puppy who became our 90lb baby and wanted to be a lap dog. A gentle giant, a white and black lab mix who looked like a huge Dalmatian, but who hid behind the chair whenever he saw a camera. He liked to be combed, and he guarded and took care of our rabbits. The rabbits got out of the hutch somehow and we found him and the rabbits lying next to each other under the shade tree. He loved our two Poms and played happily with Fang (my son's cat). He was brave, but his feet wouldn't stay still unless he really thought you needed protection, then he would stand between you and it. What we thought was an infection and old age turned out to be cancer. There was nothing to do that wouldn't make him miserable, and we had to say goodbye. It was a shock, and we still miss him. Our Poms still won't eat out of his bowl. He will always have a special place in my heart. He was a good dog.

LuDena Radford

This is the latest in a series of dedications from readers who have shared the pain of the loss of a beloved dog. For more details, check Justine's blog at justinedavis.com.

Chapter 1

Amy Clark slipped her glasses back on as she reached the baggage claim carousel. It was cool and rainy here in Seattle in mid-April, but LA had been having an early heat wave so she welcomed the change. She welcomed even more being away from everything else she'd left behind. Already the burden of her problem felt lighter.

Even after years away, this misty green place still felt like home.

It felt safe.

With your luck, you'll end up back here soon, running home because the big, bad city was too ugly, too nasty for you.

She wasn't ready to admit that it was both those things yet. She'd worked hard and loved her job as a paralegal. She wasn't ready to give up on the dream. Even if it seemed on the edge of turning into a nightmare.

Which reminded her, she was going to have to get her car fixed when she got home. How stupid to have scraped it up like that trying to escape that van that hadn't really been following her anyway. It just happened to be going the same direction, hundreds of people headed for the airport and the surrounding area every day. She was just on edge, her imagination in overdrive. She—

"Hey, stranger!"

She whirled, a huge grin spreading across her face as she saw her best friend. Hayley Cole—Foxworth, she corrected, still not quite used to the change—looked as she always did, vibrant, her green eyes sparkling. Their hug was worthy of two people who had been friends since the second grade.

The baggage carousel came alive, began to move. Hayley looked at it warily.

"I'm getting better," Amy said with a laugh. "A whole three-day weekend with only one bag and a carry-on."

"And a purse the size of Alaska," Hayley retorted.

"Well, yes. Because you never know."

"It's not really leaving home if you bring most of home with you," Hayley said, right on cue. They both laughed at the old, familiar exchange.

Amy spotted her suitcase and grabbed it as it circled past. It was heavy, but not impossible, and they were soon headed to the parking structure. She was glad she'd put on her jacket, but still welcomed the chill in the air.

"Hot in LA, huh?" Hayley asked.

"In more ways than one," Amy said, a bit of the grimness she'd pushed aside creeping back into her voice. But she didn't want to go into it now, so she diverted. "Are the daffs up?"

"All over," Hayley answered. "Mr. Elkhart planted some new ones last fall, some interesting colors."

"I'm a traditionalist—I love the yellow ones." A bouquet of daffodils was one of the most cheerful sights she could imagine.

"I know, you always did. We can…"

Hayley broke off, laughing. They'd reached her car, and a second later Amy was laughing, too. For sitting in the driver's seat, looking at them with a pleased expression, was Hayley's dog, Cutter.

"I left him in the back," Hayley said.

"Is he going to drive?" she asked with a grin.

"Wouldn't surprise me. At all."

Amy laughed at Hayley's serious tone as her friend hit

the unlock button and the compact SUV chirped oblig-
ingly. She opened the driver's door. Cutter jumped out at
their feet. He was as beautiful as Amy remembered with
his black head and shoulders and russet-brown body. He
greeted Hayley with a swipe of pink tongue. To Amy's
surprise, she herself got a more effusive greeting, a plumy
tail-wagging, nudging sort of dance that made her smile.
She set down her voluminous purse to greet him properly.

"Well, hello again, Cutter."

He gave a short yip, and she bent to pet him. The moment she stroked his dark head she felt an odd sensation
of relief, as if suddenly she knew it would all work out, it
would all be all right. All the fears seemed to not vanish
but at least recede.

In that instant, the welcoming dance stopped. The dog
leaned into her, staring up into her face. Something in the
intense gaze, or in those gold-flecked dark eyes, was mes-
merizing, and she couldn't seem to look away.

And then he moved. He turned, sat down at Amy's feet
and looked up at Hayley. And Hayley, oddly, stopped mid-
motion as she was putting her own purse in the car. Her
eyes flicked from the dog to Amy.

"Uh-oh," Hayley said.

"What?"

"Are you all right?"

Amy hadn't expected that. At least, not so soon. "Fine,"
she said. And health-wise, it was true. Otherwise, not so
much. But she needed to work up to discussing that. "I
may need your help loading this up, though," she said,
gesturing at the large blue suitcase.

"Hmm." Hayley sounded doubtful, but she seemed to
accept the answer. She looked back at the dog. "I got it,
boy. I promise."

Cutter gave a low, soft whuff and a movement of his
head that looked startlingly like a nod. Amy had no idea

what was going on. She'd never had a dog, so she was a neophyte.

Within a few minutes they were out of the airport and onto the freeway. Amy knew it would be only natural for Hayley to ask how things were going at work and she wasn't ready for that, so she turned it around.

"How are things at the Foxworth Foundation?"

"Quiet," Hayley said. Then she glanced toward the back of the SUV where Cutter was now settled in quietly. "At least, they have been. It's been nice to have a break."

"Especially since your last case was so huge. Talk about taking on the big guys!" Amy knew the Foxworth Foundation had only one goal, to help those in the right who couldn't fight alone any longer. The size of the case didn't matter, but sometimes it got both large and complicated.

Hayley laughed. "Hey, we weren't even here. That was Cutter and Brett Dunbar, with a little help from Rafe. And things are already getting fixed."

Amy studied her friend for a moment. Hayley had been through some rough times—the death of her father when she was twelve, more recently the long, slow battle with her mother's terminal cancer. And of course there was Walker, that black-sheep miscreant. Hayley was far too generous when it came to her thoughtless, selfish, cold-hearted brother. All she ever said about the guy who had walked out after their family tragedy, who had later left her alone to deal with their mother, was that everyone had to handle grief in their own way.

She supposed she might be inclined to a little more generosity herself if she hadn't had such a crush on him when she was a kid, Amy thought. She'd adored Walker Cole, and although she was just his little sister's friend, he'd always been kind. And then he'd shattered all her illusions. She tried not to remember her foolishness.

"You're sure Quinn won't mind me being here? I mean, you have only been married three months."

Hayley laughed. "He's glad you could come. He even said it was too bad you couldn't stay for the month."

"I couldn't, anyway. I have our big office anniversary party in a couple of weeks," she said, "but remind me to thank him for that."

"He knows what you mean to me," Hayley said quietly. "He knows you were there for me every time life kicked me in the teeth. You never let me down."

Unlike your idiot brother, who left you alone to deal.

She stopped herself before she could go down that path. Thinking of Walker Cole was not going to help matters. Because then she would start thinking about how nice he'd once been to her, how he tolerated her silly crush, which would make her think of how just spotting him had sent her heart racing, how she'd learned everything she could about baseball because he played it. Then she'd graduate to his crooked grin, thick, unruly hair and those amazing hazel eyes that were a golden green rimmed with a darker shade, so different from his sister's meadow green. She knew it was a trick of melanin and light scattering, had even looked it up once, but that didn't detract from the beauty of them.

And here she was, thinking about him.

She shook off the odd mood, determined to enjoy this visit as much as she could, despite the reason for it. And despite her fear that her life was going to blow up.

"What are you frowning about?"

"Was I?"

"Yes. Let me guess, you're still mad at Walker?" That was the problem with best friends; they saw things others might miss.

"After what he did? Of course I am. On top of everything else, missing your wedding without even a word except that stupid text message?"

For the first time a hint of disappointment showed on

Hayley's face. "Yes. He did. And I'm not sure Quinn will forgive him for that very soon."

"I think I'd like to see the day they finally meet, if they ever do," Amy said, thinking with a rather grim satisfaction of the powerful—and intimidating—Quinn Foxworth taking Walker Cole apart piece by piece.

"You wouldn't hate him so much if you hadn't loved him first," Hayley said.

"Schoolgirl infatuation," Amy said, even as she realized ruefully how close her friend's words were to her own earlier thought. "Believe me, I'm angry enough on your behalf alone."

This was true, but she also knew that she had loved him, with all the strength of her teenage heart. She'd loved his laugh, she'd loved the way he teasingly winked at her and she would never, ever forget the time he had come to her defense when she'd been cornered by a trio of nerd-baiting mean-girl types. He'd already been tall at seventeen, and a star athlete, and that he had bothered to step in and chase off the three—who happened to idolize him, the star pitcher on the high school baseball team—had thrilled her down to her thirteen-year-old soul. It had also insulated her somewhat from further attack. Word had gotten out that she was under the protection of Walker Cole, and while she was sure the nasty comments and thoughts continued, she was never backed into a corner again.

And then it had all fallen apart. His father died and a year later he was gone, the college scholarship abandoned along with his mother and his little sister. The mother and little sister Amy had always thought he loved.

Just goes to prove you're a lousy judge of men. If you ever needed more proof.

She shook her head sharply. This was not the time to dwell on her miserable dating track record. Not when she'd made a much more serious misjudgment than just dating the wrong men.

And this one could at the least upend, at the worst ruin her life forever.

At least, she hoped that was the worst.

Chapter 2

"You want to tell me what's really wrong?" Hayley finally asked when they were parked in line for the big ferry that would take them across the sound. "Because Cutter says something is."

Amy blinked. "What?"

"He knows you have a problem. And," Hayley added in a dry tone, "he expects action."

"What are you talking about?"

"That look he gave me, after you petted him. That's his 'fix it' look."

Amy remembered the moment when the dog had sat at her feet and looked at Hayley. Was it possible the dog had sensed her turmoil? From what her friend had told her, the dog was incredibly empathetic.

Amy drew in a deep breath, savoring the salt-tanged air, looking out over the water toward the towering, snow-capped Olympic Mountains. She couldn't wait to get into the thick trees where the fresh scent of evergreens would add its own note to the smell of home.

"I did want to talk to you about something. I need some help working something out, and you're the only one I trust."

Hayley smiled. "We always do work it out, eventually."

"Yes. Not," she added hastily, "that that's the only reason I came."

"I'm glad to see you whatever the reason," Hayley said. "So what's the problem?"

"I… It's complicated."

"I assumed so or we could have talked it out on the phone."

"No, no, I couldn't talk about it on the phone."

Something about Hayley's demeanor changed then, and the next sideways glance she gave her was different, more intent, more alert.

"Amy, are you in trouble? Did something happen?"

"No and yes. Or yes and yes, maybe. I didn't do anything wrong," she hastened to assure her friend.

"I never thought you had. Or would. Is it a personal thing? Some guy?"

Amy laughed sourly at that. "Please. My love life is as dry as LA these days. Only available men I meet are lawyers, and I've found I don't care for most of them much. Not that it matters—I'm not their type, either."

"Not shallow and flashy enough?" Hayley suggested.

For the first time since she'd started this journey, Amy laughed with genuine pleasure. "And that is why I run to you, my friend. I would have said too quiet and serious. LA legal affairs is a high-powered world."

"Their loss," Hayley said dismissively. "So, what kind of help do you need? More than just talking it out?"

"I…don't know. That's what I'm trying to figure out."

"One question, then."

"What?"

"Should we head for the house, or should I have Quinn meet us at Foxworth?"

Amy hadn't expected that to come up so soon. Hayley seemed ready to spring into some sort of action, just like that. Maybe working with Foxworth had brought that on.

"House," she said. "It's not…immediate."

She put it out of her mind for the pleasant duration of the ferry ride. They took a walk around the upper deck, outside, so Amy could take it all in again. She looked back as they crossed, seeing the dock and the buildings shrink as the ones they were heading for slowly grew and she began to be able to pick out familiar buildings amid the tall, thick trees. She looked toward the cliffs of the south end of Whidby Island to the north, always a favorite spot of hers since the day she'd seen a pod of orcas passing through the strait.

To complete her ritual, she hit the snack bar for a cup of her beloved clam chowder. Her glasses fogged up as she held the steaming cup under her nose, and they both laughed.

"I like those," Hayley said, indicating the red frames.

"So do I," Amy said. The various pairs of glasses she had were her one indulgence; since she had to wear them, she wanted options. What had been a painful necessity as a child had become almost a signature style for her now. She even thought she looked odd without them.

The ferry docked, and Amy felt the calm settle in. The pace was slower here in this more rural area, and she always felt the change. Once off the boat they chatted about other things until finally Hayley started down the familiar driveway. Amy looked around. Every day for years she had come down this driveway to meet Hayley for school, and for respite from the chaos of her own house on the weekends. Now, the empty space to the left, where another house had once stood before it exploded the night Hayley and Quinn met, made it feel almost off balance to her.

"It sounds so crazy," she said, "that that was a safe house where they were hiding a federal witness."

"Worth it," Hayley said. "Vicente was a rock at the trial, and some very bad people were put where they belong."

"And you found Quinn. Or rather, he found you."

Even as she said the name, she spotted the man himself coming out the front door. And there was no doubting the sincerity of his greeting as he grandly opened the car door and welcomed her. Tall, dark and intimidating, with that sardonic arch to his brows, Quinn Foxworth would have made her very nervous if he hadn't been smiling so widely.

At least, he was until Cutter replicated his action from the airport, turning to sit at Amy's feet and looking intently at Quinn.

"Oh?" he said with a glance at Hayley. She nodded. "Hmm."

It must be one of those husband/wife things, Amy thought, communicating without really saying anything. Or in this case, husband, wife and dog.

Quinn lifted her heavy case and carry-on as if they were grocery bags, and to Amy's relief made no comment on their weight. Hayley must have warned him.

It still got dark fairly early this time of year, so the light was already fading by the time they were settled in the comfortable living room before a fire Quinn had built, simply because she'd said she'd missed such things in LA. She liked this man, she thought, not for the first time.

"Now, what is it?" Quinn said.

Startled, Amy looked at Hayley.

"He's a get-straight-to-business kind of guy," she said with a smile.

"But how did he— Never mind. Let me guess. The dog told him."

"Actually," Quinn said, "he did."

That's his 'fix it' look...

Apparently Hayley had meant it.

"Really, I just need advice," she said. And she was suddenly having second thoughts, because once she told someone else of her suspicions, she was committed, and she wasn't sure she was ready for that.

"We're good at that," Hayley said.

Quinn studied her for a moment before saying quietly, "If you'd rather, I'll leave you two alone. But Cutter seems to think I might be of help."

She didn't know how seriously to take this. "So he not only tells you there's a problem, he tells you who should, as you put it, 'fix it'?"

Quinn's mouth quirked wryly. "Believe me, I know how it sounds. I was the hardest sell on his unique…talents."

"Hayley's told me all about his abilities," she said doubtfully, "but seeing it in person is quite different."

At her words the dog rose from where he'd plopped beside the fire. He walked over to her and rested his chin on her knee. He looked up at her intently. It was a natural thing, she thought, to pet a dog who did that. Yet it was odd how she felt as if she had no choice.

The moment her fingers touched the silky fur of his head, a strange sort of calm came over her. She stroked, gently. Again, then again.

"Crazy, isn't it?" Quinn asked. "How he makes you feel better?"

She looked up. Realized she truly did feel better. "It's… disconcerting."

"At the very least," Hayley agreed, grinning now.

"So is it personal or professional?" Quinn asked.

That straight-to-business thing again, Amy thought. "Professional," she admitted, although she still wasn't sure she should do this. But she'd come over a thousand miles, so it seemed silly to quibble now. And she was feeling better about it, she had to admit. Maybe it really was Cutter, she thought as the dog laid down at her feet, resting his chin now on the toe of her foot.

"I thought you loved your job," Hayley said.

"I do."

Quinn lifted a brow. "Problem with people, then?"

"Sort of. I mean, the support staff is great, and Kim, the receptionist, is a sweetheart, but the attorneys… Most of them are just driven types, always looking for ways to raise their profile. Becca Olson—I told you about her, Hayley, she's the one I have lunch with almost every week—is the only really friendly one. I think that's a 'we girls have to stick together' thing, since there are only a few of us. The guys are pretty cold fish, and I wouldn't be surprised at anything from them. But I always thought my boss..."

She broke off, still not quite ready to put her suspicions into words.

"You've always said you respected him, that he's tough but fair," Hayley said.

"I do. Did." She saw by their expressions that neither of them missed the switch. "But I think... I'm afraid he's involved in something."

"Something you don't like? Or something crooked?" Hayley asked.

"I'm not sure."

"I met Marcus Rockwell once," Quinn said, startling her. "He impressed me as a pretty straight arrow."

"You met my boss?"

"Through a friend, who has another law firm in LA."

"Oh? Maybe I've met him. They all run in the same circles."

"He's pretty high up in those circles himself. Alex Armistead."

Amy's eyes widened. "I'd say so. As in the very top. We like to think of ourselves as their main competition, but in truth his firm is a couple of rungs up at least. I've never met him, even though their office is across the street. Seen him now and then."

"He's a good man."

Amy had the feeling that was not an accolade Quinn Foxworth passed out lightly. "He..."

Cutter erupted to his feet with a trumpeting bark, cutting Quinn off. Amy jumped. Nearly shrieked. Even Hayley drew back in surprise.

Quinn, however, was instantly on his own feet. Amy could practically feel the change in him. Just looking at

him, he'd gone from her best friend's concerned husband
to the man she'd only heard about until now. The fighter,
the leader, the man in command. So much so that she
wasn't truly surprised when he spun to the cabinet behind
him, reached down and touched something that made a
part of the surface pop up. An instant later he had a black
pistol in his hand and was headed across the room after
the dog.

Amy gave Hayley a startled glance. "Some people
aren't happy when we're done with them," Hayley said,
on her own feet now.

Cutter was nearly to the front door when he stopped
dead and fell silent in the same instant. He gave a low
whine that sounded almost puzzled. And when he looked
back at Quinn, his expression was almost comical. The
dog looked utterly confused.

Quinn diverted to the window closest to the front door,
but kept to the edge, out of sight from outside.

"What is it, boy?" Hayley asked the dog. "A threat?"

That same puzzled-sounding whine. It might not be
words, but even Amy could interpret the canine "I don't
know."

Quinn reached out and slid the window open a frac-
tion of an inch. He leaned over, clearly listening. Then he
took a quick look.

"Somebody walking down the drive," he said. "Can't
tell who." He glanced at Cutter. "And apparently neither
can he."

"Odd, he's never reacted like this before."

Quinn leaned farther to look through the window again.
"Guy isn't trying to hide," he said. "And he's got a duffel
bag with him. Don't recognize him, though."

He looked a moment longer, glanced once more at the
puzzled Cutter, then straightened, setting the weapon
down on the table next to the door. That alone made Amy's
pulse slow a bit more. Whether he trusted the dog's in-

stincts or his own more she didn't know. But she did trust him. Something about this man she barely knew seemed to inspire that.

Quinn looked at Cutter, who was, Amy realized, staring at Hayley. With that same intensity she'd turned on herself. After a second or two the dog got up and walked to Hayley, then turned to face the door. Putting himself, Amy realized, between her friend and the door. Just as Quinn had put himself between them and the possible threat.

"Well, now," Hayley said softly as she touched the dog's head, "this is all new."

"He's protecting you, right?" Amy asked.

"He's not in protect mode. Believe me, you'd see the difference."

"He wants to be between you and whoever it is," Quinn said, "but doesn't think whoever it is is a threat? Dog, you are a challenge."

He went to the door, opened it in the instant before Amy heard a footstep on the wooden porch. Cutter leaned but didn't move, and Amy could see his nose flexing as he sniffed eagerly. Yet he didn't leave Hayley. She marveled at the workings of his canine mind even as she glanced back toward the door with building curiosity.

She heard a voice, low and unintelligible, except she thought she heard Quinn's name.

"You son of a bitch."

Quinn threw a punch so quickly Amy barely saw his arm move. She heard the thud of something hitting the boards of the porch. Someone.

Stunned, Amy froze. Cutter growled, but didn't move. At least, not until Hayley did. When she ran to Quinn's side, Cutter moved as if he were Velcroed to her side.

Amy rose, but hesitated. This might be some family thing; she should stay out of it. Obviously what threat there was Quinn had dealt with it.

But then Hayley gasped. "Walker?"
Amy's heart nearly stopped.
No wonder Quinn had clobbered him.

Chapter 3

Walker Cole rubbed at his jaw. At least it wasn't his nose, he thought, which had already been broken twice before, once in each direction. As a result it was still fairly straight, but you could feel the kinks where it had healed.

And that, he thought, was probably the stupidest thing he could be thinking about just now.

Gingerly, he got to his feet. He kept a wary eye on Quinn—he'd had no doubt from the instant the big man had opened the door who he was—but his attention was focused on the woman now beside him.

Hayley.

His baby sister.

The only family he had left.

The one person left in this life he loved unreservedly.

She was staring at him in shock. And why not? He hadn't been home in over five years now, since he'd stopped here before heading to Chicago, the Great Lakes. All had been well then, their mother healthy, Hayley happy in her job in Seattle, and he hadn't felt a qualm at moving on when the walls started to close in.

He hadn't realized he'd never see Mom again.

He hadn't planned on anything that had happened after that last visit.

"Hi, sis," he said finally, and it sounded lame even to his ears.

She shook her head as if she were at a loss for words.

And the dog. When had she gotten a dog? Or was it her new husband's? Whichever, he wasn't liking the way it was staring at him, as if it couldn't decide whether to welcome him or go for his throat.

Walker glanced at the man beside her, now with his arm protectively around her shoulders.

"If you're expecting an apology, you won't get one," her husband said coldly.

Slowly, he shook his head. He studied the man for a moment. He'd met men like this, had learned to assess them. "No. I had that coming."

Quinn drew back slightly, looking like a man whose car suddenly made an unexpected sound. Walker glanced at his sister. And she finally spoke.

"I don't know whether to hug you or slug you myself."

His mouth quirked. "I'll gladly take the latter if it gets me the former."

That did earn him the hug, and she let him hold it for longer than he'd dared hope. For a moment he simply couldn't speak. Hayley had been his most ardent defender for so long, but even her devotion had to have run out years ago. He would never forgive himself for that, and he doubted she would, either. Not when he couldn't tell her why.

But that didn't stop him from savoring every second of this. He'd never have thought this could be so precious, never thought just holding his sister close again could make him ache so much. Moisture stung his eyes, and he tried hard to blink it away. He tightened his embrace, half-afraid he'd hurt her, but again she let him. Maybe she felt the little tremors going through him, and was too kindhearted to pull away when he was shaking under the impact of a simple hug after the years of cold distance.

"Who's the furry one?" he asked when he finally had to end the contact that had warmed him more than anything in the past five years.

"This is Cutter," Quinn answered. "And I'd hold off petting him. He hasn't decided about you yet."

But you have, Walker thought. *And I don't blame you.*

"I suppose you'd better come in," Hayley said, her words and tone telling him he was far from forgiven. He'd expected that. She had every right, after all.

"Are you sure?" Quinn asked her, sounding as if he would happily toss Walker into the sound.

"He's my brother," she said simply. "I can't just throw him out."

Quinn made a sound Walker suspected was disagreement with that. But he stood aside and let Walker through the doorway.

The house had changed. It startled him, but he should have expected it. He swallowed past the sudden tightness in his throat as it was pounded home to him that his mother was truly gone. This house that she had made the near-perfect home of his childhood would never ring with her laughter again. And he hadn't treasured it or her nearly as much as he should have. And now he would never see or hear her again, except in memories.

Pain dug at him, burrowing deep. He'd thought himself prepared for this, but he'd been wrong. Very wrong.

He looked at Hayley, made himself face her even knowing she couldn't miss the wetness in his eyes. The initial shock was ebbing and she held his gaze, her expression unreadable even to him, who had once been able to read her so well. He knew there was every chance he might never earn her forgiveness, that he may have lost his sister forever.

Along with his mother. For an instant the house seemed empty despite their presence. She had always so filled this home she and his father had built together.

"Why did you stay?" he asked, barely aware of saying it aloud.

"This is home," Hayley said, her voice tight. "I feel

closer to her here. Not that you'd understand. Running away is more your style."

He winced. As far as she knew, she was right. Once, his first instinct would have been to get away from the constant reminders, as it had been when his father had died.

"That was before I realized there is no getting away from some things," he said quietly.

For an instant something shifted in her gaze, as if she'd sensed the pain behind the words. Whether it mattered to her or not, he couldn't tell. His sister had ever been kindhearted, but even the kindest heart could only take so much desertion.

Her expression went cool again, and he had to look away. He glanced around. This was Hayley's home now, and their mother's taste and Hayley's had never been the same, Mom being more the floral print and ruffle type and Hayley not. Or maybe it was Quinn's influence. But he liked the look of the blues and greens, the solids and stripes, even as it saddened him to no longer see that huge, ugly sofa on the far wall, with the big orange flowers that had always looked kind of alien to him. But mom's big chair was still in the corner, and…

There was someone else here.

He stared at the woman, who seemed familiar. Not a neighbor, he thought. Must be a friend of Hayley's; they looked about the same age. Tall, with beautiful blue eyes behind stylish red-framed glasses, long waves of shiny auburn hair, a turned-up nose and, he assessed, a great shape. Just enough curves, and those jeans and sweater hugged every one of them. And her mouth…the way she was biting her lip as she looked at him…

He felt a kick of interest. Quashed it swiftly. Not just out of habit, as something he hadn't dared risk in a long time, but with Hayley already angry at him that was hardly the way to go ten seconds through the door.

"Hi, I'm Hayley's nominee for worst brother in the world," he said wryly to the woman. "And I think I'll win."

"Walker," she said, her voice oddly tense.

His brow furrowed at her use of his name. She knew who he was? She had been staring at him rather intensely for a stranger. Belatedly, he realized what else had been in her tone. She didn't just know him, she expected him to know her.

"I'm sorry, I…"

"You don't even recognize me, do you?"

He tried to judge if there was hurt, or maybe anger, in her tone. Everybody else here was ticked at him, why not this one? When he caught himself assessing threat, trying to decide what answer would turn the situation the right way, he had to rather fiercely remind himself he wasn't in that hole anymore.

"I… You look familiar," he said, feeling a bit helpless, a sensation he didn't care for; he'd been there too often. But he wasn't there anymore, he told himself again. And here, it wasn't likely to get him killed.

Unless he pissed Quinn off enough and he went for that pistol he'd seen on the table just inside the door. He had no doubts the man could and would use it if necessary. He'd come to know a bit about that kind of steel in a man.

"She has changed a bit since you last saw her," Hayley said. "But I would think you'd still recognize your little shadow."

That quickly, an image flashed through his mind. A girl, at least six inches shorter than this one, unnaturally quiet, with unruly, bright, almost-orange hair in a clasp at the back of her neck, and big, heavy glasses that masked her eyes.

"Amy?" He knew he sounded astonished, but who wouldn't be? Who would ever have expected this dazzling creature to emerge from that shy child who tried so desperately not to be noticed? What had happened to the orange hair and the huge glasses she'd hidden behind? "Quiet little Amy?"

"Not so little anymore."

"I can…see that." He barely managed not to let his gaze slide over those rich curves. Damn, what was wrong with him?

He was off balance, that was all. He'd known this was going to be difficult, even painful if his sister reacted as she had every right to, with anger and rejection. But he hadn't expected, of all people, the girl who had been so infatuated with him in high school to be here. The girl who had, on occasion, trailed him like a clumsy but loving puppy. The girl he'd tolerated because she was his little sister's best friend and he didn't have much choice. The girl he remembered as studious, reliable, responsible and a few other things that were, at the time, the most boring attributes he could think of.

The girl whose innocent adoration, to his own considerable shock, had floated into his mind at odd moments over the years as the last purely sweet thing that had happened in his life.

"Did you expect nothing would change?" Amy asked, an edge in her voice.

"No, I…"

"Everything's changed," Hayley said, and he couldn't miss the undertone that had come into her voice; he'd grown up with her and he knew when she was on the verge of breaking. The sound ripped at him. "And you never cared."

"Hayley, no, I…" he began, but before he could get out another word his sister had turned and disappeared into the kitchen. Quinn gave him a hard look, then followed.

"I never got the chance to really thank you," Amy said, snapping his head back around.

He blinked. "Thank me?"

For the life of him he couldn't think of one thing any

of the three people in this house would want to thank him for. That he'd had no choice, and worse, couldn't explain, didn't matter in the long run. He'd shattered the one tie in his life he still valued. He doubted from the moment he'd been free to come home that it could be repaired, but he had to try. That he was feeling a bit battered at the moment didn't change that.

"For saving me from those nerd-hunters my first week of high school."

It took him a moment; it seemed so long ago. But then the memory was there—a small, quiet figure with the too-vivid hair backed into a corner, tears on her cheeks as she stared at the ground rather than the trio of girls who were jeering at her. He'd groaned inwardly when he realized it was Hayley's friend, but he'd waded in anyway, telling them to back off. And stay backed off, this girl at least.

She had just stared at him with that awestruck look that was so embarrassing. And, admit it, secretly flattering, he thought now. If he'd known she'd turn out like this, maybe he wouldn't have been so embarrassed by her tween-age devotion.

And a few months later it was all gone. Everything had changed.

He shook off the old weights. "You're welcome," he said.

"I'm glad I got this chance," she said sweetly. "Now I never have to speak to your irresponsible, cruel, heartless ass again."

She turned on her heel—giving him what normally would have been a pleasant view of a curved backside—and headed for the stairway. He stared, a bit confused by the sudden shift.

"Ouch," he muttered, feeling nearly as walloped as when Quinn had decked him. Still, this overt hostility was better than the pain in Hayley's voice.

Amy looked back over her shoulder, clearly having

heard him. "You expected a warm welcome? After you abandoned your mom and my best friend, your own sister, to deal with the aftermath of your father's death while you went gallivanting around the country on some teenage quest, with only a call or a note and a visit maybe twice a year?"

"I waited until I graduated high school," he protested. "She understood. And Mom. They told me to go, that they'd be okay."

"You left them still grieving! You think that they didn't beg you to stay makes it right? When have you ever done what was truly right, Walker Cole?"

At least once. And it may well have cost me everything.

But Amy wasn't nearly done yet.

"She had to deal with the long horror of your mother's cancer alone, you don't even come home for your own mother's funeral and you entirely skip Hayley's wedding, with nothing but a few stupid *texts*? And then turn up three months later as if you're just late to the dentist, and you have the nerve to be surprised that I'm angry?"

Quiet little Amy Clark had definitely grown teeth. Yet he couldn't help being glad of it, because it was for Hayley. It seemed he'd forgotten something on that list of her attributes. Loyal. Fiercely, completely loyal. And unchanging. People like Amy never changed.

And in an ever-changing world, perhaps he hadn't valued that enough.

"I'm sorry," he said. "You're right. About everything. All of it."

"Yes," she said flatly. "I am. And I'm leaving before I slug you myself."

She vanished up the stairs, and Walker Cole chalked up yet another casualty to the chaos his life had become five years ago.

They'd told him the price would be high.

He hadn't expected it to be everything.

Chapter 4

By the time she closed the guest room door behind her, Amy was shaking. She hadn't realized quite how much anger she'd been harboring all these years.

It was mostly for Hayley's sake, and if she was honest, it was in part because Hayley herself didn't seem angry enough. She never had.

"I don't hate my brother. He's just...Walker. Aptly named."

"That's okay, I hate him enough for both of us."

How many times had they had that exchange?

She wondered if Hayley was saying the same thing to her husband right now. She was doubly glad Quinn was here, both because he'd done what she would have liked to do in decking Walker, and because he was probably the best comfort Hayley could have just now.

If she didn't love Hayley so much she might have envied her that kind of support. Because now here she herself was, under the same roof with her adolescent crush. The perfect name for it, since he was the one who had crushed her heart. And who had come perilously close to being the last straw that destroyed any faith she ever had in the male of the species. No matter how many times she reminded herself that not all men were utterly irresponsible like her father and Walker, it was sometimes a hard belief to hang on to.

At least Walker wasn't a drunk, she thought as she

made herself finish her unpacking. Or maybe he was. He did look a bit haggard, and while all the good looks were still there, his eyes looked different. Still beautiful, with unfairly long and thick lashes, but more world-weary somehow. And that thick, espresso-brown hair needed a trim. She didn't mind longer hair, if it at least looked intentional. This looked like he'd just neglected it.

Or like her father's had, when the money for haircuts had gone for booze instead. And caused nights filled with furious arguments between her parents. That was part of the reason she'd escaped so often to the warm haven of Hayley's home. Both Hayley's parents had looked out for her, and she'd found in them the steady caring and consistency that had been so lacking in her own life. When Christopher Cole had been killed by, horribly, a drunk driver while on duty as a police officer, and then Nancy had died just over two years ago, Amy had grieved fiercely right alongside her friend.

She closed the closet door rather sharply. She hated that Walker was able to unsettle her so after all this time. That she was wasting so much time and thought on him. He didn't deserve even the anger she'd vented on him downstairs. In fact, she was a bit embarrassed about her rant. She'd hoped, if she ever laid eyes on him again, to be cool and unaffected. In fact, she'd hoped she might be able to react just as he had, puzzled, not quite able to place him. Although she'd have to pretend it; there was no way on earth she would ever forget him, no matter what he'd done. Or not done.

"When have you ever done what was truly right, Walker Cole?"

Her own words rang in her head. She stopped in her tracks.

…done what was truly right…

She sat abruptly on the edge of the bed.

"Girl, you need to listen to your own rant," she muttered under her breath.

For hadn't she been wrestling with that very problem in those moments before Walker had arrived to blast it all right out of her mind? Wasn't the question that had driven her here in the first place how to do what was right, or whether to even try at all?

You have no right to criticize him if you're not willing to do it yourself.

As for Walker's annoying presence disrupting everything, she would just have to do what she'd always told herself she'd do if she ever encountered him again.

Ignore him.

Walker had had some sleepless nights before, far too many of them in the past five years, but this was a doozy. He'd gotten through some of them then by telling himself he'd sleep when it was over—or when he was dead, which could well have come first—but now it was over, at least as far as he was concerned, and here he was. Still watching the seconds tick by in the dark.

He grimaced into the darkness of the living room, where he'd crashed on the couch. His old room was a home office now, not that he would have asked to sleep in it anyway. This was crazy. He was as wide-awake as he'd been when his life hung in the balance. When a single wrong word or step could have meant giving himself away to men who would kill him without a millisecond's hesitation.

Then again, didn't his life hang in the balance now? The rest of it, anyway? Having quiet, shy little—well, not so much any of those anymore—Amy Clark chew him out in front of Hayley and her new, intimidating husband was bad enough, but what if Hayley couldn't ever forgive him? What if he truly had lost the only family he had left because he'd done the unforgivable? He hadn't let himself think of that possibility in his drive to get here, but after this reception he knew he had to.

He didn't kid himself by saying he'd make it up to her. There was no making up for what he'd missed, what he'd left his sister alone to deal with. Amy was right about that. And the only thing that could possibly ameliorate it was something he couldn't give her.

It was barely light out when he finally gave up and staggered into the kitchen. But Quinn was up and, thank God, he had coffee on.

"You look like hell," Quinn said, sounding rather cheerful about it.

"Feel worse," he said, eyeing the coffeepot.

Quinn noticed. "Everything's where it always was."

"But this isn't my home anymore."

He was a little startled at the bleak sound of his own voice, although after last night he supposed he shouldn't be.

"You're the one who left," Quinn pointed out flatly.

For a moment, Walker studied this man his sister had chosen. He knew little about him. Nothing, actually, other than his name.

"I thought I'd let you know I'm getting married. In January. His name is Quinn. I love him the way Mom loved Dad. You'd be welcome, but I won't expect you."

That had been the entirety of the message. And the bitterest part of it was that of all the messages she'd left, that was the best one. Much better than *"Mom has cancer. It looks bad. You need to come home."*

He rubbed his fingers over the sore spot on his jaw. Quinn watched him, and Walker didn't think he was mistaken in thinking there was a certain satisfaction in his gaze. "You pack a hell of a punch."

"You deserved it."

"Yes."

"Still do."

"Yes."

Quinn lifted a brow, as if surprised at his lack of argument.

"You may find this hard to believe, but I'm really glad Hayley found someone who loves her enough to…do that to someone who hurt her."

Quinn's expression changed then, his brow furrowing just slightly, as if he hadn't expected that. "And I'll do it again, if need be. You've put her through hell. I won't let you add to it. She needs time to figure out how she feels about you, and I intend to see that she gets it."

Walker had no doubt the man meant it. He adored Hayley. And vice versa. It fairly rippled off them both. And last night he'd made it clear he wasn't going to leave Walker alone with his wife and give him the chance to hurt her all over again.

"What is it you do?" he asked, wondering if Hayley had somehow ended up with a cop. He wouldn't have thought that possible, given what had happened to their father, but then he wouldn't have thought the turn his life had taken possible, either.

"Family business," Quinn said. "You?"

He winced inwardly. "Currently unemployed."

"That why you're here? Looking for a free roof?"

Anger kicked through him. "You pushing for me to return your welcome?"

"You could try," Quinn said, clearly unconcerned.

You might be surprised, Walker thought. He'd learned a bit since he'd left here.

But then he realized that he couldn't very well be glad Hayley had found a man who loved her enough to take down anyone who hurt her, and then expect him to act any other way, given what he knew. Or thought he knew.

"I never meant to hurt her," he said softly.

"Good intentions are meaningless. Especially when you cause that kind of pain."

"Yes. But they're all I've got."

He took another sip of his coffee as he looked at Walker.

"You're her brother, so she decides what happens. If she wants you here, then you stay. If she wants you gone, then you go. But I warn you, either way, if you…"

He held up a hand. "I get it." He eyed the man who was now his brother-in-law warily. There was something about him that screamed he did not make idle threats. He reminded him, not in looks but in manner, of Tobias Cabrero, the guy who had turned his life upside down when all Walker had been trying to do was be a good citizen. "Let me guess. Ex-fed?"

"In a manner of speaking."

Walker took in his bearing, his calm manner, the air of command and competence. He hadn't been there himself, but he knew enough of them to recognize the type.

"Ex-military," he said, and this time it wasn't a question.

"You're smarter than you've acted."

Well, there was a double-edged compliment, Walker thought wryly.

"Did I smell coffee?"

Walker froze as the female voice came from behind him. Amy.

"You did." Quinn sounded much more welcoming. The man reached up and opened a cabinet door, taking out a mug and handing it to her. More than he'd gotten, but then she was a lot more welcome than he was. Amy walked past him without a glance, took the mug.

"Thank you," she said as she filled it from the glass pot.

Quinn nodded, finished his own coffee, rinsed out the mug and stuck it in the dishwasher. Then he looked at Amy, and Walker would swear he was stifling a grin. "I'm off to work. Over to you," he said to her, and without another glance at Walker, he walked out of the kitchen.

Amy frowned after him, clearly puzzled by his words.

"I think," Walker said drily, "that meant he liked the way you chewed on me last night, and is hoping you'll take up where he left off."

Her expression cleared. "Oh. Well. I could do that."

He sighed. For a moment he just looked at her. The glasses were blue today, matching her top, and it made her eyes look even more blue. And the rich, russet color of her hair was a far cry from the carrot-top she'd always been teased about. "I'm sure you could," he said finally.

And he was. For there was no denying that while little Amy Clark had grown up, she'd lost none of her intelligence, principles or fierce loyalty.

Which meant that, in her view, he was probably one step this side of the devil.

And he couldn't tell her that she was wrong, that there were much worse devils out there. And he knew some of them personally.

Chapter 5

Walker heard the steps approaching, but couldn't pull his gaze away from the framed photograph on the hallway wall. Then he sensed it was Hayley, and was afraid to look at her, anyway. After the scene in the kitchen he'd managed to avoid more encounters until now, needing time to gear up for the rest of what was likely to be another unpleasant day.

And then he'd noticed this picture, of him and Mom the day after he'd pitched his first no-hitter, him in uniform, her looking proud, happy…and very much alive. The image had once hung in his mother's corner above the chair where she so often sat, sewing, knitting or any of the other things she always kept busy with.

Had kept busy. Had. As in never would again.

He blinked rapidly, but it wasn't enough and he had to swipe at his eyes.

"You kept this," he said, still without looking at his sister. His voice sounded strange even to him, thick with the tears he was fighting.

"Yes."

"Why, when you're so angry with me?"

"She loved you."

He turned to face her then. It seemed the least he could do.

"Hayley," he began, but his throat tightened too much for more words, and he could only shake his head.

"There was a time" she said, sounding as if her throat was nearly as tight as his, "when you showing up would have been the answer to many prayers. When it would have eased my pain, soothed my aching heart."

She was killing him. And he deserved it.

"I…" He stopped when she waved a hand that was none too steady.

"You being here now has made me remember all over again how much I needed you when she got sick. How much *she* needed you."

He tightened his jaw against a new wave of pain. But he held her gaze, didn't fight it. Looking at his sister, the one who'd lived through every day of it alone, he didn't feel he had the right to dodge one ounce of it now.

"Hayley, please, let me…"

"I need some time, Walker. Time to absorb, figure out how I feel."

He sucked in a long breath. He had no right to demand more of her. No right to demand anything. He nodded. "I'll wait."

"You might want to do it elsewhere. Amy will be out in a moment. We're going for a walk."

He grimaced, thought of several things to say to that, discarded all of them. "Enjoy," he said, figuring that was safe enough.

"Doubtful." Concern flickered in her eyes. "She has a problem to deal with. It's why she's here from LA."

He frowned. Amy had a problem big enough to warrant coming over a thousand miles?

None of his business, he told himself. And took his sister's advice and vacated the hallway.

"Don't you think it's time you told me?"

Amy looked at Hayley as they walked up the long driveway. Cutter was trotting along beside them, occasionally pausing for a sniff of something, but never letting them get too far ahead of him.

"You have enough on your plate with your brother," Amy said, thinking of what Hayley had told her of their encounter in the hallway.

They reached the road at the end of the drive. Cutter's demeanor changed, she noticed. Instead of racing around, checking all corners of the yard, once they hit the road he was at their side, as if he completely understood walking along a roadway, even here where traffic was very light, was a different matter.

"Just because Walker shows up out of the blue without a word doesn't mean I'm going to drop everything," Hayley answered. "Especially when it's you. Now quit dodging."

Amy sighed. When she wanted to be, Hayley could be tough as nails. Probably a good thing when dealing with a man the likes of Quinn.

"I'm not sure it's anything, really."

"But it bothers you."

"It's just a…tiny niggle."

"You said it was your boss."

"Yes. It's something I found, by accident, when I was pulling up a file he had me working on. I wasn't snooping or anything."

"I never would have thought you were."

Amy stopped as they reached the corner. For a long moment she stood just looking at the house there, the two-story shaded by huge evergreens, and the big yard on two sides. It looked so different now, tidy and well-kept by the current owners, painted a cheerful blue with white trim.

"Do you know what my mother used to say was the best part of living on a corner?" She was barely aware, as the memories stirred, that she'd said the words out loud.

"What?" Hayley asked.

"That when Dad came home drunk he had a fifty-fifty chance of not parking the car in somebody else's yard."

For a moment Hayley didn't speak, and the words seemed to echo in Amy's head. And although Hayley had long ago told her she would go insane if she let every mention of a drunk driver bother her, Amy still said, "Sorry."

Hayley shook her head. "I wasn't thinking about that. I was thinking about the hell your life was, compared to mine."

Amy turned to stare at her. "Your father *died.*"

"Yes. But while I had him, he was wonderful. Loving, kind, supportive, always there for me. You never had that."

Cutter had come back when they stopped, and now he was standing in front of her, in fact leaning against her legs. The furry warmth of him was again comforting. And it seemed to crystallize her thinking, as well. Amy stroked Cutter's head as she looked at the house again, then back at this woman who had so often been her lifeline.

"What I knew of real fathering came from yours," she said quietly. "He always put up with me hanging around. He laughed *with* me, not *at* me. He hugged me, gave me advice, fixed my bike."

"That was Dad," Hayley agreed.

"I used to…wish he was mine, too." Amy sighed. "But you know that."

"Yes." For a long moment Hayley looked at her, then smiled gently. "So did he."

Amy didn't know whether to feel embarrassed or grateful.

"You know, he kept a close eye on you. If there had been the slightest sign of physical abuse from your father, if he'd even seen so much as a bruise, he would have had you out of there in an instant."

Amy blinked. "What?"

"He had it all figured out. He knew who in CPS he'd talk to, someone he had good rapport with. And which judge, if they needed one. He wanted it all mapped out in case he had to move in a hurry."

"I...I never knew that." Her heart ached for the loss of a man who had cared even more than she knew.

"Mom told me one day when I needed distraction, when she was sick. She'd asked how you were, and that got us started."

"My father was never that at least. Abusive, I mean." She grimaced. "Just silly, and pretty much useless. And he only argued with my mother."

"No wonder you hated going home."

"I so often wished I could just stay at your house."

Hayley looked at her consideringly. "They talked about that, too, Mom and Dad. That if he had to pull you out, if maybe you could live with us."

Amy stared at her. "I never knew that, either."

"Neither did I. They didn't tell me back then. They were afraid I'd get my heart set on it."

"And if you'd told me back then, I would have gone crazy, wishing for it to happen." She looked back at the house once more. "And I hope the people that live here now are happy. It was a nice house once, and now it looks like it is again."

Determinedly, she shoved the past aside. She didn't let it define her. "Your father told me once that bad examples could sometimes teach you as much as good ones," she said as they resumed their walk.

Hayley laughed. "That was Dad. He told Walker the same thing when his buddy Joe got in trouble for shoplifting."

Amy looked at her friend. It was, she told herself, past time that she thought about Hayley's situation rather than her own silly emotions. She was merely dealing with the reappearance of a schoolgirl crush. Hayley was dealing with something much more painful.

"I can't imagine how you must feel, him showing up like this."

Hayley grimaced. "It was a shock."

"I hope you told him off last night."

Hayley grinned then. "Actually, you did that quite nicely. I didn't have to add a thing. I think 'What she said' was about the extent of it."

"I was…angry."

"And I love you for it. I think he was more stunned that quiet, shy Amy launched on him than if I had. Well, that and Quinn decking him before they'd ever even met."

Amy smiled at that. "He had it coming."

"He did." Her voice softened. "And he knows it. He's not a cruel guy, Amy."

"Sometimes thoughtless, insensitive and selfish amount to the same thing."

"Yes. But he's still my brother."

"So you forgive him?"

Hayley grimaced. "I didn't say that."

Amy was glad to hear that, given she thought what Walker had done—or not done—unforgivable. But she didn't say that as they crossed the street at the stop sign and headed toward the water. The street they were on now dead-ended at an overlook, where some community-minded citizen had built a bench where people could sit and watch the passing marine traffic in the sound.

"And even if I did," Hayley added, "Quinn hasn't. I was afraid to leave them alone last night."

"Too bad. I would have liked to have seen that," Amy said drily.

Hayley laughed. "I had to…lure him away. Much more fun, I promise."

Amy smiled. "I can't tell you how wonderful it is to see you so happy. I'd love your husband for that alone."

Now that they were farther away from Walker's unsettling presence, she felt calmer. Although she wasn't convinced that wasn't in part due to the dog, who seemed glued to her side just now. And when they sat on the bench he sat beside her, again putting his chin on her knee in that way he had.

"Your dog is very sweet."

Hayley laughed. "He is many things, and sweet is often one of them. And," she added with a pointed look, "he is very perceptive, especially when something's bothering someone."

Amy sighed.

"Out with it, girlfriend," Hayley ordered.

"We shouldn't do this now. It can wait. You need to have it out with your brother. And you haven't seen him in so long."

"Let's see," Hayley said with exaggerated thoughtfulness, "drop everything to deal with someone who left to wander the country years ago, couldn't be bothered to show up or even call when his own mother died and then skipped his only living relative's wedding...or help the one person who has ever and always been there. Tough call."

Any smiled suddenly. "I love you, too, you know."

"I do."

"If I hadn't had you and your family for an example, I would have been seriously screwed up."

"And instead you're my wonderfully sane, beautiful best friend. So what did you find on your boss's computer?"

She sighed. "Two things. Neither one alone is anything odd, but together..." She took a breath. She'd come here to do this, hadn't she? She plunged ahead at last. "First thing, a month ago, was in his encrypted, password-protected files, where the file I needed was. A document creating a fictional corporation offshore, in the Virgin Islands. Which in itself isn't that odd—we do that all the time for various reasons. What was odd was that he had it hidden like that."

"It's not usually?"

"No. There's no reason it should be. It's a routine kind

of thing that he handles all the time. And I actually only know what it was because the file I needed was next on the list and I clicked on the wrong one by accident."

"What was the second thing?"

"I found it just last week. A record of a bank account, also in the Virgin Islands, opened in the same fictitious business name, in the same week the filing was finalized. It started issuing checks immediately to another business name in LA."

Hayley leaned back against the back of the bench. For a moment she was silent, then she asked, "What exactly are you thinking?"

"After I saw the bank statement, I did a little checking. That business that the checks were going to? As far as I can tell, with what research I was able to do…isn't a business."

"What?"

"They don't do anything. They don't make anything, they don't sell anything, not even advice or information. They don't have a website or even a business listing anywhere. There's no public information on them anywhere that I could find. Even their snail mail address is just a mail drop, one of those rent-a-box places."

"Odd," Hayley agreed.

Amy let out a compressed breath. "I know it's not much, and I didn't dare risk copying the file so I don't have any proof, although proof of what I don't even know. It may be nothing, it may be completely legitimate, but…"

Hayley was silent for a moment when she finally trailed off. Long enough that Amy wondered if she was thinking her friend had turned into some kind of conspiracy theorist. She couldn't blame her; now that she'd said it out loud it sounded very thin. There was more, but it was even more ephemeral. She had no proof at all to validate her feelings of being watched and followed, and was convinced it was only what she'd found that had brought them on.

And then she stood up. Slowly, Amy rose in turn. And Cutter, who had been plopped at her feet, happily sniffing the various breezes that wafted by, got up and looked at both of them.

"Come on," Hayley said.

"Where?"

"I think it's time to introduce you to the full wonder that is Foxworth."

Chapter 6

He hadn't gotten the prodigal son's welcome home, but he hadn't expected that. But then, he hadn't expected that uppercut from his new brother-in-law, either. But it could have been worse. He could have used that gun.

Walker rubbed at his now-shaven jaw. He'd waited until now, when Hayley and Amy had gone for their walk, to use the guest bathroom. He poked at the sore spot, wondering what it would be like to get in a knock-down, drag-out fight with Quinn Foxworth.

It wouldn't be pretty.

But then, none of this was pretty. And Quinn had been no angrier at him than he himself had been when he'd finally surfaced from his five-year nightmare and found that the life he'd left behind didn't exist anymore. When he'd learned what they'd withheld from him so he wouldn't be "distracted," he'd been angrier than he'd ever been in his life, except for the day his father had been killed.

So you left home angry, and you came back angry. Great.

But what was he supposed to feel when all they'd had to say was that they couldn't compromise the mission?

Oh, by the way, there were a couple of things we couldn't tell you, because we couldn't risk compromising the mission. Your mother's dead and your sister got married. Here's your phone with the messages.

Admittedly, it hadn't been quite that blunt or cold, but

it might as well have been. He should have suspected when they'd made him hand over his old pay-as-you-go cell phone, saying it was for his own safety. He'd learned that lesson now, that anytime the government started talking about taking things away for your own safety was the time to be wary.

At least they'd kept the phone active, ancient though it now was in technological terms. Although he doubted it was for his benefit, given that they'd used it to send short, meaningless texts to his sister, maintaining the fiction that he was still wandering. And they hadn't deleted anything, which at first had made him laugh wryly at the scruples.

And then had come the painful jolt of listening to Hayley's strained voice telling him of their mother's illness nearly five years after the fact. And later of her death, two years too late.

They'd paid him a nice chunk, enough to keep him going for quite a while. And bought his ticket home. Cabrero—who threatened to flatten anyone who used the hated nickname Toby—had even taken him to the airport after the long debriefing, but Walker thought that was mostly so he could pound home the warning one more time.

"I'll check in on you now and then. But you can't tell anyone anything. You know that, don't you? We're close to making our move, and if you let even one thing slip, it could jeopardize operations all over the country."

"Yeah, I get it."

"That means not even your sister. Especially not her. It could put her in danger."

When he stepped out of the bathroom in only his jeans, that sister was walking down the hall. She looked him up and down. For an instant he saw her gaze snag on his left arm. The tattoo, he thought. He needed to do something about that. Cabrero had told him they could have it removed, but he'd been in too much of a hurry to wait around to have it done. At least Hayley wasn't likely to recognize it for what it was—the symbol of belonging to a group of men who were brutal beyond anything he'd ever imagined.

All she said was, "I should send you to our friend Laney. She's groomed sheepdogs before."

Apparently her request for time didn't mean she wasn't going to speak to him at all, and he was thankful for that.

"I know I need a haircut. I was…in a hurry."

For a moment she just looked at him.

He sighed. "Go ahead. Say it."

"Say what?"

"That I'm way too late to be in a hurry. I know that."

Her green eyes, so like their father's, seemed to zero in on his face. "There is one thing I would like to ask."

He hadn't wanted to have this conversation standing here in the hallway, but he had the feeling dodging it now would do even more damage than he'd already done.

"Ask."

"Why?"

He'd thought of little else on the flight here, what he could tell her. Everything involved a lie of some sort. He didn't want to lie to her. He never had, had never felt he had to, because Hayley always understood. But now he did have to, or say nothing.

"There's a reason. A good one," he finally said. His mouth tightened before he added, his voice rough, "And I can't tell you what it is."

"Ever?"

"Maybe."

For a long moment his sister just looked at him. Then, "All right."

But the way she walked past him to head downstairs told him that she was far from accepting his absence through what had to be both the worst and best moments of her life. Moments she'd gone through without him, the brother who should have been with her every step of the way.

"Well, that was just a beautiful explanation and apology."

He spun around, saw Amy standing in the guest room doorway. Her arms were crossed in front of her, her mouth—when had her mouth gotten so luscious?—quirked with an emotion that looked unsettlingly like disgust.

"'I can't tell you what it is'? Really? She's supposed to just accept that?"

"She knows I wouldn't lie to her."

"No, you just abandon her and—oh, never mind. This is pointless. You are who you are." She gave him a look then that made his stomach knot. "Whatever happened to that boy, Walker? The one who rescued me that day, the one who would have stood with and for his sister through anything?"

His mouth twisted. "Life happened. Death happened."

"It happened to Hayley, too. She didn't run away."

"Is that what you think I—never mind. You're right. This is pointless."

He couldn't take this, the way she was looking at him. He turned around and followed his sister downstairs.

Amy shook off her upset at the truly pointless conversation, grabbed up her jacket and her big purse and headed down to the living room. Hayley was by the door, tucking her phone into a pocket of her much smaller purse. Walker was standing a couple of feet away. Maybe he thought she'd finally punch him herself, and so was keeping out of arm's reach.

As Amy came in, Hayley was speaking to her brother.

"We're going over to Foxworth," she said. "Would you like to come along?"

Her tone was polite, composed and almost impersonal,

as if he were just a casual guest, and the answer didn't really matter to her. No, Hayley wasn't as accepting as she'd first thought.

And right now, she stood there wishing the fact that he was still wearing only a pair of low-slung jeans didn't unsettle her so.

Amy doubted he even knew what Foxworth was, other than apparently that family business Quinn had mentioned this morning in the kitchen. She doubted he knew just how much she'd heard. What she had heard had done nothing to change her opinion on either man. Quinn was everything she could have wished for her friend, and Walker was just what she'd been afraid he was.

When Walker decided to go along, she wasn't happy about it. She doubted he wanted to know more about the work that had become a passionate calling for his sister. He was more likely already bored at being home, she thought sourly.

At least he got in the backseat, she thought, so she could ignore him more easily. And the shirt he'd put on helped, although the image of his bare chest and ridged stomach stubbornly stayed in her mind. He hadn't gone soft in those years, she thought. He still looked like the star athlete he'd been, the holder of the state high school record for no-hitters pitched.

Well, minus the odd, squiggly line tattoo she'd noticed on his arm.

Cutter, now in the wayback, apparently still hadn't decided about Walker. It was as if the dog somehow knew he was connected to his beloved Hayley, but also knew he'd hurt her. Amy wondered if he didn't like him, but held it back because of that connection. And then laughed at herself for crediting the canine with human emotions and decisions.

She focused on where they were going.

"Foxworth really helps with such small problems?"

Hayley smiled. "Foxworth may have helped to practically take down a government—in our absence, mind you—but one of Quinn's favorite cases was finding a little girl's lost locket, the only thing she had left from her mother."

Amy smiled back at that. "He was probably thinking of you and your mother." And only a little bit of that was aimed at the silent passenger in the back.

"His own, too," Hayley said softly. "He was a lot younger when he lost her. Just a child."

Hayley had told her of Quinn's parents, killed in the terrorist bombing over in Scotland, and how that event had led years later to the starting of the Foxworth Foundation.

As they passed the blackened spot, Walker asked about the missing house. As Hayley told the story of how she and Quinn had met, black helicopter and all, Amy smiled. Hayley was so clearly—and rightfully—proud of what Foxworth did. Foxworth helped people who were losing battles even though they were in the right and had nowhere else to turn. It warmed Amy all over again. And she realized suddenly that this feeling, this passion, this certainty that what you were doing was not just right but necessary, and incredibly important, was what was missing from her own life.

And yet, that feeling was exactly what she had hoped to find in her work. She thought she had found it. Her boss was—she'd thought—a good guy at heart. Kind of old-school, tough, a bit brusque, but fair. But now she wondered. Was afraid he wasn't who she'd thought he was.

Just as Walker hadn't been, she added as he reacted to his sister's tale of danger and a midnight kidnapping.

"Damn it, Hayley, you could have been killed," Walker said.

"Quinn wouldn't let that happen."

"No man's infallible."

"He's pretty darn close," Hayley said cheerfully, and

Amy liked how she refused to let her brother's supposed concern now, when it was far too late, matter. "And of course Cutter would never let that happen, either."

On his name the dog let out a sharp yip, and Amy had the satisfaction of seeing Walker's head snap around.

"He go with you everywhere?" Walker asked.

"Pretty much," Hayley said.

"He's a loyal sort," Amy said.

She didn't realize until she'd spoken the words that they could be interpreted as a jab at Walker. But he didn't react, and she risked turning her head enough to where she could see him out of the corner of her eye. He was looking over the backseat at Cutter, who was staring back at him. But from that angle she could see his jaw was tight, set.

"He's also an excellent judge of character," Hayley said, and Amy gave her friend a startled look, wondering if she was taking a shot at Walker, as well. It was hard to interpret the timing of that comment as anything else. And another glance back at Walker told her he knew it.

But he didn't protest. He said merely, "So I should be glad he hasn't torn my throat out, is that it?"

"Oh, I don't think he's made up his mind yet," Hayley said, her tone still cheerful as they reached the turnoff for Foxworth. Having visited it several times helping with the wedding, it was familiar to Amy.

"This was the perfect setting," she said as they drove down the winding drive through the trees. "You were lucky you had such a gorgeous day for the wedding," she said.

"We were. Winter's not usually so cooperative around here."

"And Cutter did his job as ring-bearer perfectly."

"He did, didn't you, my sweet boy?"

Cutter made a sound that was half bark, half whine, amazingly like "Yes," in sound and "Of course" in tone.

"And you couldn't have scripted the eagles' flight any better. That was so amazing."

"It was gasp-worthy, wasn't it?"

"Nothing like having a soaring stamp of approval from our national symbol in front of everyone," Amy said with a laugh. "Quite the salute."

Walker said nothing. But when she glanced once more as she got out of the car, Amy noticed his right hand was clenched atop his knee. And his knuckles were white with the pressure as they talked about the wedding he'd missed.

Good, she thought. And didn't feel the least vindictive for it.

Chapter 7

Well, wasn't that just a pleasant drive?

Walker had never been so grateful that a trip was over. He told himself neither woman had been sniping at him, that Hayley and Amy were quite naturally talking about the wedding because it had been held here and because that's what women did.

It didn't make him feel any better. Nor did looking out at the meadow beyond the anonymous, three-story green building, and trying to picture what it must have looked like set up for the ceremony. He'd seen the photograph of Hayley and Quinn on the table in the living room, and the others along the stairway wall when he'd gone up to take a shower. Something about every one of them had jabbed at him—how beautiful Hayley had been, the way Quinn looked at her as if she were the treasure at the end of the rainbow and the number of people there he didn't know, yet another part of his sister's life he had no place in.

And how amazing Amy had looked in the royal blue dress that had skimmed every curve and set her hair off like quiet fire. She'd worn those blue glasses, matching the dress, and he wondered if she'd bought them for that reason. And how many pairs she had. Little Amy had come a long way. Despite the difficulties of her childhood, she'd made a success of herself. In the end, she'd done a heck of a lot better at it than he had.

That it wasn't entirely his fault didn't matter much at this point.

The dog, who had been on his feet from the moment they'd turned off the road, was antsy now that they'd come to a halt. Hayley hit the button that raised the back liftgate on the SUV and the dog was out before Walker even had his door open. He watched as the animal trotted toward the door of the building.

A quick glance around showed that the dark blue SUV he'd seen Quinn leave in was parked a few feet down. At the very end of the gravel drive sat an older, rather nondescript silver coupe, like thousands of others on the road. A few yards closer, in between the coupe and Quinn's vehicle, sat an older, dark gray pickup.

"Liam's here," Hayley said.

"He's that cute Texas boy, right?" Amy said.

"That would be Liam," Hayley said with a grin.

Cute Texas boy? Walker wondered.

And then he was completely distracted by the sight of his sister's dog raising up on his hind legs and batting at something near the door. It was, he realized, an automatic door opener, like a handicapped entrance. He wondered if they had regular visitors who needed it, or if they'd put the thing in just for the dog.

The door swung open, and Cutter vanished inside in a rush.

"He's in a hurry," Amy said.

"He's never quite happy if Quinn and I aren't together."

Amy laughed, and it was a light, airy thing that made him feel as if a feather had brushed his ear. "And neither are you and Quinn."

Hayley grinned. "Nope."

He should be happy for her, Walker thought. And he *was* happy for her. It was himself he was feeling ridiculously sorry for. He'd known this would be tough; he just hadn't expected it to be this tough. He thought he even preferred his sister's anger to this nonchalance, as if he were barely there, or didn't matter to her at all.

What did you expect?

He reminded himself that he'd been here less than twenty-four hours, and it was a bit early to be giving up. He tried to put himself in her shoes, or better, in Quinn's. If he loved somebody as much as Quinn obviously loved Hayley, and he came face-to-face with someone who had hurt her so badly, what would he do?

I have no idea. I've never loved anyone like that.

He caught the door just as it was about to close behind Amy. For a moment he found himself standing stock-still, watching as she walked into the building. From behind, she looked…amazing. Snug jeans and that blue sweater that had a white tribal sort of design around the bottom edge at the hip. It seemed to emphasize her shape, that sexy curve, the taut backside. The red-brown hair fell halfway down her back in smooth waves, unlike the wild orange curls he remembered. The coloring that had drawn so much unwanted attention to her.

The freckles, he thought suddenly. They, too, had smoothed out, or perhaps she just stayed out of the sun enough that they had faded. He remembered that summer Amy had gone with them on a trip to the coast. He'd been maybe twelve, so Hayley—and Amy—would have been about eight. She'd gotten so sunburned it had been pitiful. But she'd learned her lesson and made sure it hadn't happened next time.

That was also the trip when he'd first learned of her life. He'd been amazed—and more than a little annoyed—that she exclaimed with wonder over the simplest things. "You really wouldn't mind?" was the phrase he heard most often from her when his parents acquiesced to something as simple as having another hot dog. It was his father who had finally taken him on a long walk down the

beach and explained about her life at home and what a
jerk he was being.

*"Now that you understand, I'm going to trust you to
look out for her when I can't."*

His father's words slammed back into his mind, forgotten until now. He'd promised with all the sincerity of
his twelve-year-old heart.

*And you broke that one, too. For the sake of people
you've never even met and never will? Nice priorities,
Cole.*

Then he was inside, and what he saw was enough to
push the memory out of his mind, for now at least.

To his surprise, the ground level of the utilitarian—
and conspicuously unmarked, he'd noticed—green building was furnished like a home. The room was large, the
great-room effect emphasized by wood flooring, and a
fireplace against one long wall. In front of that, around a
large, low table, was arranged a leather sofa and a couple
of chairs atop a patterned rug. Above the mantel was a flat
screen, dark now. Back in one corner was what appeared
to be a full bath. In the other corner, a small kitchen area
with an island.

Two men were there, and Cutter dashed over to them.
He greeted the taller of the two men first, a lean, almost
lanky guy with a firm jaw stubbled slightly with a dark
beard. As he bent to acknowledge the dog, Walker saw
his dark hair was nearly as long as his own was now, and
nearly as unruly.

Cutter leaned into him and, oddly, he thought he heard
the man say softly to the animal, "It's okay today, dog," as
he scratched a spot behind the dog's right ear.

Cutter then turned to the other man, a muscular guy
with a buzz cut who appeared quite a bit younger, who
crouched down to the dog's eye level.

"Hey, buddy," he crooned, "how ya doing?" As he went
for that same spot behind the ear, Walker wondered if that

would work for him even as he cataloged the man as, judging from the trace of a drawl, "that cute Texas boy" Amy had mentioned. Texas, anyway, he was no judge of cute.

Except maybe Amy. But she wasn't cute, not really. She was too serious for cute. But attractive? Oh, yeah. That had happened.

"Rafe, Liam, you remember my dearest, best friend Amy Clark, from the wedding?" Hayley asked. Walker cataloged the names and faces instinctively.

"Of course," the taller man who had to be Rafe said. "Welcome back."

"Who could forget you?" the younger one asked rather blatantly. Walker saw the dark-haired man's eyes roll slightly, but affectionately, while Amy herself merely laughed.

"Anyone," she said, "but I'm glad you didn't. It's good to see you both again."

With another woman who looked like this one, Walker would have thought the charming, self-effacing demeanor an act. But with Amy he knew it was likely for real, born of years when being overlooked had been a rare blessing.

"So," Rafe said as he took a sip from the coffee cup he held and shifted his gaze to Walker, "the prodigal brother returns."

Walker realized he was being studied, and from the man's expression, not favorably.

"Not exactly," Walker said drily. "He got a warmer welcome."

The man lifted a dark eyebrow. "Figure you deserve one?"

Okay, so no punches pulled there. "No. But your boss already decked me, so I'd appreciate it if you'd restrain."

The younger man straightened and looked at him consideringly. "I thought he looked a mite satisfied when he came in this morning." Liam's gaze flicked to Hayley. "More than usual, I mean."

"Liam Burnett, you brat," Hayley said, clearly joking but with a tinge of pink in her cheeks. "Where is he anyway?"

"Upstairs on the phone with Teague," Rafe said.

Hayley seemed to hone in quickly on that. "Any news?"

"He's onto something, yeah," Liam answered. "I think he needed to know how far Quinn wants him to go."

Hayley's gaze shifted to Rafe. "You okay with that? You did the heavy lifting on this, after all."

Rafe gave her a one-shoulder shrug. "As long as payment is extracted, I don't care who the tool is."

"As long as it's Foxworth," Liam added.

"Assumed," Rafe agreed.

Walker glanced at Amy, who seemed as in the dark as he was. Yet something about their manner kept him from asking. He doubted he would get an answer, anyway, although Amy might. Nobody here was going to trust him.

And from their point of view, they were right, he told himself. Being Hayley's brother wasn't going to win him points here. Being the brother who had abandoned her was more likely to make him a pariah. It was obvious they all liked and respected her, counted her as one of them. And he was glad of that. Even if she never forgave him, he was glad of that.

Cutter's head came up, and he trotted briskly toward the stairs. A moment later Walker heard footsteps coming down. Quinn appeared, tucking a phone into his pocket. He seemed to pause for a split second when he spotted Walker. *Maybe he'll just throw me out*, he thought.

Hayley went to him and gave him a hug. The big man's arm went around her protectively. And as far as Walker could see, the only person here Quinn would think she needed protecting from was him.

But Quinn didn't linger on him. He looked at Hayley. "So?"

"Yes, we have an inquiry, at the least."

Walker frowned. He didn't like that whatever Amy had wanted to discuss with Hayley, it was enough to get Quinn and his foundation involved. He didn't like the idea that her problem was that serious.

Quinn looked at Amy. "Your boss?"

She looked hesitant, even reluctant.

"Might be just as likely we can exonerate him," Quinn said. "We always try, if someone's not certain."

Her expression cleared. "Oh. Yes. I'd much prefer that."

Quinn nodded, then looked at Rafe and Liam. "This is sort of a family thing, if you two have other things to do."

"Hey!" Liam protested. "We're family!"

"Unless," Rafe put in quietly, "Amy would prefer it."

Liam subsided at that, looking a bit embarrassed.

"It's just that there isn't much," Amy said. "I'm not sure it's worth your time."

"Liam was right. Family," Rafe said, "isn't just blood."

The man's gaze flicked to Walker, and Walker read the look as clearly as if the man had spoken. *And blood isn't always family.*

No, there was no welcome for the prodigal brother here. No open arms, no homecoming celebration.

Just the silent suggestion that he shouldn't have come home at all.

Chapter 8

"I'm not at all sure there's anything to this," Amy said.

Quinn smiled at her. "Only one way to find out."

"But I don't want you to…mobilize Foxworth when maybe I'm just being… I mean, I've always thought my boss was a good guy, and…"

"And he may be," Quinn said. "Look, Amy, we're here, we're not busy at the moment, so let us put your mind at ease if nothing else."

"But if he finds out I'm poking around, I could lose my job. They're not that thick on the ground these days."

"That's why you let us do it. If we find anything, he'll never connect you to the search. And you can call it off at any time, if you really want to."

She looked out the expansive windows of the upstairs meeting room. They took up nearly the whole wall, and looked out over the meadow. The meadow where just three months ago Hayley and this man had taken the pledge she knew in her heart would carry them forever together. Still in the throes of winter then, it was now dotted with splashes of color, wildflowers and a stand of daffodils here and there. She wondered if they were naturalized, or if Hayley had planted them in that artful way. It had been such a beautiful day, as if winter itself had blessed their union by holding back for the ceremony.

She'd come to accept that some people—herself apparently included—just didn't have that kind of luck when it came to love. Of course, Hayley had risked her life to win in that game, a situation where she knew she herself would have been a crumpled mass of jelly. But Hayley had always been braver than she.

She managed not to glance at the man who was standing beside the window, looking out toward the evergreens and the big maple where, Hayley had told her, the eagles who had made that amazing salute often perched. He'd shaved, at least. And he was still lean, strong, with that easy grace to his movements that had always entranced her.

And before her mind could career down that unwanted path, she pulled herself back to the matter at hand. Quinn was waiting, probably wondering why on earth his brilliant, decisive wife put up with such a fool for a friend. Or assuming she'd been pondering her decision, and not wasting her thoughts and his time on his scapegrace brother-in-law.

"All right," she said finally.

Quinn nodded, as if she had answered when he'd first asked. He opened a drawer in the big table and took out a legal pad and a pen.

"Give us everything you remember from the documents. Names, dates, addresses, anything. Writing it will help you clarify it in your mind."

"All right," she said again.

"There's only one more thing you need to decide before we dig in here," Quinn said.

"What?"

He looked at Walker, who had turned back from the window. "Do you want him here?"

Amy thought she saw a wince flicker across his face. And for an instant she felt a pang of sympathy. But then the memories flooded back. No, no sympathy here, she told herself firmly.

"I'm not sure it matters," she said, looking back at Quinn. "After all, he'll be gone again soon, I'm sure."

The wince was definite then.

"I'll just go...play with the dog or something," he said.

"I'm still not sure he's decided about you yet," Hayley put in.

"Then I'll go tell him I'm grateful for the benefit of the doubt."

His voice had an edge this time, and that irritated Amy even more. What benefit of the doubt did he think he'd earned?

"You do that," she said.

"Hoping he'll go for my throat?"

"He's a smart dog."

Amy watched him go. She turned back to see Hayley smiling at her. "I'm glad you're here to say everything I'm not saying to him."

Amy smiled back, her mood suddenly lightened. "Better it's me. My bridge with him is a lot less important than yours. And I'll happily burn it down."

"Personally," Quinn drawled out, "I wouldn't want to go up against either one of you."

Amy's smile widened. She was truly starting to like him for more than the simple fact that he loved her best friend.

"Now," Quinn said, his tone brisk, "let's get this started. Then we'll turn it over to Ty. If there's anything to find, he'll find it."

With the feeling she'd started the proverbial snowball down the mountain, Amy picked up the pen and started to write.

"At least you don't appear inclined to chew on me," Walker said to the dog as he brought back the tennis ball yet again. He took it and gave this throw his all, since he was well warmed by now. It sailed across the meadow toward the trees, but the dog caught up with it easily.

"I need a baseball," he muttered as he watched the dog start back. He could throw it farther, make him work harder.

Cutter stopped suddenly, his head turned toward the Foxworth building. He seemed so intent Walker looked himself, wondering what had caught the dog's attention. Nothing had changed that he could see.

Correction, he thought as he turned back in time to see the dog move again. Limping. *Now you've hurt Hayley's dog. Just great.*

He ran out to meet the dog, hesitated, but then knelt to look at the right front paw he seemed to be favoring. He couldn't see anything, no visible injury, but he supposed Cutter could have strained something in his energetic pursuit of that fuzzy yellow sphere.

It didn't seem so bad that the animal couldn't walk at all, which was a relief since he wasn't sure the dog would take kindly to being carried by a man he wasn't too sure about, anyway. But Hayley wasn't going to be happy. With a sigh he wondered if she'd blame him for this, although he wasn't sure what he could have done to stop it other than not indulge the dog at all, when it was clear he played like this often.

He walked beside Cutter as he half hopped his way to the back door, his right paw never touching the ground. Maybe she wouldn't be so mad if he paid the vet bill, he thought as he pulled the door open and followed the dog inside. Maybe if he...

The limp vanished. The moment the door swung closed behind them, that right paw came down and the dog walked forward as if it had never happened.

What the hell...?

Cutter looked back over his shoulder as if to be sure Walker was following. He gave a low woof that, added to the body language, sounded for all the world like "Come on." Feeling a bit like one of the sheep he supposed the dog's brethren herded, he obeyed. The dog scrambled up the stairs at a pace that made Walker think he'd been played beautifully.

He hesitated, knowing the gathering he'd been pointedly excused from was still going on, but he also couldn't deny he wanted to know what was bothering Amy so much she called this meeting. So he followed the dog.

Cutter stopped in front of the three occupants of the room. Once he'd made eye contact with all of them, he looked back at Walker, almost pointedly. Feeling the gaze of the others, Walker thought about explaining, but since he had no idea how, stayed silent. Then the dog came back to him, walked behind him and nudged his legs as if to urge him forward.

"Well," Quinn said, "it seems he's decided you need to be in the loop."

Walker blinked. Stared at the dog, who now crossed the room to a large, cushy dog bed beneath the big windows, and curled up on it with an air of satisfaction. Then he looked back at Quinn, who didn't look overjoyed, but didn't move to throw him out, either. Hayley looked thoughtful, while Amy didn't look at him at all.

Thanks, dog, he thought. He didn't have a clue what had been in that canine mind, but he'd take the result. He couldn't do anything if he wasn't even allowed on the field. And Cutter had fixed that.

Chapter 9

Amy looked at the large flat screen on the wall, at the face of the young man Quinn had introduced as Tyler Hewitt. He'd been talking for a while now, explaining the twists and turns of what he'd done, and while he occasionally lapsed into tech speak she couldn't follow, she got the gist.

Hayley had told her that, like Liam, Tyler had once been on a wrong path, using his tech skills for questionable purposes. But then he'd run afoul of Quinn, and had come out of it converted.

"It sounds," Quinn said now, "like that corporation was formed specifically to shell money out."

"That's the only function it's got as far as I can see. Of course I just started looking."

"Keep going," Quinn said.

"Limits?" the young man asked.

"It can never be traced back to Amy, which means us."

Amy felt a warmth blossom inside her at the easy inclusion. Quinn had never hesitated to take this on, simply because she was Hayley's best friend. What must it be like to be loved like that, by a man like that?

You'll never know, as long as you keep falling for guys like Walker.

She managed not to look at him, knowing it would only confirm the realization she'd ruefully had some time ago, that many of the men she'd dated over the years reminded her of him in some way. The fellow paralegal had had a similar grin, the photographer had hair that fell the same unruly way, the cop she'd truly thought was the one had walked with that same easy, tight-knit grace. After that string, when she'd finally figured it out, she'd taken a long vacation from dating at all. Not that she had guys knocking down her door.

Nevertheless, it had been a jolt when she'd realized what she'd been doing, subconsciously looking for a replacement for Walker.

If you want to replace a Cole male, you'd be better off looking for someone like his father, she had told herself the night that realization had hit. And that had been what she was thinking about when she'd stumbled across that bank data.

"...dig into Leda Limited. The people behind it," Quinn was saying. Amy pulled herself out of her useless musings. They were doing this for her, after all; the least she could do was pay attention. She wasn't thrilled with Walker being here, but it wasn't like he was going to be involved. "Find out where the checks are going. If we can find out who that money's being shelled out to, then maybe we can figure out where it's coming from. And why this way."

"Without a trace," Tyler said, grinning. The screen went blank, the connection severed abruptly, apparently on his end.

"Bit in his teeth," Hayley said with a smile.

Amy hesitated, glanced at Quinn, then back to her friend.

"Out with it," Quinn said mildly.

"I... You didn't tell him why."

"He didn't need to know. And there are reasons for him not to."

"Like not going in with a preconceived idea of what's going on?" Walker said. They all turned to look at him in surprise. "Yeah," he said, his tone wry, "he speaks. He even thinks now and then."

"He's even right now and then, it seems," Quinn said, and Amy thought she saw a flicker of gratification in Walker's eyes at the words.

"It happens."

After a moment Quinn nodded.

"We don't want Ty focused on what we think might be happening. He might miss what really is happening if we're wrong."

That made sense, Amy thought. And Walker had seen it right away. She needed to remember how smart he was.

"Plus," Quinn added, turning to Amy, "it's another layer of protection for you."

She'd still been looking at Walker, so she saw him stiffen at the word *protection*. Of course, Quinn had meant insulating her from the inquiries Ty was making, not actual physical protection. Hadn't he?

Walker shifted his gaze to her, and she had the strangest feeling that he knew she was hiding something. Well, not really hiding, just not telling them about her silly paranoia. But there was no way he could know.

And besides, he'd been right. She didn't want to plant any ideas; she just wanted the truth.

She had known it was real, that what Hayley had told her about Foxworth and what they did was true, simply because it was Hayley. But it was somehow different to see it in action in person. And this was just the investigative end, with Tyler Hewitt. But there was no doubt in her mind they would handle anything more strenuous that came along. Just looking at Quinn and his quiet, solid strength, made her sure of that. After all, she'd seen Quinn put Walker Cole on the ground with one blow. And a satisfying one it had been, almost as satisfying as doing it herself would have been.

She glanced at Quinn, who was making some notes on

the laptop. She had the feeling he would say that in itself made it worth it. He, and all the men of Foxworth, had truly renewed her faith that not all men were selfish, heedless of the damage their own chosen path did to others.

The cell phone on the table near Quinn rang, something that sounded like a marching band in a parade. Startled, Amy glanced at Hayley, who grinned back at her.

"Charlie," she said as Quinn excused himself to answer, rising and walking toward the window. "A marching song seemed appropriate."

Amy laughed.

"Charlie?" Walker asked, reminding Amy that he knew very little about his sister's life now. Oddly, instead of sparking the usual anger, it only made her sad.

"Foxworth's COO, among other things," Hayley answered him evenly. "That things here, and in every other Foxworth facility in the country, run so smoothly is in large part thanks to Charlie."

Amy looked over at Quinn. "He looks quite serious."

Hayley nodded. "We finally have a good line on the mole who nearly got us all killed during the operation with Vicente."

Walker swore, low and harsh. This must be what Quinn had been so serious about earlier. If he'd bought Hayley's earlier assurance that Quinn would never have let her get hurt, he was doubting it now.

"After all this time?" Amy asked.

"Rafe was so antsy about it, Quinn finally sent him to DC a while back to poke at various hornets' nests. One of them turned up the stinkbug we were looking for, so now we know where he works at least."

"But not who he is?"

"Not yet. But Foxworth won't stop until they find him. For all we know, he may have actually gotten others killed. Three federal agents died in the initial hunt for Vicente, and according to one of Rafe's sources, it was because they knew they were coming. That was why Vicente called Foxworth in."

Walker was staring at his sister. Amy guessed he'd had no idea the kind of thing Foxworth occasionally dealt with. For the first time she found herself looking at things from his point of view, how it must feel to come home to find everything so changed and unfamiliar. Whatever his supposed "good reason" was, he was paying a high price for it.

Quinn ended the call and came back to them. He did not look particularly happy. "Another possibility eliminated," he told Hayley. "Waterman was into something, all right, but not this."

Hayley let out a sigh. "I thought we had him this time."

"So did I. He had all the signs. But turns out he was only colluding with a senator who has some…unacceptable appetites he apparently shares. They were consumers only."

"How did Charlie find that out?"

Quinn gave a half shrug. "You know Charlie. Connections. Teague's info ended up with someone who knows someone who knows someone who knows the senator has a predilection for little boys."

"Nice," Walker muttered, but he was shaking his head in shock, probably at the ease with which both his sister and her husband tossed around stories from the highest halls of power.

Amy grimaced. "No wonder I try to avoid the news these days."

"We'll find him," Quinn said. "And in the meantime, the information on the senator and his buddy has been passed along to someone who isn't afraid of the guy, who won't let it be buried."

"I have faith in Charlie's connections," Hayley said with a smile.

"I have faith in Liam's chili," Quinn said prosaically. The moment he spoke Amy became aware she had been smelling something appetite-whetting for a little while now.

"You know he won't let us eat it yet," Hayley said.

"I know, I know, too green," Quinn said, but he headed for the stairs anyway.

"Green chili?" Walker asked.

Hayley laughed. "Not color-wise. Too young. He says it has to mingle for at least a day before it's edible. But we usually steal some, anyway, because it's still good. But tomorrow it will be amazing."

"Do you guys cook here a lot?"

"Sometimes," she said. "Wait until you have Quinn's spicy chicken."

"Oh, my God," Amy said, "he cooks, too?"

"They all do. Although Teague runs more to just grilling."

"And—I'm almost afraid to ask—Rafe?"

Hayley grinned. "Big, bad, scary Rafe makes the best, fluffiest omelets known to man. Not to mention a wicked homemade barbecue sauce that would make roadkill taste good."

That thought was enough to make Amy both laugh and gag slightly.

"Ty, on the other hand, does not cook. But he should be back with something soon," Hayley said.

Amy lifted a brow. "So quick?"

"He's not only good, he's fast. But in the meantime, let's go steal some chili," Hayley said.

As they headed down the stairs, the tempting aroma getting stronger, Amy again had the wistful feeling that this, this feeling of doing good work with good people, was what was missing in her life.

And by the time they were downstairs, she had herself convinced that that was even more important than what she thought she'd been missing. What she'd been thinking about since last night, the absence of any kind of steady relationship in her life.

And that train of thought had, she told herself, nothing to do with the presence of Walker Cole.

Chapter 10

"So, have you guys ever made a mistake?" Walker asked after he swallowed the last mouthful of chili that he couldn't really believe would be better by tomorrow, as the young Texan indeed had insisted.

"We may have made one today," Quinn said, looking at him rather pointedly.

Walker met the intense gaze steadily, although it took more nerve than he would ever have expected to stare down his new brother-in-law.

"You may have actually started that one last night," he said, brushing a finger over the sore spot on his jaw. He saw Quinn's eyes narrow, as if he hadn't expected that.

Good.

He'd learned a great deal in the past five years about people and how to read them. You tended to pay attention when your life depended on it. Quinn didn't like him being here in his domain.

Quinn didn't like him, period.

The irony of it all was that if it were someone else, and he was standing on the outside watching, he'd be cheering Quinn Foxworth for it. If it were someone else, he himself would be ready to do worse than deck the man who had so hurt his little sister.

But it wasn't someone else. It was him.

The way things stood, he realized his relationship with

Hayley would never be the same. That hurt more than anything. And he knew he would never have Quinn's liking.

But he would have his respect. Even if it took that knock-down, drag-out battle. He'd taken that first hit, because he had it coming. Probably more, to be honest. But he wasn't about to let his brother-in-law pound on him, no matter how much he might deserve it. He'd learned a lot of ways to fight in the past five years, and as he held Quinn's assessing gaze, he thought he wouldn't be averse to using some of them.

And you'd have to, with this guy.

And again he was in that bitterly ironic position of being glad his sister had found a man who wanted to beat him up at best, kick him out of her life forever at worst.

"Everybody makes mistakes," Hayley said. She said it without any undertone, so he didn't think it was aimed specifically at him, just an answer to his question.

"Some more than others," Liam said, but he seemed to be contemplating the taste of the chili more than anything. Then he shot Walker a sideways glance that told him the Texan was just as aware of his huge mistakes as the others.

"We've made them," Rafe said, leaning back in his chair and eyeing Walker with the same sort of intensity. And even though it was almost as threatening as Quinn's steady gaze, he found himself appreciating this, too, and laughed inwardly at himself at landing in this sea of irony, liking that his sister had people around her who would fight for her, even if it meant the one they'd like to put in the dirt was him. "But most times we fix them."

At least he hadn't said bury them, Walker thought. And the word didn't seem like an exaggeration with this man. With that instinct honed during too much time with men the opposite of these, men with evil intent, he sensed this man might be the deadliest of all of them.

"And not many since ol' Cutter showed up," Liam added.

The dog, who had been dozing in a cushy bed near the fireplace, lifted his head at the sound of his name. He seemed to study them for a moment, then put his head back down and closed his eyes. He either was oblivious of the undercurrents in the room, or trusted his people to handle them, Walker thought.

Hayley laughed and the others smiled. "He does do a good job of picking them, doesn't he?"

"Picking them?"

She explained the cases Cutter had led them to. It seemed beyond unbelievable, yet they were all adding bits, as if the stories were all familiar and accepted. Walker wondered if this was part of it, if they were playing some kind of purposeful game with him. For an instant he risked a glance at the one person he'd been trying to avoid looking at. Amy.

He wasn't sure why her disdain stung more than anyone's. Hayley was bad enough, but she, being who she was and his sister, seemed to be reserving judgment at least a little.

But not Amy. She'd made herself crystal clear from the first moment she'd laid eyes on him. She would never, ever forgive him for what he'd done to the woman who was like a sister to her.

Why should she? She's been a better sister than you've been a brother, blood or no.

Amy seemed to feel his gaze, and looked at him. A chill went through him at the coldness of it. Little Amy had grown into a tough cookie, as his mother used to say.

His mother.

It hit him again, hard, and he had to look away as the pain of loss swamped him. He'd learned to hide every emotion the hard way, but this one was too raw, too deep, too personal.

"Walker?" Hayley said it as if she cared. Or maybe it was just curiosity.

He stood up abruptly. And made himself look at his sister. "Mom's been gone two years for you," he said, his voice rough with the effort not to say it even as the words tumbled out, "but for me it's been two days."

He walked out the back door before he let anything more slip.

"What the hell did that mean?" Quinn muttered.

"I don't know," Hayley said, staring after her brother.

Amy looked at the others, saw each one registering a trace of the puzzlement she was feeling.

"Two days?" Quinn said.

Hayley was shaking her head. "I don't understand."

"That makes no sense," Amy said.

"Not with what we know," Rafe said.

Was he implying there were things they didn't know? Of course there were, but things that would make sense of that odd statement, those words Walker had clearly fought letting out at all?

As if she needed something to do, Hayley got up, went to the kitchen and began to clean up the dishes. Amy flicked a glance at Quinn, whose expression was troubled, and at his slight nod followed her. Her mind was racing, down what she suspected were mostly blind alleys.

She started to help with the cleanup. After a moment she spoke the only thing she'd been able to think of.

"Maybe…maybe he just didn't really believe it until he got here."

Hayley paused. "You mean maybe he had to be here where she was, or in her house?"

"I don't know," Amy said. She hesitated; then, still trying to figure out what Walker had meant, quietly asked Hayley something she'd always meant to. "With all this at your beck and call, as it were, why didn't you ever turn it on your brother?"

"Hunt him down, you mean?"

Amy nodded.

"Thought about it. And Quinn would have done it. I think he would have liked to, so he could have delivered that punch sooner. But every time I got close, I'd get some silly text from him, saying pretty much nothing, but letting me know he was alive at least."

"How thoughtful," Amy said sourly.

"I know, I know. And I still worried, but he's been for the most part gone since he graduated high school, so I'm used to it. Sure, he'd drop in now and then but... Besides, what was I going to do or say when we found him? Walker made his own choices. And he says he had a good reason."

"And you accept that?"

"All I know is the Walker I grew up with was never heartless or cruel. So I can only hope that the reason he can't tell me is good enough." Hayley in turn gestured around them, at the Foxworth surroundings. "I have learned, since I've been here, that there are many reasons for many things that I never would have thought of before."

Amy didn't answer. For some reason all she could think of was that look on Walker's face that had made her think of all this from his side. And suddenly she needed to know.

She put down the bowl she'd just dried and announced, loudly enough that Quinn looked at her, "Why don't I just go ask him what he meant?"

She was nervous about all this, now that she'd seen the scope and capabilities of Foxworth. She had the feeling she truly had started that snowball down the mountain, and she feared she might regret it.

She knew she was nervous because even talking to Walker seemed a good distraction.

Plus she was angry with herself at the effort it had taken not to look at Walker across the table.

She hated him, didn't she? It should have been easy. And yet it seemed like every few seconds she'd had to stop herself from stealing a glance. And even when she managed not to look at him, images filled her mind, as if sparked by his very presence. Images from long-ago childish daydreams of some fantasy day when Walker Cole would look at her and see something other than his sister's shy, garishly haired best friend.

And like most childhood fantasies, when she'd finally gotten that day she'd dreamed of, she hadn't wanted it. Walker had been truly stunned when he'd finally recognized her last night, and it had meant nothing to her. In fact, it had even irritated her more.

Everything about him irritated her more.

She stood up.

"Amy," Hayley began.

She smiled rather tightly at her. "My bridge, remember. Don't worry, I won't kill him. Yet."

She saw Quinn's rather sardonic lift of a brow. "Deadlier than the male," he quoted, but she thought she saw approval there. She turned on her heel and followed the man who'd once been the boy she adored.

She found him in the meadow, staring out at the trees. She looked, thought she saw something perched in one of the upper branches of the maple tree. One of the eagles, maybe? The tree was leafing out for spring, and it was hard to tell. "There's a lovely video of the wedding, including the eagles. You should watch it."

He hadn't looked when she'd come up behind him, but he didn't jump when she spoke. Clearly he'd known she was there.

"Since that's as close as I'll ever get?" he suggested with a sideways glance.

"Actually, I was only thinking of how beautiful it was."

He looked back at the meadow. "I'll bet it was," he said almost wistfully. He glanced at her again. "I'll bet you were beautiful."

There had been a time when she would have killed for a comment like that from Walker Cole.

She wanted to say, "You could have seen for yourself," but something, she wasn't sure what, stopped her. But instead, she asked what she'd originally come out here for.

"What did you mean, for you it's been two days?"

The glance he shot her then was sharper, more assessing. Was he deciding what to tell her? Or whether to answer at all? She had the oddest feeling his mind had suddenly kicked into high gear, and he was trying to decide just what and how much to say. If anything.

And she wondered why it was apparently such a complex decision. He'd said it, after all. But perhaps he hadn't meant to.

She waited, more than willing to let the pressure of silence come to bear. And the silence spun out until she thought he was going to just leave it hanging there. But finally, he answered her. Sort of.

"I can't tell you why, but that's when I found out."

She stared at him. "What?"

He grimaced. "I knew you wouldn't just accept that."

"Are you saying you actually only found out about your mother two days ago?"

It was ridiculous. Absurd. His mother had become ill five years ago, and had died over two years ago. She knew personally that Hayley had tried many times to reach him before finally giving up. And yet he was saying he'd only learned about it two days ago?

"Yes. And the wedding."

Even more ridiculous. "But you texted her. That stupid, one-word text."

He blinked. "What?"

"I mean, really, Walker, your only sister, your only living family, gets married and the best you can do is a one-word text saying congratulations?"

He looked stunned, bewildered, in fact, almost as if he'd truly forgotten, even though it had only been a few months ago. Then he frowned, and she could almost feel his mind racing.

"I…"

"Amy?" Hayley's voice came from the doorway. "Come on in. Ty's back with what he's found so far."

Efficient, she thought, at the same time noticing that Hayley didn't invite her brother.

She walked away and left him standing there. As he deserved, she thought, and put him out of her mind.

Chapter 11

For a moment, Walker stayed where he was. His emotions had been in overdrive since the moment he'd arrived—if they hadn't, he wouldn't have slipped up like that—and he needed a moment to process.

He'd known he wouldn't be welcome anywhere here, and he'd come anyway. Because somewhere, deep down, he'd known he had to make peace with this, his old life, before he could move on. He hadn't come here expecting a miracle, which was what forgiveness would be. He'd given up on those long ago. But if he didn't at least try, it would hang over him for the rest of his life. And that life was going to be miserable enough without adding that to it.

And once more it went to war inside him, the certainty that he'd done the right thing versus what it had cost him.

I wonder how Cabrero and the other guys who do it for a living survive?

He fought down the old wish. It was useless, wishing he had never gotten sucked up into it. He had been; he'd been the wrong person in the right place at the right time. And he believed—he had to believe—Cabrero when he said lives had been saved thanks to him. Lots of them. Because that was the only way he could live with essentially the loss of his own.

Determined to shake himself out of pointless rumination, he followed Amy back inside.

"…the only outgo."

The voice was coming from a young man whose image was on the flat screen on the wall over the fireplace.

"Hold on for a second, Ty," Quinn said, apparently instantly aware he'd come in. He looked at Amy. "Want him out?" Quinn sounded as if he'd relish making that happen.

She barely flicked Walker a glance. "He's irrelevant."

Quinn turned back to the business at hand, obviously taking her at her word. He was indeed irrelevant. She hadn't just grown teeth, she'd grown fangs, Walker thought with an inward grimace.

"So every transfer into that offshore account was for just under ten thousand?" Quinn asked.

"Exactly," the guy with the spiky hair and small patch of beard under his lip said. "Just enough to avoid the reporting requirement." His brows rose exaggeratedly. "Screams shaky, don't it?"

"Structured deposits do," Quinn agreed. "Do we know yet who the principal on that fictitious business is?"

"Still tunneling on that." The young man shifted his gaze, and even through the monitor Walker saw the appreciation in his expression as he looked at Amy, who was sitting on the couch next to Hayley, watching the screen intently. "Going in cloaked takes a bit longer," the young man explained to her. "But you'll never be connected to it."

Instincts Walker had never had when he'd last been home were firing. He'd learned that, too, how to put small pieces together, and how eventually, if you survived long enough, the small pieces made the big picture. And sometimes those pictures were horrible, even bloody, mosaics.

He didn't like these pieces.

Amy had a problem.

It apparently involved her boss.

And a bank account he'd set up to make payments to a fictitious company.

An offshore bank account.

And Amy didn't want to be connected to Foxworth's digging.

No, he didn't like the sound of it. He'd seen too much of life's dark side now to shrug this off as nothing.

He took advantage of her being focused on the monitor to study her for a moment. Hayley had gone from cute to pretty to beautiful, but Amy had started out on an entirely different playing field. And not just in looks but in temperament and background. Which made the transformation all the more amazing. He wondered if that shy little girl was still in there somewhere, if you ever really got over the scars of being an odd one out as a child.

He was so lost in his thoughts he was almost startled when the screen went dark.

"He'll find whoever's behind that fake name," Quinn was saying to Amy. "Then we'll have a better idea of what we're dealing with."

Amy looked troubled. "But you think there is something?"

"There could be an innocent explanation. But it is suspicious."

"And then some," Walker said. "That would take a lot of explaining."

Amy glanced at him, and to his surprise there was no anger in her expression. He doubted she'd changed her mind about him, but at least the active dislike had ebbed. Or maybe this was just more important to her.

"Enough to keep going?" she asked Quinn.

Quinn didn't hesitate. "Yes."

"Unless you want to stop," Hayley put in. "It's still up to you. We pull the plug anytime you say so."

Amy shook her head. "What next?"

"We see what else Ty turns up," Quinn said.

"And keep Amy out of it, right?" Walker asked. "If this is what it looks like, it could get ugly."

Quinn raised an eyebrow at him. "Without saying."

"Good."

He glanced at Amy to find her staring at him. Was she really so surprised that her safety was a concern to him? Or had she just not thought of herself being in danger as a result of what she'd discovered? Either way, she'd best take it seriously.

Or maybe he would.

"Ugly?" she said after a moment.

"Wherever that kind of money is getting tossed around, there's always the potential," Walker said.

"He's not wrong," Quinn said, studying his brother-in-law with renewed interest.

If you only knew, Walker thought.

"Maybe I can help," he suggested.

Quinn made a sound that sounded like he was suppressing a snort. "I wouldn't hire you as janitor."

Walker looked at him, forcing his face to show no emotion, but his voice was full of a bleakness even he could hear when he said quietly, "Too bad. From you, that's a job I might take."

Quinn drew back slightly, studying him yet again. But after a moment he said only, "I'm thinking we may fire up Wilbur and head south."

Amy blinked. "Wilbur?"

Hayley grinned. "His precious airplane. Liam named it."

Amy laughed.

"It gets worse," Quinn said glumly. "He named the helicopter Igor."

"Wright and…Sikorsky?" Walker guessed.

"Exactly," Hayley said. The smile she gave him was still a bit impersonal, but he'd take it gratefully.

Amy was still laughing. It was a great sound; he liked it. He liked it too much. "He makes a habit of naming things, I gather?"

Yes, she sounded altogether too amused, Walker thought.

"That cute Texas boy..."

Well, why shouldn't she be amused? And attracted, if it came to that. The guy was a bit young, but what did that matter? He realized he had assumed, since she wore no ring, that she wasn't married, but that wasn't always a certainty. And she could be with somebody, even if they hadn't tied the knot yet.

He was glad no one was looking at him. He was sure his shock at the odd sensation of being punched again, this time in the stomach, must show. He looked at her again. She was still smiling, and it nearly took his breath away.

He shook it off. Or tried to. It took him a moment of staring out the window. Somehow picturing the wedding ceremony he'd missed steadied him. That was the wedding he should be thinking about. He had too much to atone for here to let…whatever this was get in the way.

"…hate to make you go all the way to LA on some skimpy information," Amy was saying when he tuned back in.

Hayley glanced at Quinn. "It will give him a chance to break out his second favorite toy."

"The plane is second?" Amy asked.

"First is the helicopter," Quinn said with a look at his wife that seemed to heat the air in the room a couple of degrees. "Funny, it used to be the other way around."

It didn't take much of a jump to connect that look to the story she'd told on the way here, that the helicopter had been how they'd met.

"Some things change," Hayley said quietly, looking back at Quinn with that same heat. It was a little disconcerting to see his little sister look at a man like that, but it told him a great deal.

"And some things," Quinn replied just as quietly, "never, ever change."

It was no sappy declaration of love with flowery words, but it was the most intense affirmation he'd ever seen.

He heard a tiny sigh and looked at Amy. She was also watching Quinn and Hayley. She was wearing a different smile, a smile of happiness for her friend, but touched with what looked like a bit of wistfulness. But not a trace of envy, he noted. Amy loved Hayley too much for that, and there wasn't a jealous bone in her; he was sure of that.

Of course, not so long ago he would have said he was sure she never got spitting mad, either. Or outspoken. Or would have had the nerve to confront someone the way she had him. So clearly he needed to reassess his assumptions about Amy Clark. Especially the ones that had kept her, in his mind, in the category of his sister's shy, studious, quiet, carrot-topped best friend.

"...can do some other things down there, too," Quinn was saying, and Walker realized he'd tuned out again. Crazy, since not so long ago doing that could have gotten him killed. "Charlie finally settled on a location for the southwest office. I should check it out."

"You're moving?" Walker asked, startled. He hadn't thought Hayley would ever leave her beloved Northwest.

Quinn looked at him. His gaze wasn't warm, but it wasn't quite as contemptuous as it had been, either. "No," he said after a moment. "Just opening a new branch."

"The fifth," Hayley added proudly. "We'll have one in every region in the country when it's done and staffed."

Walker stared. Hayley had said they were headquartered in Saint Louis, and that's where Charlie and Tyler were, but he'd had no idea Foxworth was that big. "And they all do the same thing?"

"Yes." Quinn obviously didn't feel the need to expand.

"How you'd end up in this one?"

Quinn flicked another glance at Hayley and smiled that smile again. "More luck than I deserved."

"After the Middle East," Hayley said, apparently more willing to explain, "I think he wanted the coolest, greenest place he could find. And Alaska was a bit too far from everything. Thankfully," she added as she returned that smile to her husband. If nothing else, Walker thought, he could rest easy on that count. His little sister would be well taken care of. And about time, since he surely hadn't been doing it.

No choice, no choice, no choice...

The old mantra that had somehow gotten him through echoed in his mind. But sometimes, no matter how often he told himself he'd done the right thing, he couldn't quite make himself believe it. Couldn't stop that other part of his brain from pointing out that the right choice was to take care of your own, and leave the big-picture stuff to those trained for that kind of thing. People like Cabrero.

Or Quinn Foxworth. Because he had no doubt his new brother-in-law was one of those. There was something about his assessing look, something even more obvious when he was focused on something distant, that he was seeing much, much more than what was immediately in view.

And if it had been the other way around, if Quinn had happened into the mess Walker had stumbled onto, he would have made the same choice. Walker was sure of that, too. Oh, he would have done it much better, no doubt, and could have skipped the intensive training because he'd already had it, but he would have done it.

Of course, he never would have ended up in the same position, at least not as he looked now. He was too obviously a straight arrow. None of the brothers would have let him get anywhere close, whereas Walker looked like just the kind of footloose, rootless guy who fit right in. The kind they looked for, to use and discard. Which was what had landed him in that mess to begin with.

Quinn was looking at him again, with that faintly curious expression. He'd come here hoping to regain at least some piece of the old loving relationship with his sister. But now he realized he wanted something else, too. He would like very much to have this man's respect, and for more than just taking a punch. And he knew instinctively that if Quinn knew the truth, he might just get that respect.

And he'd get that right after Hayley forgave him. Meaning never.

Chapter 12

"I wish you could have known the old Walker," Amy said.

Quinn, who had just called someone about readying the airplane, put his phone back in his pocket and leaned against the island of the small kitchen, where he'd gone to top off his coffee. He gestured at her mug with the pot, but she shook her head. She was already wound up enough; she didn't need to pour the fuel of too much caffeine on top of it.

"Their dad dying really devastated them all. But especially Walker."

"And you, too," Quinn said softly. She gave him a startled look. "Don't worry, she didn't tell me anything. She wouldn't. But it wasn't hard to guess he was the father you wished you'd had."

"He was," she agreed. "If it wasn't for him, I might have grown up thinking all men were like my father." She clasped her hands around the fading warmth of the mug she held. "And I thought Walker was just like him. He *was* just like him, until it happened. And then he just…left."

"Hayley said he walked away from a baseball scholarship, that he'd been good enough he had a shot at turning pro."

Amy nodded. "And he loved it. Or I thought he did. But the minute he graduated high school he took off. Said he couldn't stay here another minute." She grimaced; the coffee had just crossed the line into too cool to enjoy. She set the mug down. "We never knew where he'd call from next."

"But he did call."

"Yes. Regularly, at first. And came back to see Hayley every year on her birthday, and the occasional holiday. But then he stopped. Stopped even calling. Started just texting. Right when Hayley needed him most, when their mom was diagnosed."

"He abandoned you, too."

She waved a hand as if brushing away a persistent gnat. "I was just a silly schoolgirl with a crush. Which died pretty darn quick when I saw how much Hayley was hurting. What good reason could make up for that?"

Quinn frowned. "Good reason?"

She lifted a shoulder in a rather dismissive half shrug. "He insists there is one. But that he can't tell us what it was."

"Can't? Or won't?"

"Good question," Amy said. Quinn looked thoughtful, as if he were pondering possibilities.

She knew the feeling.

"She's...changed."

To Walker that seemed safe enough, since it was undeniably true. Amy had changed. A lot.

"Only on the outside." Hayley watched Cutter as he investigated the large field across from the bench overlooking the sound. The leash she carried was more for anyone else they came across, she'd said. He was a perfect gentleman and utterly reliable, but he wasn't small; he was very intense, and some people got nervous.

"She's changed at least a little on the inside." His mouth quirked. "She used to like me."

"She used to adore you," Hayley corrected. "And she was heartbroken when you left."

He shifted uncomfortably on the bench. They'd walked down here after they'd found themselves up and looking for coffee early on this Sunday morning. He'd half expected Quinn to stop them, but at a look from Hayley he'd backed off. Walker was thankful for that. Now that she seemed willing, he'd wanted to talk to her away from the house and the chance of interruption by Quinn or Amy. Especially Amy.

"She was thirteen," he said.

"And no one can get more heartbroken than a thirteen-year-old girl over her first crush."

He sighed. "I never knew it was that bad."

"What did you expect? You were her hero, after you got the mean girls to leave her alone." Hayley looked away. "And I was so proud of my big brother."

She said it so regretfully his stomach knotted up. "But you're not anymore."

To her credit, he thought, she didn't say, "What's to be proud of?"

"I just don't understand you anymore," she said instead.

"Neither do I," he muttered.

She looked at him then. Studied him for a moment. Cutter, as if sensing her mood, abandoned whatever it was he'd been sniffing at in the field and came back to them. She reached out and scratched behind his right ear as she said, "You *could* just explain. But you won't."

"Or can't."

"That's a rather minute difference."

"It's the difference between choice, and none."

This time she turned to look him straight on. "Do you remember Dad's funeral?"

"I remember every second of that day." The ceremony, the long parade of vehicles and police motorcycles, the mournful bagpipes—he remembered it all.

"Do you remember what Captain Malone said to you?"

Like acid etched it into my brain. "'See to your mother and sister, boy. It's your job now.'"

"And you swore you would."

"I know."

"You were there for my high school graduation. Then college. Mom's fiftieth birthday. And I always knew if I needed you for something else, you'd come home. Because you loved me."

"Yes."

"What happened, Walker? Why did it change?"

"It didn't."

"But you didn't come."

And there they were again. The question she had every right to ask and get that honest answer. Every right.

For an instant he hovered on the verge. Hayley could keep a secret, he knew that. Hadn't she held her peace when she'd caught him sneaking back into the house after that ill-advised joyride? She'd even washed the mud off Dad's car, under the guise of watering the flower bed, before he'd had a chance to. And more importantly before Dad saw it. Even when confronted—idiot kid that he'd been, he hadn't realized their father would notice the mileage—she hadn't given him up. He'd done it himself.

When Dad had told him his punishment was going to be pushing back the day he could get his own much-coveted driver's license by six months, he'd let out a shocked groan of protest.

"Quiet," his father had said sternly. "It would be a year except that you didn't let your sister take the heat. You manned up. I'm proud of you for that."

You wouldn't be proud now, Dad. I really let her down.

"Tell me something," Hayley said, and he wondered how long he'd been sitting there silently, lost in the memories.

"I told you I can't…"

"I don't mean about why. Not directly, anyway."

"What, then?"

"You say it's a good reason."

"Yes."

"Then why is it eating you alive?"

His sister had lost none of her smarts, or her perceptiveness in the past five years. He turned it over again in his mind, even though he knew it was pointless. He'd tried every way he could think of to explain, but couldn't come up with one that didn't violate his promise. And Cabrero's explanation of what could happen if he talked was always uppermost in his mind. And if it wasn't, the man reminded him each time he'd called to see how he was doing.

At last he answered her in the only way he could. "Because I love you and I can't tell you the one thing that might make you love me back again."

Hayley drew in an audible breath. "I never stopped loving you, Walker. I'm just…disappointed. That you don't seem to be who I thought you were."

His stomach churned. He wasn't sure he wouldn't have preferred she just agree she hated him. His jaw clenched, and he closed his eyes, feeling the sting of moisture. After all he'd been through in the past five years, he was going to break down now and cry in front of his little sister? Like hell.

He felt a touch on his knee, and his eyes snapped open. He found himself staring into a pair of dark eyes flecked with amber.

Cutter.

The dog had silently gotten up from Hayley's side and come to sit in front of him. It was his chin he'd felt, now resting atop his knee.

There was something compelling about that canine gaze, and suddenly the tales he'd heard from the others of Foxworth didn't seem so crazy.

What was crazy was how he inexplicably felt…not better, really, but calmer. Slowly, still caught by that stare, he

She turned around, saw in her face that Hayley had heard enough.

"Amy, please, it's all right. Set it aside, for now at least. Let's focus on your situation."

"All right," she said. Somehow it was easier to agree after that glimpse of what he was hiding.

"Thank you," Hayley said. "Now I've got to get Cutter's things together."

"He's coming, too?" Amy asked.

"Of course," Hayley said. "He's one of the team. Sometimes the most important one."

Amy smiled, but her friend looked utterly serious as she left them and walked into the kitchen.

She looked back at Walker, aware Hayley hadn't directly acknowledged his presence.

"You know," she said softly, "if you let her see a bit of that hurt, it might start to change her mind."

He didn't try to deny what she'd seen, and she felt a grudging respect for that.

"I don't want to…manipulate her with emotion."

Amy laughed at that. "Women are all about emotion. Besides, it's letting her see *your* emotion I'm talking about, not you playing with hers."

His brow furrowed. "Why so generous all of a sudden?"

"I'm always generous," she said airily, rather guiltily pleased that she had him puzzled. "And I promised Amy."

"So just like that, you put down your weapons?"

"Oh, I haven't put them down. I've just holstered them. For the moment."

For an instant she thought she saw his mouth quirk, almost as if he were trying not to smile.

Hayley came back into the room, a small tote bag in one hand. She held a zip-top Baggie in the other that appeared to be full of peeled baby carrots.

"Carrots?"

Hayley laughed. "They're his favorite treat. Crunchy."

"Um…dog biscuits?" Amy suggested.

"He likes them, too, but these he asks for."

Walker finally spoke. "Asks for?"

Amy watched as Hayley looked at her brother. And once more she spoke to him as if he were a casual acquaintance, not her closest and only remaining blood relative. "Yes. He has a way of making it quite clear. That and many other things."

Her expression changed somehow, and Amy thought she saw a trace of the same kind of pain she'd seen in Walker's eyes.

"Like this morning, at the bench."

Silence spun out as brother and sister looked at each other. Amy felt as if she should go, leaving them alone. No matter how angry she was with Walker, she knew he was right; it was Hayley's decision to make.

And if Hayley decided to let him back into her life, then he was going to be back in hers, as well. The possibility hadn't really occurred to her until now, which she supposed was a measure of how stunned she'd been when he'd turned up on the doorstep, literally.

Walker broke first. He lowered his gaze, and Amy saw the tightness of his jaw. Perhaps he'd taken her suggestion, and let his sister see a bit of that black pain. Hayley's expression had certainly softened.

"So," she said, now that the moment had passed, "where is the furry one?"

It took a moment for Hayley to refocus. "Quinn took him out for a fetch session. He's going to be cooped up in the plane for a while, so he needs to work off some energy now. They should be back momentarily."

On the words the back door opened. Amy heard Quinn say something, and then Cutter appeared in the doorway. He paused there, seeming to study the three of them, looking from one to the other as if assessing. Seemingly satisfied with whatever he saw or sensed, he went to Hayley, nosed the bag of carrots, then trotted over to his dog bed and picked up what appeared to be a fresh chew bone. Then he came back and sat next to Walker's duffel, as if to indicate he, too, was packed and ready to go.

Amy shook her head. "I know you've said he communicates, but it still amazes me."

"Us, too, sometimes still," Hayley said.

"Just talked to Mick at the airport. Plane'll be ready by the time we get there," Quinn said. "We're going into Orange County, since that's where the new office is and I need to check it out, anyway. Charlie will have a car waiting for us."

Amy stared at him. "I didn't expect you to get all of Foxworth involved."

Quinn smiled at her. "You get one of us, you get all of us. Besides, I think Charlie's bored. Only two or three crises going on."

Amy, who had met the legendary Charlie at the wedding, didn't find that at all hard to believe. And it warmed her. She'd been afraid she might lose Hayley, at least a little bit, when she found Quinn. But instead, she found she had gained more, an expanded family of sorts, who only needed to know she was important to Hayley to make her important to them. It was an amazing feeling for someone who had grown up so uncertainly.

While Walker had merely gained more people angry at him, for Hayley's sake. And while her brain said he'd earned that and more, her heart couldn't help remembering those moments of pure, unadulterated pain.

She hadn't thought about it until they headed out to Quinn's SUV, but obviously she was going to end up sitting in the backseat with Walker. Unless she sat in the cargo area with the dog. For a moment she actually considered the idea, thinking she'd find Cutter much less disturbing.

But she'd promised Hayley to set it aside, and so she

climbed into the backseat with every appearance of unconcern. She plopped her big purse on the seat between them. If he noticed or thought anything of the makeshift barrier, it didn't show as he settled in on the other side.

And she was not going to obsess about it, or him. She had other things to think about, a lot more important than Walker Cole. Like whether her boss was not just crooked but criminal.

Chapter 14

"Nice," Walker said with a low whistle.

Normally she would have made some teasing observation about boys and their toys, but Amy couldn't deny this was a very pretty airplane. From here on the ground it seemed large to her, although it would be dwarfed by the commercial jet she'd flown in on. But she liked the look of it, and the way the ribbons of dark and light blue flowed over the sleek white body from the bottom up to the tail, sweeping along as if in the wind. Even on this damp, rainy day the plane looked as if it was eager to fly.

"Yes," Quinn said. He was still acting cool toward Walker, but even so apparently couldn't resist this urge. "She's different in light aviation. A prop plane with a pressurized cabin."

"Not quite the jet you wanted," Hayley said, clearly teasing, "but she does nicely. Although I'm surprised you haven't pushed for a seaplane, too. They're so common here."

"The thought has occurred," he admitted with a grin.

Amy watched the man who had been fueling the plane detach the big hose, fiddle with what she supposed was the airplane equivalent of a gas cap, then give a thumbs-up to Quinn and start reeling the hose back onto the fueling truck.

She glanced into the open hangar the plane had clearly been pulled out of, probably by the small tractor she saw sitting to one side. Across the back was a row of what looked like storage rooms or maybe offices, the one in the corner having windows that looked out into the main part of the hangar.

"For emergencies," Hayley explained when she saw where she was looking. "We could run Foxworth out of here if we had to."

"Have you ever?"

"No. But Quinn believes in being prepared for anything."

"Saves a lot of worry," Quinn said. "You want to get them settled in while I do the preflight?"

"Or I could do the preflight," Hayley suggested.

"Yes," Quinn said agreeably.

Amy had heard every step of Hayley's progress toward her own pilot's license, so she wasn't surprised by this. Walker, on the other hand, seemed a bit startled.

Amazing how people's lives go on, even without you.

On the heels of that uncharitable thought, the memory of what she'd seen in his eyes came back once more, and she felt a qualm. Somehow that moment had changed everything, and she found herself wondering yet again where he'd been, what he'd been doing that had done that to the carefree boy she remembered. Only now, it was without malice.

"I'll get them settled, cap'n," Hayley said with a grin.

With an effort, Amy was able to enjoy the novelty of it all as the clamshell door in the side of the plane opened. Cutter, clearly familiar with this, went up the steps without hesitation, then Hayley led them after him into the surprisingly spacious cabin.

Amy glanced forward into the cockpit, where the array of electronics and screens looked beyond intimidating.

"So how are the lessons going?" she asked.

"Good," Hayley said. "Not much longer."

"You're really learning to fly this thing?" Walker asked.

His sister arched an eyebrow at him. "Think I can't?"

"Never said that. It just looks pretty daunting. To anyone," he added.

Hayley let it go. "Pick a seat," she said.

In response, Cutter jumped up into one of the comfortable-looking seats, then turned to neatly face front. Amy and Walker both laughed in the same moment.

"He sits there for takeoff, so we can strap him in. After that he gets the run of the cabin."

"Taught him to fly yet?" Walker asked drily.

"He could probably learn," Hayley said with a ruffle of the dog's fur.

Amy took the seat opposite the dog and tried to focus. She still had great trouble believing Marcus Rockwell could be involved in something sketchy. Anything sketchy. She would have sworn he wasn't that kind of attorney, that kind of man. And if she was wrong, which it was starting to appear she was, then she would have to question her own competence, both in judging people and dealing with them.

But she still couldn't quite make herself believe it. She...

"Amy?"

Hayley's voice broke through, and clearly she'd said something before that Amy had completely missed.

"Sorry," she said. "I was just thinking."

"We'll figure this out," Hayley promised.

"I don't know whether to hope we do or not."

Hayley sat in the seat beside her. "You're really torn, aren't you?"

"Yes." She let out a compressed breath. "Remember when I found out last year my father had finally drunk himself to death?"

"Of course," Hayley said quietly.

"My boss found out, probably because I was so scattered. He called me into his office, and I thought I was in trouble because I'd messed up a couple of things, including an important procedural motion. Instead, he told me about his own father being an alcoholic, and how it had affected his whole life. And that when he died, he was angry at himself for feeling anything."

She paused, starting to wish she hadn't begun this. She wasn't sure she wanted Walker to hear it. But she was in it now, so she kept going.

"That was exactly how I was feeling. I had expected, when the inevitable happened, that I wouldn't feel a thing. That I'd just shrug and move on. My father had never really been a part of my life, so why would it matter?"

"And yet you were grieving," Hayley said, reaching out to gently put a hand over hers.

"Yes. And he explained it. That I was grieving the loss of what now would never be. It made so much sense."

"Sounds like the voice of someone who's really been there," Walker said, his voice quiet.

"A very kind and understanding someone," Hayley added, zeroing in on the crux of it as she so often did.

"Yes," Amy agreed. "He didn't have to do it, but he did. And he never got upset over my mistakes that entire month. In fact, he fixed the big one himself and never mentioned it again."

"No wonder you're having so much trouble believing he's gotten into something illicit or crooked," Walker said, still in that same tone. Amy was afraid to look at him, because just the way he was speaking made her feel quaky inside.

"One thing I've learned from experience with Foxworth," Hayley said, "is never to assume guilt too quickly. We may turn something up that explains everything."

"I hope so," Amy said fervently.

"Do you apply that everywhere?" Walker asked, his tone just a bit too innocent.

What did he expect? Amy wondered.

"That depends on the evidence," Hayley said evenly, and without waiting for him to reply, turned to see that Cutter was safely belted in.

And the evidence against you is insurmountable, Amy thought as she fastened her own seat belt securely. And wondered if the apparent fact that his own decisions had caused him great pain came anywhere near ameliorating what he'd done.

Quinn came up the plane steps and nodded at Hayley. She turned and made her way up front, into the copilot's seat. Quinn looked at Amy and smiled, nodded at her fastened belt, then walked over to Cutter and scratched that apparently favorite spot behind his right ear.

He glanced at Walker. "Buckle up," he ordered.

"Not going to toss me out at altitude?"

"The thought occurred," Quinn said drily. "But if it comes to that, I'll manage."

Amy smothered a laugh as Quinn headed up front, since the words didn't seem to have much heat. Even Walker's mouth quirked, albeit rather ruefully. But then, he'd once had a great sense of humor. Back then.

"You wouldn't hate him so much if you hadn't loved him first..."

And, oh, she had. Despite her easy denial to Hayley, she knew she had adored Walker with all the power of a young heart that had never been broken in that unique way. And for years he had lived up to her imaginings, along the way becoming the most beautiful male human being she had ever seen.

And damn him, he still was. It wasn't just that lean, athlete's body; it was those eyes, those dark rimmed, hazel-gold eyes. Or maybe the unfairly long lashes. Or the thick, silky hair that still tended to fall forward as it did now, making him shove it back with an impatient hand.

"I'm sure Hayley has some dog clippers. She could fix that for you."

She made sure her tone was nothing more than amused. He looked surprised at first, but answered in the same way.

"That's the second offer of a clipping I've had. Tempting."

"No barbers where you were?" Again she kept it light.

He looked at her across the small space. "No time. For that and a couple of other things. I wanted to get here as fast as— Never mind."

She wondered if he'd stopped because he feared she would start in on him again. She wouldn't, she thought with renewed determination. Hayley had asked her to set it aside, and she would.

Selfish of you, she thought. She'd been so incensed at first that she hadn't thought enough about how much harder her own anger would make things on Hayley. It couldn't be pleasant to have your best friend and your brother snapping at each other all the time, no matter how you felt about him. And Hayley was the one who had the real stake in this. And if by some miracle, although she couldn't imagine what it would be, she and Walker made up, she didn't want to put Hayley in an even more awkward place.

So she would pretend that she cared nothing about it. She would take her lead from Hayley, and act as if he were someone she had just met, a casual acquaintance.

"Everyone ready?" Hayley called back to them. Cutter woofed softly as if in answer, and Amy laughed. So did Walker, and the sound caught at her. She had so loved his laugh...

The plane began to move, and Amy turned her head to look out the large, rectangular window. They quickly reached the end of the main runway. She could see that the small airport cleared out of tall trees wasn't much more than a couple of airstrips laid out at angles to each other. No control tower, yet Quinn had a headset on and was speaking into it. When an even smaller plane touched down, slowed and rolled past them, its pilot giving them a wave as it went by, she realized that was who Quinn must have been talking to. She looked upward then, but couldn't see any other planes.

On that thought they started to roll. It was a much quieter and gentler process in the small plane than what she was used to. But cutting through the thick cloud layer was a bit more tension-inducing. Maybe the bigger windows, she thought. You could really see how much you couldn't see. Which was the silliest sentence she'd come up with in a while.

They finally broke through and into the sunlight. It streamed through the windows into the plane's cabin. And suddenly the flight was exhilarating, and she understood Quinn's affection for the nimble little plane.

She glanced over at Walker, who was looking out his own window. The light poured in over him, making the lighter strands of his hair gleam. She could see every plane, every angle of his handsome face, the strength of his jaw and the softness of his mouth.

Tempting.

The word he'd spoken in response to her quip about the dog clippers echoed in her head. But looking at him now, sitting in the golden glow, her unruly mind was putting an entirely different connotation on it.

At least you're consistent, she said to herself. *Consistently idiotic.*

Hayley came back and unbuckled Cutter, letting the dog down on the cabin floor. He promptly went to a flat cushion that lay opposite the door—or was it a hatch on a plane?—and plopped down with his bone, obviously completely at ease.

Amy was grateful for the distraction. And had the thought that she could do worse than model herself on the dog's unconcern.

Too bad that seemed impossible for her with Walker

around. Which was ridiculous, since what she should be worried about was the very real possibility she was about to blow up her entire life.

Chapter 15

If this trip so far was any indication, Walker thought, Foxworth was a very efficient operation. The promised car had been waiting at the hangar they'd taxied to on the private side of the busy airport, once they'd finally gotten clearance to land in between the big commercial jets. Quite a difference from the quiet, rural airport they'd left from.

There are airports and then there are airports, Walker had thought as he'd helped offload their bags. The heat, even now in early spring, was a shock after the still-cool and rainy northwest. He'd been here once in his travels, but it had been years ago and the place had grown. He could see the now-bigger expanse of airport buildings from here. Cutter was also looking around curiously. The dog stayed close, though, seemingly dividing his attention between Hayley and Amy, with an occasional glance his way.

He was a very different sort of dog, Walker thought, and not just because of those moments when he'd come to him and given him an odd, unexpected sort of comfort. That had been, he thought, one of the strangest sensations he'd ever known. It had made him think of the stories of the wonders therapy dogs accomplished. He'd always assumed it was simply mental, that humans had such an affinity for their furry brethren on this planet that just interacting with one did them good. Especially when they were in distress.

Now he was wondering if there wasn't something more to it.

"You two could stay with me," Amy said to Hayley as they waited for Quinn to get the plane secured. "And Cutter. There's even grass in the courtyard for him."

"Thanks, we would, but Quinn needs to check out the new office, anyway."

Walker noticed he was not included in that offer. Which was, he told himself, only to be expected. He didn't think Amy realized yet just how much danger she could be in. But he did, and he wasn't going to let anything happen to her. He'd lost a battle like this once; he wasn't going to lose this one. Not with Amy. He wasn't going to let anything happen to her.

He'd spent far too much time on the flight down here sneaking glances at her, watching how the sunlight streaming through the window lit up her hair, and marveling at how it had changed from that clownish orange she had always hated to this rich, beautiful shade. On its own or with help, it didn't matter; it was beautiful.

She was beautiful.

At one point during the flight she had taken off the blue-framed glasses and cleaned them. He was startled at how different she looked, like someone else, and more startled to realize he felt better once she put them back on.

She was, if he was remembering right, nearsighted. He had a vague memory of seeing her younger, bookish self reading intently along with his sister, without glasses, and then having to grab them up when something happened across the room.

The lenses had darkened in the bright sunlight, hiding the clear blue of her eyes. They were obviously the kind that did that automatically, removing the need for sunglasses like the ones he'd pulled out of the side pocket of his bag as soon as he had it off the plane.

He wondered why she didn't wear contact lenses. And

on the heels of that thought came an odd bit of appreciation that she didn't. The image of that girl who had hated wearing glasses flashed through his mind again. She'd clearly gained the self-confidence to make the most of it now.

"Problem, Mr. Cole?"

Her voice held that sweet tone that, with his sister, warned him a shot was readied, just awaiting a trigger pull. He suspected it was the same with Amy. They'd probably learned it together.

"I was just thinking glasses have come a long way."

She considered that for a moment. "They're a style choice for some these days. Which is very useful."

"Why do I get the feeling you don't just mean for correcting your vision?"

Surprise flickered across her face for a moment, as if she hadn't expected him to get that. If she knew how often his life had depended on reading people lately, she wouldn't have been.

"I don't," she said. "It says something about people who wear them when they don't need them."

"Like people who wear cowboy boots who have never met a cow?" He knew he saw a smile threaten. It pleased him far beyond what it should have.

"In a way, yes. For them it's all about image. Which is telling. And they're useful in other ways. For one thing, people focus on them instead of my eyes, so they…miss things."

"Funny, I can still tell when you're looking daggers at me."

She did smile at that. "Good. I'd hate to think that was wasted."

"You said, 'For one thing.' What else?"

"Categorizing," she said.

He blinked. "What?"

"The people who buy into stereotypes. Who think it automatically means you're smart."

"But you are."

The smile was genuine this time. "Yes."

"What else?" he asked, realizing with a little jolt how much he was enjoying this simple thing, talking with her minus the anger, the sniping and those daggers.

"It helps keep the male of the species at bay."

He drew back slightly at that. "How?"

"Some truly can't look past them. The old joke still has truth—some don't like girls who wear glasses. It helps weed out the ones who are that shallow."

He just looked at her for a moment, standing there with the California sun lighting up her hair, the bright blue top she wore clinging subtly to curves that still startled him, looked at the delicate line of her jaw, the softness of her mouth...

"They're the ones who need help seeing, then," he muttered, his voice a little harsh.

She looked genuinely startled, and then her gaze narrowed at him. God, he'd gone crazy. This was Amy. Little Amy, his sister's best friend. He couldn't be reacting like this to her. It had to be that he was just off balance, coming home after all this time. He was just messed up, that was all.

Besides, there was the little matter of the fact that she hated him.

Quinn came back then, the keys to the small SUV in his hand. *Small* meaning they'd be even closer in the backseat this time. Great. Maybe there wouldn't be room for the dog in the back, with four bags, and he could sit between them. That might help.

And then Quinn startled him by handing the keys to Amy.

"You're the local," he said.

Walker remembered then that she had lived down here, south of LA, until the commute into the city had gotten to be too much and she'd reluctantly had to move closer.

Hayley gestured at Quinn, then the front seat. "You'd better stay up here. You're too tall to be comfortable back there."

No concern for him, of course, even though he was nearly as tall as Quinn. But he hadn't expected any. At least it meant he'd be in back with Hayley, not Amy.

The irony was not lost on him. The one person he'd been most afraid to see was now the one he feared least. At least his sister wasn't likely to resort to physical violence with him, and she didn't glare at him, either.

Of course, that sad, disappointed look she gave him was no better. In some ways it was worse than Amy's glare. Because it seemed a lot closer to not caring, to writing him off.

He'd take anger over that.

"How'd Foxworth end up down here?" Amy asked as she negotiated what were familiar paths to her. Since it was Sunday, the traffic wasn't nearly as bad as it would have been on a workday, and they were in the south part of the county fairly quickly. Quinn had gotten a call, then he and Hayley had had a quick, private conversation, and then they were on their way.

"This is where Charlie finally found the right place," Quinn answered, adding with a grin, "*Picky*, I think is the right word."

"There are living quarters, too. You will stay with us while we're here?" Hayley asked.

"I'm supposed to be back to work tomorrow. And my car's at home."

"We'll get you there, and to work and back the next few days. This way you and Hayley can have some time together. Plus it will make things easier if you're handy in case there are questions," Quinn said.

"All right, then. Once I get my car I can commute for

a while." She rolled her eyes. "I did it for a long time be-fore I moved."

Quinn nodded, apparently satisfied, since he moved on. "Be a pain to deal with traffic, both air and ground, if you had to use that airport all the time."

"Rethinking that jet?" Hayley teased.

"Maybe you just need another helicopter," Amy sug-gested. "One you could land anywhere."

Quinn grinned at her. "I like the way you think."

Hayley had struck gold here, no doubt, Amy thought. Kind of made up for her brother. Who hadn't said a word since they'd gotten in the car. Not that she wanted him to. She much preferred he stay quiet. She didn't want to get drawn into another long conversation with him.

Because you enjoyed that one too much?

Way too much, she thought in answer to the little voice that had popped into her head. And it had shocked her. It should have annoyed her that someone she was so angry at had been so perceptive. She didn't want him to be per-ceptive, to understand, to see her point, any of that.

"They're the ones who need help seeing, then..."

And she especially didn't want him saying things like that, in that low, rough voice that had sent a shiver down her spine and made her tingle in places that had been safely asleep for a very long time now.

"Turn right in one hundred feet," the GPS prompted.

Good thing, she thought, or she probably would have driven right past the street they needed.

There was no excuse for this silliness. She shouldn't be wasting any time wondering where he'd been, or what he'd been doing. Hayley had said he hadn't been in the military, and he'd always sworn he could never be a cop. And it didn't matter, anyway. Unless he was telling the truth about having only found out two days ago. But that seemed impossible. Ridiculous even.

So why would he make it up? He wasn't stupid; far from

it, so if he was going to make up an excuse, why wouldn't it be something more believable? Then again, hadn't she seen people in her work whose real-life, genuine reasons sounded just as implausible? Becca had told her about one of those, a gang leader accused of a gory murder, who had a convoluted, complicated but in this case genuine alibi.

"He's probably committed murder," Becca had said wryly, "but he didn't commit this one."

Which was why she worked for Mr. Rockwell, even though she liked Becca better personally, Amy thought. She didn't think she could deal with those kinds of people, let alone help defend them. So she stayed safely away from the criminal defense side of the business as much as she could.

"Destination ahead one hundred feet on the right."

Amy slowed, looking around. The entire block looked like it had once been residential and now was converted to a business zone. There were old oak trees lining the street, casting a pleasant shade. She wondered idly if the infamous Charlie had a tree thing, and if every Foxworth location was surrounded by them.

"I think that's it," Hayley said, "the one with the Spanish tile roof. It looks like the picture Charlie sent."

Amy nodded and slowed as she spotted the building up ahead on the right. It was a bright white adobe-look building with arched windows on either side of a heavy wood front door, and a driveway to one side that went past the building.

"Take the drive to the back," Quinn said, and she made the turn.

The front building was the size of an average large house on the block. Midway along the side there was a sturdy gate across the driveway. It looked new, and she wondered if it had been added to give Foxworth an extra measure of security; she hadn't forgotten what Hayley had said, that by the very nature of their work powerful people sometimes got angry with them.

To the back, where the driveway curved toward the garage, was what apparently was a guesthouse, in the same style as the one up front. She stopped the car in front of the garage that sat to one side, next to a tiled courtyard with a fountain, dry at the moment. There was a grassy area shaded by a second large tree alongside it, between the two buildings. That, she guessed, would be a nice haven from the heat in summer.

Quinn's cell phone rang. He pulled it out and looked at the screen.

"Ty," he said. He answered, then said, "Putting you live for everybody."

Then he set the phone on the dash so they could all see the screen.

"Hi, all." The young tech's voice was cheerful. "You're not driving, right?"

"Just arrived," Quinn said. "What have you got?"

"Something I should have seen before," Ty admitted. "But I kind of went past it. Then the numbers came together in my head."

"What numbers?"

"Different ones, but what tripped was the total is almost the same. There were a string of smaller cash deposits in Rockwell's account that total the same amount as the money he used to open that offshore business account in the first place, within a couple hundred dollars. And again all under ten thousand dollars."

Quinn frowned. "So he sets up this business and the attendant account with his own money, it immediately starts shelling out money to another business and then he starts collecting deposits in cash, and all under the reporting limit, from another source totaling the same amount?"

"Kind of circular, huh?" Ty said.

"Like a washing machine," Quinn muttered.

And Amy suddenly got what he meant.

Washing machine. Laundering.

A chill swept her as she realized what she might have gotten herself into.

Maybe she hadn't been imagining being watched. And followed.

Maybe she hadn't only found out her boss was crooked. Maybe she'd gotten herself into a whole lot of trouble.

Chapter 16

"She could be in real danger."

Quinn looked up from a canvas bag he was unpacking as Walker strode into their room after a brief knock that had been a signal, not a request; he wasn't taking no for an answer just now. Walker could see the bag was full of not clothing or toiletries but gadgets. The kind of things that might or might not be needed, but would be nearly impossible to find in a hurry. Especially, he guessed, since this office wasn't even up and running yet. So Quinn had come prepared.

"Yes," Quinn said.

Walker heard his sister make a small sound at the quick and simple agreement. She had to have realized this when they'd found out what Amy had likely stumbled onto.

"You were right," Quinn said, surprising him. "Any time there's lots of money and the potential that something illicit's involved, it's best to tread carefully."

"You heard what she said in there," he said, gesturing back toward the room where Amy had explained. "She was being followed."

"She thought she was, yes."

"Enough to scrape her car on a light pole trying to get away. I don't want Amy left alone."

Quinn raised an eyebrow once more. "I would ask why you think you have any say in this at all, except that I happen to agree."

Walker let out a breath of relief at that. He glanced at his sister, saw her watching him with an odd sort of speculative gleam in her eyes.

"We'll discuss it," Quinn said, and then picked up another, smaller bag, turned and walked into the bathroom that joined this bedroom and the one on the other side.

Hayley stood silently for a moment, still looking at him. When she spoke, it was a non sequitur, but welcome.

"I don't know how good your reason is, but I do believe you can't tell me what it is."

He drew back slightly. He hadn't expected that. "Why?"

"For all your sins, Walker Cole, you've never lied to me. And besides, as Amy said, if you were going to lie, wouldn't you come up with something better?"

He blinked. Had to swallow before he could speak. "Amy…said that?"

She nodded. "And she's right. I know that, in my head. Just give my heart some time to come around."

Walker let out a long, harsh breath. "All the time you need, Hayley."

"Do those birds really come back, or is it all tourist hype?"

Walker was looking at the framed print on the wall, showing the fiesta celebrating one of the local traditions, the day the swallows came back to the nearly two-hundred-fifty-year-old mission just a couple of miles south of where they now were.

"Oh, they come back," Amy said. "They just don't consult a human calendar to do it."

"You mean they don't all show up on the appointed day?" Hayley asked, her tone so exaggeratedly aghast Walker couldn't help smiling.

"Birdbrains," he said.

"At least they…"

Amy stopped, an expression of disgust flashing across

her face. He sensed that it was aimed inwardly. Because she'd promised to set it aside? Because he was certain she'd been about to say, "At least they come back."

And there was nothing he could say to that. So instead, he got up from the table where they'd eaten delicious carnitas from a local place Amy had recommended that was named after those same proverbial swallows. He began to gather up the debris from the meal. And not for the first time caught Quinn studying him, as if he were some creature in an experiment who had done something unexpected.

Walker stifled the spurt of longing for the days before he'd thought like this, the days when he'd been able to take people at face value, heedless of what was behind the facade, or more important, not looking for it and expecting evil. He wondered if there would ever be enough time back in this world to make him get over that now-automatic reaction.

Walker held Quinn's gaze. "She needs somebody to watch her back."

Quinn arched an eyebrow at him. "A bodyguard?"

"I don't need…" Amy's protest faded away, as if what she'd really happened across was getting through to her.

"I don't disagree," Quinn said mildly.

"It can't be you," Walker pointed out. "You said you've met her boss. He'd know why you were there."

"He might not remember me."

Walker laughed. "Even I know that's ridiculous. You're not the kind of guy anybody with a brain or instinct for survival forgets."

"I can't argue with that," Hayley said, making them all, even Amy, smile.

"I'm considering the options," Quinn said.

"Consider them all," Walker said pointedly.

Quinn returned his steady gaze. "I will."

Message received, Walker read, and nodded.

Needing to move, he carted the trash to the can just outside the back door.

"This is quite a setup," he said when he came back, calmer, "for an office that isn't even open yet."

He'd been amazed, walking into the larger building and seeing already in place an arrangement similar to what they had up north—a couple of private offices, computers, monitors and bigger screens, a meeting table. Also there was the gathering place, this time in front of corner fireplace that looked as if it were as old as the mission they'd been talking about, although the building was of recent vintage. A good replica overall, he thought.

Homey. Welcoming. Not that he was welcome, of course.

Walker drew in a deep breath, for a moment facing the hopelessness of it.

If there's no hope, why are you even here?

He knew why. Knew he was—foolishly, no doubt—drawing that hope from those moments with Hayley this morning, sitting on that bench overlooking the water. And those moments just now, in the next room. In those moments the anger, the hurt, had been put aside, and she had looked at him as she had before, with concern.

If she could do that now, even for a moment, surely there was hope?

And Amy, had she really said that? While it didn't mean anything except that she thought he'd tell a better lie if he was going to, it was something, wasn't it?

God, you're an idiot. Don't you remember optimism is a fool's game?

He had to get out of here, needed to get away at least for a minute, from the pressure, the strain of the feeling that the entire rest of his life was hanging in the balance. That it was the truth only made the feeling worse.

"I'm going to get some air," Amy said in the instant before he turned to head for the door.

Damn.

"Shall I take Cutter with me?" The dog, who was sprawled on the tile floor as if savoring its coolness, lifted his head at the sound of his name. "I'll just stay here in the yard."

"He'd like to explore the outside, I'm sure," Hayley said.

Amy turned to the dog. "Will you come with me, sweet boy?"

He was on his feet in an instant and came to her eagerly.

Lucky dog.

He swore silently at himself, at the suddenly idiotic turn his brain had taken. This was Amy, little nerdy Amy. Except she wasn't, not anymore. And she'd chosen her place in this, and that was loyally beside her dearest friend. As it should be.

He just wished it wasn't against him. And in that moment he was more tempted than he'd yet been to come out with it, to say to hell with it and pour the truth out. What could it possibly matter? It wasn't like his sister or Amy would give anything away, and Quinn sure as hell wouldn't. He was cut from the same cloth as Cabrero— the only difference appeared to be in their approach to the problems of the world today.

He was closer to the door, so he walked over and opened it. "I was headed out myself," he said, giving Amy a sideways look. "But don't let that stop you."

She shrugged as she started out, Cutter close beside her. "It's a free country," she said as she passed him.

Free country.

And that easily, that unknowingly, Amy Clark gave him back his resolve. Because that was why he had to keep his mouth shut. Because there were those who wanted to change that.

He'd just never expected to play a part in seeing that that stayed the truth.

Chapter 17

Amy's heart leaped as she heard voices outside Mr. Rockwell's office. She'd been going through the protected files again, looking for anything else that would prove or disprove her suspicions. She quickly signed off and put the system to sleep. She grabbed the file folder that was her cover for being in here, put it squarely on the desk and was in the middle of writing a note when her boss came in.

She straightened up. Looked at the man she had, sadly, always respected. Marcus Rockwell was a tall, straight-spined man with dark hair graying at the temples. He was handsome, but imposing enough in both stature and demeanor that she'd also always felt more than a bit intimidated. He wasn't a warm, jovial kind of boss; he was all business. She hadn't minded that at all. But she'd always thought it was honest business, and she hated the idea that he was crooked.

She buried her thoughts, afraid they might show in her face. He might not be the most social of bosses, but he was far, far from a fool, and he hadn't gotten where he was by not being able to read people.

"Oh, good, you're back," she said, pleased that her voice sounded normal. "Now I can just tell you."

She wadded up the piece of paper and tossed it into his wastebasket. If he was suspicious and looked, he'd see only a legitimate message that she would now tell him in person.

"Here's the transcript of my interview of Mr. Jackson's employer. I should have the background research on the case done in time for you to go over it before your meeting with him in the morning."

Her boss smiled at her and nodded. "Good. What's your sense of him?"

That was another thing she liked about him. He asked for her opinion, and gave every evidence he took it seriously. In this case she definitely had one; she didn't like their client much.

"He seemed to me to be a good guy." *But then, I thought you were, too.* She quashed the thought for fear it would show. "Through no fault of his own his company just got into financial trouble, like so many others these days."

"So you think he just had to make a choice."

"Yes. And Mr. Jackson was the employee with the least time on, and a history of problems."

"So you think he was justified?"

"Not my decision," she said. *Thankfully.*

"But if it were?"

This was interesting, she thought. He usually didn't push for quite this much from her in the way of her opinion.

"If I had to choose between Mr. Jackson and the woman he kept, who'd been with him from the beginning and had a stellar record, I would have done the same."

"As," Mr. Rockwell said with a nod, "would I." He picked up the file. "I'll go over this, but I'll be discussing with Mr. Jackson the questionable wisdom of proceeding. And that if he insists, he will need to find other representation. Thank you, Amy."

As she walked back to her desk she found herself doubting it all. How could he be involved in what they suspected? Could she really have been so completely wrong about him?

And there had been no sign of any suspicion, not a trace

of change in his attitude toward her. Could he conceal it, if he suspected she'd found those files, had looked at them? Was he that good of an actor? All attorneys who did court-room work were, to some extent, but Marcus Rockwell had long ago eschewed the dramatics of the big criminal cases. He never took them these days.

But he had made his name there. He'd become famous after three consecutive high-profile cases. She'd never asked, and she was sure he wouldn't tell her if she did, but she had the distinct sense that he'd walked away after that last trial because he was certain he'd just success-fully defended a man who was in fact guilty of a rather heinous crime.

And how that reconciled with money laundering, she had no idea. And whose money was being laundered, if it indeed was happening?

She thought about getting out the phone Quinn had given her and making a call to let him know what she'd found. Or not found, in this case. But she would leave it until lunchtime, when she could go out and make the call unobserved. It had unsettled her a little when he'd given her the phone, not when he said that although it looked or-dinary it was unique to Foxworth and heavily encrypted, but when he showed her there was a panic alarm built into it, which would instantly let them know she was in trou-ble and where she was with the push of a single button.

"You'll probably never need it," Hayley had said reas-suringly, "but you need to know so you don't hit it by ac-cident. And if you do, you just key in the phone ID—this is number FW6—to cancel it."

She frowned as she reached for the computer keyboard, remembering her puzzlement this morning when she'd arrived to find it sitting at an odd angle. She never left it there; at the end of the day she always slid it into the cubby below her monitor. She supposed the cleaning crew could have moved it, but they were the main reason she always put it out of the way in the first place, so they wouldn't have to move it.

She grimaced inwardly at herself. If she tried, she could work that into an entire scenario of her office having been searched. A sign of how this all was affecting her, she supposed.

Looking for distraction, she pulled up the firm's client list. She wasn't sure what she was looking for, but something might trip if she went over it. For lack of a better idea she sorted the list chronologically and worked her way back in time. Several of the names she knew, many she did not. Caden and Rockwell was a large firm, and she dealt only with Rockwell clients.

She bet Foxworth's Ty could have deep background on every one of these people in a day. But to hand this list over to him would be an ethical violation so big she couldn't even seriously contemplate it. Besides, what if she was wrong? She was going to feel bad enough about wasting Foxworth's time, but if it was found out she'd violated one of the most basic tenets of the legal profession, she'd never work in the field again.

"Hey, girlfriend, did you forget we were going to have lunch today?"

Amy looked up to see Becca Olson standing there smiling at her. Dressed in a trim, navy blue suit with a pencil skirt that was neither too short nor too long, the tall, attractive woman projected success. A carefully put together image she used to the fullest advantage, thanks to a very quick and clever brain behind the facade that was all some people ever saw. Amy had always admired the way she did it, and figured if people were too shallow to see beyond the surface, that was their problem.

"Oh! No, sorry, I just got distracted."

"Spike's, my treat," Becca said. "I'm celebrating."

The expensive little café was the newest hot spot, and

Amy doubted she would ever go there on her own. Her salary was sufficient—Mr. Rockwell had given her a nice raise at the first of the year—but her practical bent prevented her from lavishing it on overpriced bistros.

"The Lancaster win?" Amy guessed.

"Got it in one," Becca said cheerfully. "Nobody expected it, but I had that jury in the palm of my hand."

Amy had seen the woman in court, and couldn't deny she had a way. She struck the perfect balance between smart, knowledgeable lawyer and "I'm just one of you," with a dash of "I only think what any reasonable citizen would think" thrown in.

"How was your trip?" Becca asked as they walked the short distance. Amy knew she loved her sleek, flashy new Mercedes, but even she wouldn't drive it a mere three blocks just to show it off. She chided herself at her thought. Becca had earned every bit of her success with hard work and determination. That she was an attractive woman had made it harder in some ways, but it was also a tool she never hesitated to use if it would get the result she wanted.

"Fine," she said. "It was good to see my friend again."

"She just got married, didn't she? How's it going?"

Amy was always a little amazed, and more than a little charmed, that Becca remembered the small details of her life. As a full partner, the woman had to have as much going on as Mr. Caden, her boss and the founding senior partner who headed the criminal side did, and yet she took an interest, offered friendship even, to a lowly paralegal. True, Amy was the closest to Becca in age, but still, it was flattering.

Amy smiled as she answered. "Wonderfully. Quinn is an amazing man. I think he might just be good enough for her."

Becca laughed. "I admire your optimism."

Becca, Amy knew, had been married once and it had

ended messily, so she supposed she understood her sour view on the institution. "They might brighten even your outlook on it," she said.

"Early days yet," Becca said, the words ominous, but her tone teasing.

"They're going to make it," Amy said confidently. "Absolutely no doubt."

"I think I'd like to meet these paragons," Becca said.

Amy nearly opened her mouth to say that might be possible, that they were in the area at this moment, then caught herself.

"Maybe you will someday," she said as they reached the café down the street from the office. There were at least three law offices on the block, so the place was often full of legal types. But even amid this larger pool Becca was a big fish. She was making a name for herself in criminal defense circles. She wasn't a senior partner—yet—but Amy knew she was getting big cases because of her win record.

Amy grimaced inwardly when the waiter brought the menus. The string of too-clever names for ordinary dishes seemed forced, but she supposed they were catering to a clientele that liked to toss around names that sounded exotic. The food, when it came, was edible, but not a lot more, and she wondered as she often did about trends and what caused them.

"So what else?" Becca said as she sipped at her iced tea; no lunch cocktails for her. Amy couldn't imagine her willingly surrendering that much control. She wanted her wits about her at all times, she'd once said. Amy understood that, better than Becca could know. "How's your love life?"

Amy hated that the first thing that popped into her head was an image of Walker. Up early this morning for the long haul to LA from Orange County, she'd walked sleepily toward the kitchen of the Foxworth living quarters in search of coffee. Walker, sleeping on the couch in a tangle of blanket, was stirring restlessly, and she tiptoed to avoid waking him. Only common courtesy, she'd told herself, not that she didn't want to face him or talk to him. She'd be seeing enough of him, since he'd insisted on being one of them to, as he'd put it, watch her back.

And then he'd muttered something and she was afraid she had awakened him, anyway. It took her a moment to realize he was in the throes of a dream, and from his muttered pleas, "Don't, don't," she gathered it wasn't a pleasant one.

"Aha!" Becca exclaimed now, pulling her out of the memory. "So there is someone? Have you broken into that box of condoms I gave you yet?"

"No," Amy denied quickly, blushing anew over the joke gift Becca had dropped on her desk on her birthday a few months ago.

"On the horizon, then? Because someone certainly popped into your head."

And that, Amy thought, *is why Becca was so darned good at what she did.* She missed nothing, and interpreted accurately.

"Just my friend's awful jerk of an older brother, who showed up unexpectedly while I was there. I used to have a huge crush on him when I was thirteen."

"Sorry. About the jerk part, I mean," Becca said sympathetically.

"Me, too. He was a good guy, once."

Thankfully, Becca let it drop there.

By the time they finished the meal there was a line at the front door, so they left via a side exit that opened to the small parking area. A short, rather stocky man Amy recognized as another on the criminal defense side, was opening the door to a flashy red coupe—he obviously had no problem driving three blocks for lunch—parked just outside. He looked at them as they came out, then a smile broke across his wide face.

"Becca," he said. "Congratulations. That was a nice job on the Lancaster case."

Becca smiled prettily. "Thank you, Alan."

"Maybe we could do dinner, you know, celebrate."

"Maybe," Becca said with a wave. But she never stopped walking. And the moment they were out of earshot she muttered, "Clown thinks because we work and live in the same buildings we're destined to be more than friends."

Amy had noticed the distinctive parking sticker on the windshield of the car, a twin to the one on Becca's car. The stylized swan of the Cygnus Towers was a subtle declaration of success and an exclusive home address.

"I can't picture you with him somehow," Amy said drolly.

Becca laughed. "Even if he was in the least attractive to me, I'm six inches taller than he is."

Amy wondered if Becca Olson had always been beautiful, if that's what it took to have such easy confidence in her looks. But she wasn't obnoxious about it at least. Some women were.

"Do you know he asked me if I wanted to open a partnership of our own?"

"I'm not surprised," Amy said. "You're a hot property, Ms. Olson."

Becca smiled at her. "And you are sweet, Amy Clark."

"I would miss you if you left."

"Not if you came with me," Becca said.

Amy blinked. "What?"

"Not saying I'm going to do it now, and certainly not with Alan, but someday I'm going to be a partner somewhere. And when I do, I'd like you with me."

"I'm...flattered."

"I'd take you now, if you wanted to leave ol' stick in

the mud Rockwell. We girls need to stick together, you know?"

Amy felt a rush of warmth inside. And relief. If this all fell apart on her, it appeared she might have somewhere to go.

Chapter 18

"That's your boss?" Hayley asked.

"Yes." Amy looked at the video playing on the large monitor on the wall. It was of her boss's most famous criminal trial, the one she had always thought had made him quit criminal law. "That was a few years ago. Dante Soren." Her nose wrinkled involuntarily, and the Chinese takeout they'd ordered suddenly wasn't sitting very well.

"Is that expression for your boss or Soren?" Hayley asked.

"Definitely Soren," Amy said. "His street nickname was 'the demon,' and it fit. He was a horrible human being."

"From what we could find," Quinn said, "he still is."

"So your boss got him off?" Walker asked.

She didn't look at him, but answered, "Yes. Murder, attempted murder and several drug charges. He walked on them all."

"Quite a performance," Quinn said as the screen went dark.

"Yes. Yes, it was. I'd forgotten how...effective he was in those cases."

She felt a cold knot settling in her stomach. Because that video Quinn had found reminded her of the answer to her earlier question. Yes, her boss really was that good an actor. He might be stiff in person, some would say unyielding, but in a courtroom he was a master. At speaking, phrasing, dramatic pauses, at simply holding the room captive.

And if he could do that for someone she knew he thought was guilty…

She looked at Quinn, saw by the look in his eyes that she didn't have to explain, that he knew perfectly well what they had just seen. Proof that Marcus Rockwell was more than capable of putting up a perfect facade.

"He could know I found those files," she said, "and I'd never be able to tell."

Quinn nodded. "He's good. Very good."

"I'd like to know why he put them there in the first place," Walker said.

Three heads turned toward him. Four, counting Cutter. He'd said little tonight, but she had never forgotten he was there. He was like a pesky gnat, always flitting around the edges of her consciousness, and no matter how many times she tried to swat him away he kept coming back.

And she was sure Walker Cole wouldn't appreciate being likened to a tiny bug. Even if he deserved the comparison.

"I'm just saying," he said with a shrug, "why would he put them there when he knows Amy has the password and pretty much free access to those files? In fact, if they're that damning, why put them on that computer at the office at all?"

She had fleetingly wondered that. Judging by Quinn's expression so had he, although he seemed a little surprised that Walker had. But then, he probably didn't realize just how smart he was. Amy did. What he'd done tended to overshadow the fact that that baseball scholarship hadn't been his only one; he'd won two academic ones, as well.

And he'd dumped those, too, when he ran away.

She made herself focus. "I never snoop. I only saw those by accident."

Hayley nodded. "And I'm sure he knows that."

"Still risky for him," Quinn said.

"He trusts me," Amy said, aware of the irony even as she said it. Being trusted by a man involved in something like this wasn't a thing to be proud of.

"So he isn't worried you'd look at them," Hayley said.

"Or," Quinn said rather ominously, "he wanted you to access them, so there would be a record of it."

"Setting me up, so he could blame it on me somehow?" Amy asked with a shiver as the possibility hit. "He has access to everything. He could have even done it from my computer after-hours or something."

"Or," Walker said with a bit of a bite, "you could all go against your apparent grain and wonder if maybe he simply isn't worried because he doesn't know those files exist. You know, the old innocent until proven guilty thing."

Amy stared at him. Was he defending her boss…or himself? And yet, he had a point, she supposed. It seemed flimsy, but it was there.

They were all staring at him. He let out a disgusted breath and turned away, again gathering up the debris from the meal, including the leftovers in the traditional white cartons, and headed for the kitchen. And Amy wondered if that's how he really felt, that he was innocent.

"There are many reasons for many things that I never would have thought of before."

Hayley's words came back to her. Was it loyalty to her brother that tempered her anger, or was it that she truly thought there was a reason, any reason, that justified his desertion? Should she laugh at the idea that he thought himself wronged, or contemplate the possibility that there was even an iota of truth in it?

Most of all, she wondered how, when they were supposed to be focused on her boss and the probability of him being unethical or worse, she had once again ended up pondering the painful mystery that was Walker Cole.

* * *

"Don't. Don't..."

"She is my daughter. Mine to dispose of."

"For looking at a children's book?"

"Females have no need to read. It gives them dangerous ideas."

Amaya reached out to him, tears welling up in her frightened eyes.

"Don't interfere," her father ordered.

The same order he'd been given last night, by the man in the suit. "Don't interfere. It could blow everything."

"They'll kill her," he'd protested. "She's just a child."

"One life against thousands. This is war, Cole. Sometimes you have to let bad things happen so you can stop even worse things."

"Walker. Walker, wake up."

Odd. Amaya never called him that. She didn't even know that name.

He felt the touch on his shoulder. Real. He shot to the surface. Jolted upright, nearly colliding with...

"Amy."

She was there, crouched beside the sofa. It was dark; he sensed it was very late—or very early.

"Amy," he said again, still feeling groggy. He shook his head sharply, as if that could clear away the miasma that dream always left behind.

"Nightmare?"

"I wish it was only a nightmare."

She tilted her head slightly, looking at him consideringly. What faint light there was glinted off glasses, black businesslike frames this time. He noticed then she was wearing only a loose T-shirt with the University of Washington logo and a pair of matching leggings. Sleepwear. Realization struck at last.

"Was I... Did I wake you?"

"I was awake. I wouldn't have heard you otherwise."

He tried to suppress a shudder, only half succeeded. "I didn't yell this time, then."

"No." She seemed to hesitate, then went on. "It must have been a really bad dream."

"It wasn't a dream. It was a memory."

"Must be an awful one."

He couldn't tell her, of course. It would give too much away. But she had had the grace to awaken him from the torture, so he couldn't help feeling he owed her at least some explanation.

"A little girl. Who died." *Because I didn't stop it.*

"You knew her?"

He nodded, slowly. "She was…special." *And she adored me, just like you once did. And now she's dead. Because I chose to follow that order.*

"I'm sorry."

He believed she meant it. She was kind, along with loyal. Staunchly loyal Amy. Except to him. He'd destroyed her loyalty to him. And he was beginning to realize what a major, if horrible, accomplishment that was.

"Thank you for waking me," he said. "I wouldn't have expected you to bother."

She brushed off his thanks. "I wouldn't let anybody suffer like that."

She straightened and walked back to her room without another word.

He didn't even try to go back to sleep. He knew it was pointless; his mind wouldn't let him, fearing it would only start again. After a few minutes of staring into the dark, he finally got up, dressed and went outside. He doubted the strange surroundings would be enough of a distraction, but it was worth a try.

Hard to believe how he had once had the world in front of him, and a loving family standing beside him. And he'd left it all behind. But he knew to this day that life-altering decision had been the only one he could live with, the only thing that got him through the pain of losing his father, the man he'd loved and respected above all others.

He knew Hayley hadn't really understood, but she'd been so young when he'd left. And he'd come back to visit often in those early days—birthdays, holidays...

And then five years ago he'd stumbled into chaos. And doing the right thing about it had cost him everything. Even things he didn't know he'd had. Or wanted.

Like Amy.

The realization of that truth hit him hard and low. He sank down to sit on the rim of the dry fountain. He wished it was running—maybe the sound of running water would calm his frenetic thoughts.

Amy. He wanted Amy.

How the hell that had happened didn't matter. Not when it was obvious she wanted nothing to do with him. The girlhood crush had long ago been seared to ash. And he didn't kid himself that she'd pulled him out of the depths of that nightmare because she cared. She'd have done the same for anyone. Probably even the dog. In fact, if it came to it, she'd probably wake Cutter up first.

He stood abruptly. If he'd learned nothing else in his life, he'd learned you didn't always get what you wanted. And he knew damned well he wasn't going to get this, any more than he'd gotten his father back, or the chance to see his mother again.

And he couldn't help wondering if, had he known, truly known, what this was going to do to his life, what it was going to cost him, he ever would have made that second life-altering decision. No matter what the stakes.

He supposed that doubt was what made him shake his head in disbelief when those guys in the suits called him a hero.

Chapter 19

"Either I'm paranoid or he's watching me. Closely."

"More than usual?" Walker asked.

Amy nodded, taking the glass of flavored water he handed her. She appreciated the gesture; she was tired, and not cut out for this cloak-and-dagger stuff. "He's never been one to hover, but this week he's asking questions. Often."

"Personal things?"

"Just if I'm all right."

"If he's asking if you're all right," Walker said, "he's noticed something that made him think you might not be."

She wanted to ignore him, but what he'd said made sense, just like the other times that he'd weighed in on what was going on.

"I never claimed to be any good at sneaking around," she said defensively.

"It wasn't a criticism," he said, his tone weary. "You're not a trained operative. No one would expect you to be able to cover perfectly."

The wording caught her attention, and she gave him a sideways look. Was she revising her assumptions? Was that why she was finding it harder each day to hang on to her anger? Or was it just the remnants of that silly crush? On the outside, after all, he hadn't changed, except perhaps to become even better-looking. He still had that easy charm, that dimpled smile and that endearing way of making you feel as if every bit of his attention was on you.

A memory flashed through her mind, of the first time she'd ever seen him. She'd been coming to their house after school for a few days at Hayley's invitation. She'd been wary, but Hayley's mother had welcomed her, and she'd felt more warmth from this woman she'd just met than she'd ever felt at home. Her eight-year-old heart had ached with the sweetness of it, without her really understanding why, other than the realization that not everyone's home and family was like hers—loud, unpleasant and chaotic.

She'd been sipping happily at the hot chocolate Hayley's mother had made them, still marveling at the woman's kindness, when the slamming of the front door made her jump. The mug went flying, hot chocolate splashing all over, until it hit the tile floor and shattered. She was so terrified she barely felt the heat; in her house, this would earn her an hour-long screaming session and days of verbal retribution. But she'd been more upset that she would now be banned from this refuge she'd only just found.

But Hayley's mother was soothing her, seeming more worried that she'd been scalded than anything. And then a boy had run in, skidding to a halt just inside the kitchen, staring at the mess.

Walker had been twelve then. She'd barely had time to realize he must be Hayley's brother before Mrs. Cole turned on him.

"Walker Cole, what have I told you about slamming that door?"

The boy looked sheepish. "Um…not to?"

"You made Amy jump," Hayley accused him with a glare.

He looked at her then for the first time. That had been the first time she'd noticed his eyes, those gold-flecked green eyes with the dark rim around the iris, eyes that were striking now, and would be devastating when he grew up. They were fastened on her, noting the wet chocolate stain on her shirt.

"Sorry," he said.

"And?" his mother prompted, gesturing at the puddle and mug fragments on the floor.

Walker had sighed. "I'll clean it up."

"You certainly will. And you'll replace that mug out of your allowance."

Another sigh. "Yes, ma'am."

He'd set about the task with determination if not enthusiasm. And his mother made no move toward him, didn't even try to hit him, and she wondered if he was going to escape physical punishment. Or maybe that was their father's job.

"Mom, can we clean Amy's shirt? She'll get in big trouble if she goes home like that."

Even now Amy felt a burst of warmth at the memory of Hayley's worry. She hadn't told her a lot about what things were like at home, but somehow her friend seemed to guess at what she hadn't said. And her mother had instantly taken over, ushering them to Hayley's room to find something for her to wear while she handled washing and drying her clothes.

She'd been still nearly shaking with relief and amazement at how different it was here when Walker had stuck his head through Hayley's doorway.

"I really am sorry. I didn't mean to scare you."

She'd stared at him, speechless. The first apology had been surprise enough, but his mother had been standing there. This was on his own, and was all the more sincere for it.

That was the moment when she'd first fallen for him. And she'd loved him with all the devotion of her childish heart, wishing, dreaming, until the day he'd gone away.

Even then it had lingered for a while, until her practical brain and her hard-won acceptance of what was had made her put away the fantasy.

And she wasn't about to succumb to that fantasy again.

With an effort, she looked away and went back to the matter at hand. "I'm wondering if maybe he's not just keeping a closer eye on what I'm doing, working on. Maybe hoping to catch me looking at things I shouldn't."

"You think he knows someone saw those files, but not who?" Walker asked.

She sighed. "I don't know. Besides the partners, I'm the only one who has the secure system password."

"I talked to Quinn. Ty's looking into that list of names you gave us, but it's taking time to do it under the radar."

"I'm going to feel really stupid if this turns out to be nothing," Amy said. "Wasting all this time and Foxworth resources."

"I may not know Quinn well, but I know he won't think it wasted if it puts your mind at ease," Walker said.

He was right. She knew that. And realized that she had somehow come to the conclusion that while Walker wasn't the voluble kid she remembered, when he did speak, it was usually worth hearing.

"My sister," Walker murmured later as they watched Hayley and Quinn play a crazy sort of tag with Cutter outside on the grass, "did well."

She doubted that was meant for her ears, but she couldn't seem to stop herself from adding, "As did Quinn."

"That," Walker said without looking at her, "goes without saying. Hayley's the best."

"Yes. She is."

He glanced at her then. Looking for a sign that that had been a jab? She met his gaze evenly, for this time there hadn't been a trace of that even in her mind, only appreciation for her dearest friend.

After a moment, a trace of a smile curved his mouth.

And nearly took her breath away. Every alarm she had went off in her head in warning.

Cutter suddenly changed course midromp, picked something up from the grass and trotted toward them. He had the new baseball Walker had bought him in his mouth now and, tail wagging and ears up, he offered it to him. Obviously the dog had decided he was all right. If the baseball had been a bribe, it had worked.

Still reeling from the unexpected reaction to that smile, she grimaced as much at herself as at him. "Funny. Hayley says he's an excellent judge of character."

For an instant that pain flashed in his eyes again. But when he spoke, his voice was quiet. "So he's wrong about me and Hayley's wrong about him?"

She hadn't thought of it in quite that way, but she saw his point. "Maybe your DNA is throwing him off."

To her surprise, he let out a wry chuckle. "Maybe," he said, and let it go.

He looked back at the dog. "I was worried at first that the baseball might be too hard on his teeth, but he seems to realize the difference. He handles it differently than the tennis ball, anyway. No midair catches, he lets it hit and roll."

She liked that he'd thought of that. "Smart dog."

He took the ball the dog offered and walked out onto the grass. Hayley and Quinn seemed content to let him take over after their energetic game of doggy tag.

"He remembered who gave him that?" Amy asked.

"Or he knows who played baseball," Hayley said with a smile.

And then Walker started throwing the ball for the eager animal, and she was flooded with memories once more. She'd become a passionate fan of the sport because of him, never missing a game he was in, learning all about it so she could at least talk to him about something without fumbling and stammering. Her young heart had thrilled to watching him, just the way he moved, the way he stared down the batters, the power behind the fastball that had major league scouts hovering even then.

"Don't stay mad at him on my account," Hayley said softly.

She gave her friend a sideways look. That was like Hayley. Generous. Forgiving. "Maybe it's on mine," she said, looking back at him, but she couldn't seem to summon up the anger to make the words bite.

It really wasn't fair. He hadn't gotten any less graceful. Or powerful. And when he threw the ball hard enough to bounce it off the adobe-look wall surrounding the yard, and Cutter practically bent himself double to turn back to get it on the rebound, she found herself laughing and cheering along with Hayley. For the dog, of course.

It had all seemed so…normal, she thought the next morning as she settled in at her desk. Like some sort of family on just a regular evening, playing with the dog, laughing together.

But it wasn't, and the sooner she got that silly idea out of her head, the better.

And yet her mind kept drifting back to it the moment her guard was down. Walker had been already up this morning when she'd come out for coffee, and Quinn had been on the phone. She'd wondered if it had been something about her situation, but Walker shook his head as if he'd guessed she'd be wondering.

"It's about this place and staffing it, I think."

"Oh." Then almost as an afterthought, she added a polite, "Thanks."

"Don't hurt yourself," he'd said wryly.

She once more pulled herself out of the memories and made herself focus on her job. She had case law to research and write up for the Marcourt case, the Douglas family trust to work on and some loose threads from other things to finish off. More than enough to keep her occupied, if she could just keep her mind in the groove. And she would, she told herself firmly.

She had the draft of the trust papers done by late morning and sent them to print. She liked to go over things in hard copy, since she caught mistakes she read right past on a computer screen. Then she got up to walk over to the printer across the office; it wouldn't start until she was there and keyed in her ID code, another layer of security and confidentiality Caden and Rockwell insisted on.

When she was done, corrections made and entered, it was lunchtime. She fed the printed pages into the crosscut shredder, emailed the finished document and, when that was done, signed off her computer and locked it down.

As she headed toward the elevator she ran into Becca just arriving, but her friend was with a client so their greeting was kept to merely a nod and smile in passing. As Amy rode the elevator down to the parking garage under the building she dug out her car keys, mentally planning her tasks to get as much as possible done in the time she had. And somewhere she had to find time to at least get an estimate on getting her car's fender repaired; she didn't like driving around with that big scrape on it.

When the doors slid open she found herself unexpectedly face-to-face with her boss. And he did not look happy. But then, his resting face was rather stern anyway.

"Amy," he said, seeming to collect himself. "Off to lunch?"

"Errands, I'm afraid."

"Take your time, then. My afternoon appointment is canceled, so I'm going to go up and close out, then head home and catch up on some reading."

She hadn't expected that. "Oh. All right. The Douglas trust file is in your in-box."

He smiled. He really did have a nice smile when he bothered to use it. "Ever efficient, aren't you? I'd be lost without you."

For a moment after the elevator doors closed she just stood there. Fought with her imagination, wondering if he'd said that, made that compliment, because he'd been contemplating doing without her. Because she'd been snooping where she didn't belong. There hadn't seemed to be any underlying meaning in his tone, but that video of him in the courtroom had proved he was more than capable of concealing his thoughts and intentions.

The sound of voices pulled her out of her reverie. Two, it sounded like, both male. Harsh, but quiet, as if they were trying to keep their voices down. She glanced that way, saw two men in the shadows of the far corner of the garage. If sound didn't carry so well in here, she would never have seen them, never even known they were there.

She couldn't hear their words, not well enough to understand, but she could tell they were arguing. Or rather, one of the men was desperately trying to explain something, and the other was having none of it. She hastened toward her car, hoping that realizing they weren't alone might calm things, and wanting out of here quickly if it didn't.

She was halfway there when it escalated. She heard an odd thump, risked a quick glance.

Her heart kicked into overdrive. One of the men was up against the side of a dark van, the other, taller one had a forearm jammed against his throat. The thump, she realized with a little shock, had been his head slamming against the wall.

The aggressor's voice was even fiercer now. Any louder and it was going to be impossible for her to pretend she hadn't heard them. Even if it only was every third or fourth word.

"...dare...me? I have...in my pocket...you..."

She couldn't make out the words in between. She was tempted to hightail it back to the elevator and go back inside, but the two men might hear her. And the elevator was likely still up on her floor.

Then she realized if they hadn't seen her yet, the beep as she unlocked the door was going to draw their attention. This was the parking garage of her own office, yes, but it was also Los Angeles, and things happened.

She risked another glance. Her breath caught. The taller man had something in his hand, something he was holding to the other man's throat. And that something glinted metal in the dim light of the corner of the underground garage. A knife? A gun?

Forget the lock release button. She covered the last few steps to her car as quietly and quickly as she could. It took her a moment of fumbling to get the key in the lock, so used was she to using the more convenient button on her key.

She heard the sound of footsteps, running. She made herself focus on getting the door open so she could get in and get it locked again. Her mind was racing, remembering what Hayley's father had said once that a car was a deadly weapon. Could she do it? Could she use it that way?

She felt the key turn. Then froze, uselessly, as the other man walked out of the shadows. Toward her.

He stopped, looked her up and down so thoroughly she felt a shiver go through her. He was handsome, in a slick kind of way, tall, slim, dark blond hair gelled straight back, but the overdone three gold rings and the almost-shiny suit destroyed the look for her.

"Hey, sweet thing," he said. When she shot him a wary glance, he laughed. It wasn't a pleasant sound. "Now, don't be frowning at a man, make him feel disrespected."

"I'm leaving," she stated firmly.

She yanked her car door open and got inside, slamming it shut and locking it immediately. To her relief, he made no attempt to stop her. The man laughed again, and this time it did sound amused, even through the closed window.

"Little girl scared?" he asked. The laugh was dismissive this time. "You should be."

His first two fingers in a V, he pointed at his eyes, then at her. *I'm watching you...*

And then he was gone, fading back into the shadows of the garage. Moments later she heard an engine start, and a sleek, flashy black European sedan with wheels so large the tires seemed no more than a couple of inches thick rolled by.

The scene kept playing back in her head as she sat there. Something was niggling at her, something about that man. She hadn't gotten the best look at him in the dim light, but still... And that voice. She knew that voice. She closed her eyes, hearing it again in her mind.

And then it hit her. She'd seen that man. Recently. Not in person, but on a video screen.

Dante Soren.

The case they had been watching, the one that had made her boss famous in criminal defense circles.

The case that, she was convinced, had made him walk away from what could have been an incredibly lucrative career.

Or had he?

Possibilities tumbled through her mind. Had he been meeting with Soren? Was that the reason he'd been down here? The reason he'd had that look on his face? Was it even possible, that kind of coincidence, her boss just happening to be in the garage where his most notorious client was lurking, with another man he had clearly threatened enough to send him scurrying away in apparent terror? Likely with some kind of deadly weapon?

They'd read off a list in that courtroom video of the weapons taken off the suspect at the time of his arrest, a list that had sounded like an armory to her. Knives, handguns, some kind of stunning device. He could have had any one of those at hand today, ready to use on that other man.

And then turn on her, she thought with a shiver.

She wondered briefly what the man had done to so displease Soren that the demon of his street name appeared. Wondered if he worked for him, or had just been in the wrong place and crossed him somehow.

Wondered what would have happened if Soren had taken more of an interest in tormenting her.

But she wasn't the issue here. Her boss was. Had he only seemed to quit? Were the calm, dry trusts and wills and business documents he dealt with now only a cover? Behind the scenes, was he still working for this piece of human debris?

She sat there, shaken, her list of errands forgotten.

I have...in my pocket...

I have a lawyer in my pocket? Is that what he'd said?

She reached for her purse to get the phone Quinn had given her. Realized that she'd never even thought of it when Soren had been towering over her. She should have. Quinn had said they—including Walker—would be within close reach all day. Even so, she'd likely have been dead if that had been Soren's intent. For she had no doubts about his ability and capacity to do just that, if he wanted to. She knew as surely as she knew her eyes were blue that he'd committed those murders. And probably more.

Instead, he'd just teased her, tormented her and then laughed. She was clearly no threat to such as he.

Or so he thought.

She pulled out the phone. And realized she felt oddly better about this whole thing.

Because now she was sure it wasn't just paranoia. Something was definitely going on, and it was getting smellier by the moment.

Chapter 20

"No wonder you were rattled," Hayley said.

"It was scary when I realized who he was," Amy admitted. "And when he did that 'I'm watching you' thing."

"Especially if he was armed."

"I'm only guessing, I couldn't really see. But...he had something jammed up against the guy's neck, and it was metal. Part of it, anyway. And the van they were next to, it looked like the one that I thought was following me. My first thought was I should call the police, but..."

"You did the right thing, calling Quinn first. He'll handle it."

"She should have called me first," Walker said. "I was closer."

Quinn, who had been on the phone across the room, ended his call and came back. He'd been at her side within a minute or two when she'd called, showing her he'd meant what he'd said when he promised he'd be close by.

She was a little startled at how good it felt to come home to people who cared, especially now, in the middle of...whatever this was. And no part of that feeling good had anything to do with the fact that Walker had just come into the room.

He didn't speak, but then he often didn't. He just quietly waited until he got a feel for what was going on. This was a marked change from the gregarious boy she remembered, and she wondered what had caused it.

One of the multitude of things she wondered about him. All of which were a waste of time, she added to herself firmly.

"A friend of Brett's," Quinn said as he put the phone back in his pocket.

"He's originally from LA," Hayley elaborated, "and still has a lot of contacts down here."

"I met him at the wedding, didn't I?" Amy asked. "The one Cutter decided he was going home with while you were gone?"

Hayley laughed as the dog at her feet yipped. "That would be him."

"And look where that got him," Quinn added with a grin.

"Happy at last, you mean? Our little matchmaker," Hayley said with a laugh, ruffling the fur on the dog's head, then going for a scratch behind his right ear that had the dog's head lolling blissfully. Then she looked at her husband. "What did you find out?"

"I told him what happened. He'll call me back if they need a statement, but for now it's just SOP for Soren. And apparently he isn't happy with local law enforcement. They won't leave him alone."

"I'm not surprised," Amy said.

Quinn nodded. "Brett's friend says the narcotics division sets up on him periodically—in fact, they tailed him for a couple of days last week—just to remind him they're still around, even if he walked on the best case they'd managed to put together. They don't, by the way, care for your boss much."

Amy sighed. "I imagine not."

"They're sure he's still dealing, but think he's put a couple more layers of deniability between him and the actual business."

"He'll end up a politician," Walker said.

And yet again Quinn gave him a sharp look. Then

down exactly what's going on. And this commuting alone stuff has to stop. You're too vulnerable. Anywhere you go, I'm with you."

She stared at him in disbelief. "And just where did you get the idea that I take orders from you, Walker Cole?"

"Same place he got the idea he's part of that 'we,' I imagine," Quinn said drily.

Walker turned on Quinn. "You think I'm wrong?"

"Didn't say that. Just wondering why you're even offering." Quinn said.

"Amy," Walker said simply.

Something about the way he said her name made Amy's chest tighten. Which was silly. She didn't want this, didn't want him to have the power to do this to her, make her feel like this. She might not be furious at him any longer, but she still wasn't happy with him, and that's the way she wanted it to stay. But at this moment, when he'd given her name as the only reason he needed to volunteer to protect her, it was annoyingly difficult to hang on to.

"I can call Liam to come down," Quinn said.

"I'm already here," Walker pointed out.

"And Liam is a trained operative," Quinn said. "What makes you think you could handle it?"

Walker's jaw was tight as he faced his brother-in-law. "Try me."

The moment the words left Walker's lips, Quinn moved. Without warning. He punched out at Walker's set jaw. Amy nearly gasped out loud at the unexpected speed of it. Faster even than the first time. Yet Walker reacted as if he'd expected it, throwing up an arm just in time to block the blow. She instinctively took a step toward them, although she wasn't sure exactly what she intended to do. Hayley held her back. Amy flicked a glance at her friend, read her expression quickly. Quinn had a plan, and it needed to play out. Reluctantly, she gave in.

Quinn struck again. This time low and from the side.

Walker blocked him again with a perfectly timed elbow. Quinn advanced. And while Walker ceded some floor to him, Quinn never landed a really solid blow. And once or twice Walker tagged him.

"Well, well," Hayley said.

Amy recognized the feeling. Her own mind had been racing since the instant Walker hadn't gone down when he should have. Somehow he was holding his own against a man she would have thought would have him on the floor begging for mercy in mere seconds.

So why was he? How? *Who the hell was Walker Cole, anyway?*

And then Quinn connected with a solid right. Walker went down this time. But as he did he swept out with one leg, catching Quinn behind the left knee. Quinn staggered, almost going down himself. And by the time he regained his balance, Walker was back on his feet, practically on him. He smacked Quinn's right hip as if they were playing tag football.

Then Walker stopped. Stepped back. Eyed Quinn. "If you'd been armed, you'd be dead."

Quinn, steady now, stared back. After a moment he said, "Surprise is on me. You've had some training."

"And I've picked up a bit here and there."

Amy's brow furrowed as he didn't deny the training comment. Training by who? Where? When? Ideas careered through her mind once more, from possible to outlandish.

"Can you handle a weapon?"

"Not quite as good with sidearms as long guns, but yes."

Amy knew they'd grown up with weapons, and their father had seen to it they knew how to safely use them.

"He is good," Hayley said.

"You won't have the element of surprise with Soren or his henchmen," Quinn warned.

"I won't need it."

As Amy studied Walker the memory of his fight with Quinn played in her mind, and she wondered if he would have had the same outcome with Soren. She found herself half-convinced he would have managed it. Somehow.

She had the feeling a lot more was going on in Quinn's agile brain than merely the assessment of Walker's capabilities. And she was very much afraid she knew what it was.

"All right, then. Come with me."

The two men walked out, headed toward the front building. Quinn pulled some keys out of his pocket as they went, isolating two. One was a door key, the other smaller.

The weapons locker. Hayley had said it was in the office.

"Oh, no," Amy said. "Not happening."

Walker looked back at her. There was more than just satisfaction at having at least matched Quinn in his eyes. There was an edge, a cool toughness she'd never seen there before.

"Live with it, Amy," Walker said, in a voice that matched that expression. "I'm your new bodyguard."

Chapter 21

"Your brother," Quinn said, pulling a beer out of the refrigerator, "is...surprising."

Hayley looked at him. "I noticed."

Amy glanced up from where Hayley was dicing onion as Quinn popped the top and took a drink. She knew from Hayley that he wasn't a big drinker, and wondered if the puzzle that was Walker had driven him to it.

Please. You're the one he's driving crazy.

"What did you mean when you said he'd had training?" she asked. "Do you mean formal training?"

"He moves like someone who's been taught. But that last move, that feint, that was street-survival, think on your feet stuff." He looked at Hayley. "You said he never took martial arts, or even boxing, growing up?"

Hayley shook her head. "He was all baseball, all the time."

"Interesting. And he also handled that Sig I gave him with some familiarity," Quinn mused.

"But he still won't say how or why, on any of it," Amy said, irritation spiking through her voice.

"No. Still says he can't." Quinn shrugged. "At this point, I think we have to accept that. For now at least."

"I'll never forgive what he did to Hayley," Amy said as she added her own sliced tomatoes to the bowl Hayley had placed the diced onions in.

"I didn't say anything about forgiveness," Quinn said.

"Just acceptance, in the sense that there's no use wasting energy pumping him about it."

"Well, that I agree with," Amy said. "It is a waste."

She heard Cutter bark from outside, where Walker had taken him for some more romping in the yard, probably with Cutter's treasured new baseball. Just as he'd begun taking him out early in the morning for a run, saying he wasn't sleeping, anyway. Avoiding nightmares? she wondered.

"He's certainly accepted him," Hayley said.

"Yes, he has," Quinn agreed. "And normally I'd take Cutter's word for it."

"Seriously? The dog?" Amy asked.

Quinn smiled wryly. "Sounds crazy, I know, but he's got a hell of a track record."

"You don't think he's…accepting him just because he can tell he's related to Hayley?"

"There is that," Quinn said. "Which is why I'm withholding final judgment. Because I agree, I don't think I could ever forgive what he did to Hayley, either."

Amy smiled at him, letting her gratitude for his presence in her friend's life show.

"You two do realize it's whether *I* can forgive him that really counts?"

They both looked at Hayley. "Of course," Amy said. "But until then we're going to be angry on your behalf, so you don't have to feel bad about it later."

Hayley laughed. "How noble of you both."

The door swung open, and Cutter trotted into the room. Walker came in after him, shutting the door—not slamming it, Amy noted—behind him. The dog came over to them, greeting each in turn, as if he'd been gone for days instead of a little less than an hour.

"Thanks for running him," Hayley said.

"You're cooking," Walker said with a shrug.

Amy was seized with the sudden, fierce wish that the

cozily domestic scene be real, and lasting. Almost instantly, she quashed it. The combination of wishing and Walker Cole had already taken up far too much of her life. And it wouldn't do to forget that he would be off again, probably sooner rather than later, indulging his wanderlust and leaving them all behind once more.

Gone.

Amy stared at the screen. It was undeniable now. She'd checked three times, her certainty that she must just be looking in the wrong place fading as each successive try rendered the same results.

The files that had started all this were gone. The file on Leda Limited and the bank record, both gone.

Quickly, in case her boss returned from his afternoon client meeting early, she ran a search of the computer's hard drive, then of the office local network. Nothing.

She thought rapidly as she quickly ran a series of other, expected searches to move the ones she'd done off the autofill field. Someone could still find the search terms, but only if they went looking.

It was clear the files had either been deleted, moved or renamed. They could have only been intended to be there temporarily in the first place. Or worse, he could know they'd been seen. It wouldn't take much, just checking the date and time the file was last accessed, but would he? Would he bother?

Only if he really was hiding something, she thought. So if she was right that something was going on, she had to assume he would check, and thus would know the files had been accessed by someone other than himself. And the only people who had access to those files were the partners...and her.

She knew where suspicion would likely fall.

And why would he move or delete them, unless he knows? The answer seemed clear.

"Amy?"

She nearly jumped. She was not, she told herself sourly, cut out to be a spy. She managed to compose herself and turned to look toward the office doorway, where Becca was standing.

"Sorry," she said, rising.

"No prob," Becca said. "Just wanted to ask if you'd have time to go over my file on that big embezzlement case. You've got such a good eye for inconsistencies and problems."

Amy smiled, steadier now. "Of course."

"Thanks, girlfriend. I'll get it to you when it's done."

"Becca?" she asked as the woman turned to go. She looked back. "Have we had any more dealings with Dante Soren on your side?"

Becca drew back, as if she'd surprised her. "Soren? Not that I know of." She smiled then. "We got him off, isn't that enough?"

"Yeah, I guess."

"I have to say, your boss was a master. Why on earth he quit criminal cases is beyond me."

When she'd gone, Amy sank back into her chair for a moment, pondering that. Why would he have quit if he was dirty? Wouldn't he want to stay where he'd be coming across people of like mind?

"Amy?"

Again she almost jumped, and chided herself for it as she looked over to see Kim, the receptionist, standing where Becca had been.

"Your ride's here," the young woman said.

Amy's gaze flicked to the antique clock on the wall, the one Mr. Rockwell had told her had been made by his great-great-grandfather. She was startled to realize it was indeed almost six o'clock. The time at which she had reluctantly agreed her "bodyguard" could come inside to get her.

"Nice work, by the way," Kim added. "He's a hottie."

"Mmm," Amy said noncommittally, fighting the urge to answer, "He's a jerk." Hardly an appropriate response, given the cover explanation they'd come up with, that he was giving her a ride because her car was in the shop.

Besides, that wouldn't really be fair, or right. Walker had been anything but a jerk. He'd been scrupulously polite all day, from the moment she'd stumbled out to the kitchen and he'd had her coffee ready and waiting—just as she liked it, two sugars, without even asking—to the moment he'd walked her inside. She'd tried to get him to just stop at the elevator downstairs, but he'd insisted on escorting her all the way. She had the feeling that if he thought she'd stand for it, he'd have been sitting in the corner of her cubicle all day long.

"He's just a friend," she said.

"Dare I hope he's a friend with benefits and your weekend is looking bright?" Kim asked.

Why was everybody so worried about her sex life? True, she hadn't had much of one for a long time, but that was her business, wasn't it?

"No," she said, wincing a little at the sharpness of her tone.

"I'd work on that if I were you. That is some prime real estate."

Amy opened her mouth to tell Kim, who went through men on a weekly basis, to give it her best effort. Then she stopped, a little startled at the visceral reaction she had to the thought of another woman going after Walker.

She managed a flat "I'll be right out," and left it at that.

And wished it was as easy to cut off the thoughts Kim's teasing had brought on. It was that "with benefits" part…

For a long moment she just stood there, feeling the sudden speed of her pulse, the heat of her skin as the imaginings tumbled through her head. There were echoes of childhood infatuation there, but she wasn't a child anymore. And that made it worse, because now her imaginings were based on knowledge, not fantasy. Not that her experience was so extensive. She'd tried, but…

A sudden memory shot through her mind. Of Hayley, years ago, commiserating with her on the end of the longest relationship she'd ever had with a man. She'd broken it off—new job, not enough time being her excuse, but with that perceptiveness coupled with two decades of friendship Hayley had seen past the pretext.

"You compare them all to Walker, Amy. But not the real Walker, a fantasy you've built up in your mind. And nobody can live up to a fantasy."

Hayley had said it with love then, for it was in the days when her brother still made the effort, when he would call, show up on her birthday, when he still acted like a brother who loved his sister.

Before he'd hurt Hayley so badly Amy had known she could never, ever forgive him.

"Amy?"

She spun around. Stared in shock. Not just because he was there, in the doorway, probably having charmed Kim into letting him through. Because when he chose to exercise it, Walker had an abundance of charm. And this was probably Kim's way of making her point, because what woman breathing could look at Walker Cole and not want him?

And this Walker Cole would fit right in this office.

His hair was still too long, but he'd brushed it neatly now, until it fell silkily to one brow in that way that always made her want to run her fingers through it. In fact, it looked like part of a carefully crafted image, a man too busy or too successful to have to worry about such things.

And the suit. God, the suit, a light gray thing that looked as if it had been custom-tailored for him, made him look broad of shoulder and trim of waist. Which, unlike many others, he actually was. The crisp white shirt and amber-colored tie were the perfect complement. The tie, in fact, set off his eyes, making them look more gold, more dramatic, than ever.

He looked as if he not only belonged here, but in the corner office.

No wonder Kim had let him through.

A shiver went through her as she fought down responses she'd thought were ancient history. But now there he was, standing there, all lean and fit, looking at her curiously, looking at her with those fascinating, dramatically colored eyes, and she was going weak in the knees.

You're going weak, period.

"What have you done?" she asked, hating the almost-rough sound of her voice.

"Cleaned up?" he suggested. "Hayley pointed out if I'm going to be seen around here, I should at least look like I belong in your world."

He looked like he owned her world.

"Ready?" he prompted, and she realized she'd been standing there gaping at him for...she didn't know how long.

"Sorry," she muttered. "Didn't mean to keep you waiting."

"Take your time. I was just checking to make sure you're all right."

"Of course I'm all right."

It sounded snappish, but he only tilted his head slightly, as if she were a machine that had made an unexpected noise. Kind of like Quinn had been looking at him lately. And he'd somehow blasted her discovery that the files that had started all this were gone right out of her mind.

"Let's go," she said, still with an edge despite her effort to tame it. She might as well admit it: this man got to her in a way no other ever had. That it was sometimes to make her furious didn't change but probably enhanced that fact. And noticing that everyone was watching them as they left, no doubt speculating like mad and egged on by Kim, didn't help any.

She wasn't sure anything could help right now.

Chapter 22

Walker didn't say another word until they were in the car. She seemed more edgy than ever, and he didn't want to risk having someone overhear something and wonder. He was supposed to be a friend, a close enough friend to be chauffeuring her every day, after all.

They were driving the vehicle they had picked up at the airport. Charlie had another car being outfitted already, Quinn had said, and in the interim they would use hers if they had to. And Quinn had explained to him exactly what "outfitting" meant in Foxworth terms, showing him the secure communications functions now built into what looked like a simple interior light and garage door system.

He was beginning to realize he'd only seen the tip of the Foxworth iceberg.

"It's a good thing my job is just to keep you safe," he finally said as she fastened her seat belt. "If it was to keep you happy, I'd be a failure."

He saw her mouth tighten, but when she spoke, her voice was even. "I'm not sure the former is necessary, and the latter is my problem, not yours."

"After what Quinn's guy found out about Soren, seeing that history, it is necessary," he argued. "You could end up…"

He broke off as the speaker in the overhead console suddenly came to life with Quinn's voice. Amy didn't seem startled, so apparently she'd already had it explained to her.

He reached up and pushed the green button to transmit.

"Here. Just getting ready to leave her office."

"Everything all right?"

"Fine." Protection-wise, anyway. Personally, not so much.

"Not really," Amy said.

Walker flicked her a sideways glance. Was she going to tell Quinn she didn't want him around again?

"Quinn, the files are gone. They've been deleted, or renamed. I looked as much as I could without getting caught, but I couldn't find them."

Walker's relief that she wasn't asking to get rid of him was quickly vanquished by her words. He frowned as Quinn's voice came over the speaker again. "No new files that weren't there before?"

"I only saw one that was added since I last looked, and it was a new case file from another partner. But I could be missing something. There are at least a hundred files in that secure partition."

"Leave it," Quinn said decisively. "Don't go poking around there anymore. If we need in, I'll have Ty tackle it."

"We have very good security on that system," Amy said.

"And Ty's very good."

"But…"

"Amy," Walker said, "if he doesn't already know you've seen those files, why give him another chance?"

She fell silent, her expression troubled. Walker sensed she was still having trouble with the idea the boss she had once so liked and respected was dirty. He could tell her that sometimes the most charm hid the most dirt—he knew that all too well—but he doubted it would help her much just now.

"You called for something?" he asked Quinn instead.

"Yes. Amy, Ty found something I need to ask you about. Does the name Theo Marquis mean anything to you?"

She frowned, thought for a moment. "It doesn't seem familiar, no. Why?"

"From what Ty was able to track, that seems to be where the money being run through this labyrinth ends up."

"That's who the checks from Leda Limited are going to?"

"He named the company after a Greek myth?" Walker asked, seemingly bemused. Amy glanced at him, startled. "You know. Leda, Zeus in the form of a swan, resulting in Helen of Troy and the twins whose names I can't remember." He finished with a shrug. "Just seems kind of whimsical, that's all."

Amy couldn't deny it was a bit fanciful. But at the moment something else was tickling at the edge of her memory, distracting her. She tried to focus.

"Sorry, go ahead, Quinn."

"A couple more levels down from Leda. The checks are going from the Leda account to another business account, where it then goes to Marquis. The trail ends there, so we assume he's just cashing the checks."

"So he's not just trusting what Rockwell set up for laundering, he's adding his own additional layers?" Walker asked.

"Or Rockwell set this up for him, too, and there's just another record that Amy didn't see."

They were talking, Amy realized, like equals. As if they were two professionals. With respect. Somewhere along the line Quinn had gone from decking his brother-in-law to respecting him, at least in this. One little mostly mock fight had accomplished this? Men, Amy thought, were very strange sometimes.

And the one sitting a foot or so away was one of the strangest.

She stayed silent for a while after the conversation with Quinn ended. There was traffic, as usual, in the area, and it took a while for them to make it to the freeway south, which wasn't moving much faster than the city streets had been.

"Nice suit," she said when they were finally settled into the flow, slow as it was, knowing how inane it sounded even as she said the words.

"Thanks."

"Expensive looking."

He glanced at her. "Worried about my wallet?"

"Foxworth's."

His gaze narrowed. "Don't bother. They didn't pay for it."

She realized then she'd never thought of this aspect of his wandering, that no matter how low-key it was it still took money. How had he survived, let alone accumulated enough to buy a suit she'd guess even off the rack wasn't cheap?

"Where did you go when you first left?" she asked.

For a moment she thought he wasn't going to answer. Then, as if it had been no struggle at all, he said easily, "Wyoming. Yellowstone and Grand Teton. Climbed a lot of that. Then Denver. Climbed Pike's Peak. Then to South Dakota. Mount Rushmore. Didn't climb that."

She smiled in spite of herself. And something niggled at the edge of her memory, something she couldn't quite pin down. "And then?"

"Banff. The Black Hills. Niagara Falls. The coast of Maine. The Florida Keys. The Alamo."

Amy's breath caught as it finally hit her.

"Your father's list."

He glanced at her, then looked back at the road ahead. Or rather the car, since they'd slowed to a turtle's pace. It was plastered with bumper stickers and decals for various causes, a couple of which were amusingly contradictory.

"You were doing his bucket list," she said.

She remembered so well that night when, around the Cole dinner table, the conversation had turned to what they wanted to do before they died. The kids—Hayley, Walker and she herself, thankful as ever that they included her as if she were one of them—thought the idea of a bucket list something only old people thought about, but the idea of all the things to do had intrigued them enough to participate. And it was his father who'd had the grandest, longest list of all the places he'd wanted to visit, all the iconic things he wanted to see.

And then he'd been killed before he could do any of it.

But his son had apparently decided to do it for him.

"Hayley knows this?"

"I told her, eventually. When she was old enough to really understand."

"She was fourteen when you left. Wasn't that old enough?"

He sighed. "Probably. But I didn't get it myself, not yet. Not until I got to Mount Rushmore did I realize what I was really doing. I thought I was just trying to get away from all the reminders."

"And going everyplace he wanted to go didn't remind you?"

He chuckled at that ruefully. "Of course it did. But I was eighteen. I still thought I could run away from the pain."

That memory came back to her again. "Hayley and I talked the other day about whether it was worse to lose a parent you deeply loved, or to never have had one at all. She thought never having one was worse. I thought having one and losing them would be a million times worse."

"So each of you thought the other had it worse."

"Yes."

"I think that says more about you two and how much you care about each other than it does about the original question."

She stared at him, impossibly moved by his words. He kept his eyes on the stop-and-go traffic ahead, allowing her the chance to study him. He looked like any successful businessman—or lawyer—who would be at home in this crazed, upscale environment. There were still traces of the boy, but the line of his jaw and the corded tendons of his neck, the taut muscles of arms and size and power of his hands, it was all uncompromisingly adult male.

And somehow it made this realization of why he'd left, that he'd been a boy setting out to fulfill his dead father's dreams, impossibly poignant.

"Why didn't Hayley tell me? Did you ask her not to?"

"No." He glanced at her again. "Maybe she did tell you. Maybe you just didn't want to hear it."

She opened her mouth to deny that, then stopped. She had been so crushed, and so very, very young. And by the time he'd told his sister, she herself had been finally getting over his abrupt departure.

"I think," she said slowly, "she may not have told me because she didn't want me to fall for you all over again."

That drew her more than a glance. "Are you saying you would have?"

"If I'd known what you were doing?" She sighed. "Probably. It is rather appealing. Romantic. Emotional. All those things teenage girls find so hard to resist."

They'd come to a complete stop, sitting behind a large truck that blocked any view of the lane ahead. He turned slightly then to look at her head-on.

"But that doesn't make up for the rest, does it."

It wasn't a question, which told her he already knew the answer. "Do you really think your father would believe you fulfilling his own dreams was more important than being there for your family, when they needed you so much?"

To his credit, he didn't hesitate. "No. Nothing was more important than that to him." He turned back, and she wondered if he was using the still-unmoving traffic as an excuse to no longer hold her gaze. "But there were a couple of things just as important to him."

"Such as?"

"His duty. As a cop, and an American."

It sounded a bit high-flown, but she had to acknowledge the truth of his words. Christopher Cole had been a dedicated police officer who loved his country and took the job very seriously, and gave each of the two parts of "protect and serve" full weight. Wasn't she herself proof of that?

If he had not, her own life would likely have been a very different—and grim—thing.

But something in Walker's voice, some undertone that seemed both tense and weary at the same time, coalesced with all her theories about where he'd been and what he'd been doing in those missing years, and she knew that answer had more levels than she might ever know.

What she did know was that she didn't, couldn't, hate him anymore. In fact, were she honest with herself, she'd have to admit she was as drawn to him as she'd ever been.

Amy glanced at the bedside clock once more, despite promising herself she wouldn't. She sighed, seeing it was nearly dawn. She hadn't imagined that it was getting lighter in the room. How could she be so tired her head hurt, yet be unable to fall asleep? If only her brain had an off switch, she thought. But then she'd be tempted to never turn it back on. Besides, how could you turn a switch if your brain was off?

Taking this ridiculous train of thought as conclusive evidence that she had slipped from merely tired into insane, she rolled over, turning her back to the clock, and set about thinking of something else, anything else.

No, not Walker. *Don't think about him.* He's even more unsettling than learning her boss was likely a criminal. And he'd been right, the fact that he'd left his life, his family—including her—for what could even been considered a laudable reason, a tribute to his father, didn't make up for the fact that he hadn't been there when he was desperately needed. And yet that she was even thinking it only told her she was already in trouble. They'd spent too much time together; she was weakening, in serious danger of falling for him all over again. He was just so damned... unexpected. Not the ogre her anger had made of him, not at all. He was still Walker, and she was still...

No. No, she was *not* going down that rabbit hole again.

Cutter, she thought suddenly. Yes, that was safe. She'd think about the dog, with his happy grin and that uncanny way he had of sensing people's feelings and expressing his own. He...

Almost on the thought she heard the faint click of toenails on the tile floor of the bathroom between her room and Hayley and Quinn's. The door on her side inched open, and moments later the dog was there, his chin resting on the edge of the bed as he looked at her.

Stared at her, more like. She lifted her head to look at him, could see the faint gleam of his eyes even in the darkened room. And she couldn't deny his stare was pretty intense.

"Do you read thoughts now, dog?" she asked in a whisper. "Did you hear me thinking about you?"

He inched a little closer. Instinctively, she reached out and stroked his head. Then again. And, that quickly, her inner turmoil seemed to ebb a little. Hayley had told her Cutter had a knack—one of many—for soothing troubled souls, even aching bodies. She'd doubted that, too.

Now she wasn't so sure.

"Did you want up?" she asked.

On the last word, the dog jumped neatly up onto the bed, barely disturbing it despite his weight. He lay down beside her, his chin now resting on her shoulder. She put her head back down, smiling in spite of herself. She'd never been allowed a pet—and had been afraid one wouldn't survive her father's capriciousness—so this was a new treat to her. She shifted so she could reach that spot behind his right ear that he seemed to love to have scratched. And something about the action, or the dog himself, slowed her racing mind down another notch.

She could sleep now, she thought with no small amount of wonder. It was almost here; she could feel it. She closed her eyes.

"Thank you," she whispered to Cutter. She let it come, her weary eyes anticipating the relief, her body the warmth, her heart and mind the respite. The daytime business tried to intrude, but she was drifting now, sweetly numbed, nothing could...

Amy jolted upright, the covers falling away. Because in the instant before sleep had claimed her, that last moment when she felt almost like she was floating, an image had glided through her mind.

A man, coming out of a shop with a cup of coffee, walking down the sidewalk toward a flashy black car.

Dante Soren. The cold, arrogant, drug dealer. Murderer. Looking so very different. So very...normal. Ordinary. Holding a cup of coffee from a shop so busy they had to scrawl names on the cups. Had scrawled a name on his.

Theo.

Chapter 23

The proximity of others had made quiet necessary, and somehow that heightened their always passionate love-making, as if what they couldn't express in sound channeled into the physical, making it even more intense.

"There's something to be said for having to stay quiet," Hayley had whispered as she lay collapsed atop her husband in the faint light of dawn.

"Speak for yourself," Quinn had muttered, shoving away the pillow he'd used to muffle his cry of her name as this woman he loved to the ends of the earth had driven him to near-madness. "I think I breathed in a feather."

"And I think I nearly bit through my lip," she admitted.

"Want me to kiss it and make it better?"

"You're liable to end up with another feather."

He grinned at her. "Worth it."

For a long time they had just lain there in silence, savoring the warmth, the closeness. Until Cutter, on the floor beside them, stirred, rose and padded over to the bathroom.

The door had apparently not been latched, because he nosed it open just enough for his lean body to slip through. They'd heard him walk across the tiled floor, and then the faint creak of the door into the other bedroom.

"He went to Amy," Hayley whispered finally when he didn't come back.

"I think she was pretty upset today," Quinn whispered,

as well, now that both doors were open. "He probably sensed that."

"Or he's bored with us," Hayley teased, "because we're always doing this."

"Tough," Quinn said. "That's not going to change."

"I certainly hope not."

More silence, easy, comfortable, necessary.

"I hope he's able to help her sleep," Hayley murmured, sounding close to slipping away herself.

"He has the knack." He hesitated, knowing this might destroy the mood, feeling the need, anyway. "Your brother has nightmares."

"I know. I've heard him." He'd done it now, he thought. She was wide-awake again. "He's changed. More than I would have expected, even after all this time." She lifted her head to look at him. "You trusted him with Amy."

"Yes."

"Are you changing your mind about him?"

"I wouldn't go that far. He still hurt you badly."

She sighed. "Yes. But…"

"He's still your brother. And there's more to him than I expected. I'm starting to think there might really be a good reason he can't or won't tell us."

Hayley shifted, snuggling deeper into his arms.

"This will sound crazy, but in a way he's reminding me of…" She trailed off with a grimace. Obviously, what she was thinking seemed too crazy to put into words.

"Rafe?" Quinn suggested.

Hayley sighed. "Yes. You see it, too?"

"I see shadows," he admitted. "No idea what kind. Rafe is…"

"A hero. I know. And those shadows he lives with are the price he pays for it. But Walker… I don't know."

"He's obviously determined to have some kind of relationship with you, because he's still here even though he hasn't exactly gotten a warm welcome."

"You mean because Amy verbally eviscerated him and you put him on the ground?"

Quinn grimaced. "He nearly returned that favor. And I haven't been surprised like that in a long time. I wonder where he…"

He broke off at the faint sound of Cutter's nails on the tile floor of the bathroom again.

"Time for a session with Laney's nail grinder," Hayley said as the dog slipped back into the room. "I should have…"

She stopped as a light tap came on the door to the bathroom.

"Hayley?"

They were sprawled diagonally across the bed, naked, covers long ago kicked aside. Hayley grabbed hastily at the sheet while Quinn righted the pillows.

"Amy, are you all right?" Hayley asked when the essentials were covered.

"I'm sorry, but Cutter, he practically dragged me over here."

Quinn and Hayley exchanged a glance. "Hmm," Quinn murmured, then nodded.

"Come on in," Hayley said. "What is it?"

If Amy guessed from the tangled state of the bed what they'd been doing, it didn't show. She seemed far too unsettled to care anyway.

"I…remembered something," she said.

"What?" Hayley prompted when she stopped.

"When I saw Soren coming out of the coffee shop next to the mailbox place…he was carrying a cup of coffee."

Quinn lifted a brow at her when she stopped again. Waited.

"There was a name written on it, you know, how they do when they're busy?"

Quinn drew back slightly. Amy looked up then, meeting his gaze.

"It was Theo."

"Well, well," Quinn said.

"I thought it was just a coincidence that he was there. That it was some sort of… I don't know, alter ego, since he looked so different. If it hadn't been for the car, I might not even have recognized him. But I know it was him."

"So the guy on the receiving end of this laundered cash is the drug dealer your boss got off on multiple murder charges?"

Amy nodded, looking miserable.

"And he's using an alias the police don't seem to know about," Hayley said. "There was no 'Theo' or 'Marquis' on the list Brett's friend gave us."

"A clean one, perhaps?" Quinn mused. "Maybe he looked so different because it really is an alter ego."

"The drug trafficker hiding in plain sight as normal citizen?" Amy shivered visibly.

"Best camouflage sometimes," Quinn said.

"Now what?" Amy asked, sounding more distressed than she had in a while.

"Now we plan," Quinn said.

"Good thing we've got the weekend to do it," Hayley said brightly. "Amy, you want to put the coffee on, and we'll get started?"

Quinn saw his wife's tone calm her friend as surely as if she'd steadied her with a touch. Women, he thought, were amazing. And his wife was the most amazing of all.

Chapter 24

Walker watched her from the couch as she prepared the coffeemaker and started it. She looked sleepy still, in an endearing sort of way. She was wearing a different T-shirt and snug leggings, and when his first thought was how easy it would be to peel them off those long legs, his body woke up fiercely.

She reached up to shove back the tangle of her hair, messing it even more. The just-out-of-bed look only nudged his response up a level, and he realized if he was smart, he wouldn't be standing up himself for a couple of minutes. Somehow he doubted Amy would appreciate his physical condition just now. Just now, he didn't appreciate it himself, since there was less than zero chance it was going to get eased in his choice of ways.

She yawned widely. It inspired an answering one he couldn't stop, and she heard him.

"You're up early," he said when she looked over. "Really early for a Saturday."

"Yes. Sorry."

He sat up in a tangle of blanket and the sweatpants he'd been sleeping in. The sweats were loose, but not loose enough to hide what just looking at her had done to him. He kept the blanket over him.

"Wasn't a complaint. Been awake for a while."

"Nightmares again?"

"I think they call them something else when you're

not asleep," he said ruefully. And awake he'd been, since long before dawn had started to lighten the sky. "Mind just won't stop."

"I call it anxiety chaos."

He blinked. "What?"

"Anxiety chaos. It's when you're worrying about a lot of different things and your brain refuses to settle on one and deal with it, but keeps bouncing around from one to the other like a billiard ball."

He laughed. "Yes, that. Exactly that."

She smiled. And it was ridiculous, he told himself, how much just that warmed him.

"Coffee?" she asked, lifting the pot and gesturing in his general direction.

He assessed how much control he'd regained, decided it was enough and got to his feet. "Thanks."

By the time he got there she had a mug poured for him. It was the friendliest gesture she'd made, and he dared to hope Hurricane Amy's winds might be ebbing. He added a packet of sugar, as much for the energy hit as the sweet, then leaned against the kitchen counter and looked at her as he took a sip.

"A little anxiety chaos of your own?"

She hesitated, then nodded. "I remembered something."

"Oh?" Again, she hesitated. He set down the mug. "Amy, if I'm going to keep you safe, I need to know. Everything."

She looked him up and down. It took her long enough that he was glad he was in pretty good shape, and he was foolish enough to hope she was seeing something she liked. But then she focused on the tat on his inner forearm, her brow slightly furrowed, and he wished he'd taken the time to get it removed. Or given how long that took, at least get it changed, worked over into something other than the ugly reminder.

"Where did you learn to fight like that?"

"Here and there."

"Quinn said you'd had training."

Obviously, he was going to have to work to get that answer. He picked his coffee up again and took another sip before saying, "I didn't sign up at the local dojo, if that's what you're asking."

Her mouth quirked. "Were you ever anyplace long enough?"

"Some places more than others. I stayed until I had enough money to move on. Once it was a year before I had enough. That's why it took so long to get the list done."

"What did you do? To earn money, I mean?"

He grinned at that. "What didn't I do? I shoveled manure, I stocked shelves, rented kayaks, and in one place I sold rain gear. That felt like home."

She studied him for a moment, and when she spoke, he got the feeling it was to ask a question she'd had in that agile mind of hers for a long time. "You never…wanted someplace to settle and not move on?"

"It was a long list. Dad had a lot of places he'd wanted to see in a lot of states."

"And you were determined to finish it."

"I needed to finish it." He didn't enjoy talking about it; in fact, had quite gotten out of the habit, since it had been five years since he'd been forced off the path he'd chosen. "It seems crazy, I know, but I felt closer to him in those places he'd always wanted to see than I did standing at his grave."

Amy cupped her mug as if drawing warmth from it. The little dwelling was fairly cool at night, even in the California heat, building already in early spring. They'd known what they were doing, those early folks who'd built their homes with thick adobe walls.

"Maybe he was there," she said. "With you."

That surprised him. He didn't recall Amy ever having a whimsical turn of mind. She'd always been pretty much a literalist, and he'd always thought it had come from the chaos of her home life; she tried for order and reality and predictability everywhere else.

Perhaps that she'd had this thought now was a sign of how far she'd come from those days.

"It felt that way sometimes." He hesitated for a moment, then decided this quiet moment was too precious to waste. "When I finally got to the Alamo, last on the list, it felt… different. You know he always had a fascination with it. When I got there, when I was standing there, in that place, it felt…as if it was time to let go. Let him go, I mean."

"Maybe that's where he wanted to be," she said quietly. "With the spirit of those other brave men like him."

He smiled, pleased at her characterization. "Maybe."

"But you kept moving after that."

He shrugged. "By then I liked it. Was used to it. New places, different people."

He picked up the coffeepot and, when she nodded, topped off her mug, then his own. The caffeine was beginning to work; he was feeling almost human again.

"What I remembered…" she began abruptly.

So he was finally going to get an answer. He listened intently, silently, liking it less with every word. She had just finished, and he was turning it over in his mind, when Quinn and Hayley walked in. Quinn made a beeline for the coffeepot.

"She told you?" Hayley asked.

Walker nodded.

"Sounds ugly," Quinn said.

"That the fictitious company is shelling out money to a killer and major drug trafficker? Worse than ugly. Amy needs to get out of there."

"Amy can make up her own mind, thank you," Amy said in that too-sweet tone that was as much a warning as a fire alarm.

"Depends on what the goal is here," Quinn said, then took a long sip of coffee.

"The goal?" Walker asked.

"If the only goal is keeping Amy safe, then yes, she should get out of there."

"Wait a minute," Amy exclaimed, sounding as if she felt a bit betrayed. Quinn held up a hand and she subsided, waiting.

"But if the goal is finding the truth, then she needs to stay. She's our only way in." Another long draw on the mug, then Quinn set it down.

"What about the cops?" Walker asked.

"I believe what we have would be called skimpy at the very best. Especially now that the evidence has been removed. And they're not likely to give Cutter's instincts much credit, either."

"I want to know the truth," Amy said. "If my boss is scummy, I want to know. I can't work for someone like that."

"Some would say it's a given, if you work for a lawyer," Quinn said drily.

"I thought he was different. I really did."

Amy sounded so disheartened Walker wanted to hug her. He doubted she would welcome it.

"So what do we do?" Walker asked.

Quinn glanced at Hayley. "We plan," she said.

"Plan what?" Amy asked.

Quinn looked at his wife with a satisfaction that Walker envied even as he appreciated it, for his sister's sake. Not to mention he appreciated that he was apparently now included in that "we."

"A trap," he said.

Chapter 25

"You can't do it."

Amy turned her head, gave Walker her best shot at the intimidating down-the-nose look she'd seen Becca give antagonistic witnesses. "I beg your pardon?"

To her chagrin, Walker just laughed. "Come on, it would never fly."

"And why not?" she asked, trying not to sound as indignant as she felt. They'd been hashing this out all afternoon, and she'd assumed from the beginning that she would be the one who set the bait.

"Because nobody who knows the first thing about you would ever believe you'd turn bad," Walker said.

She supposed she should be flattered by that. But she couldn't help pointing something else out. "A lot of people would say that about Mr. Rockwell, too." Then, added sadly, "Including me."

"Walker does, however," Quinn said rather carefully, "have a point."

"But it has to be me. I'm the one who has the in," Amy said. They'd agreed they would lure her boss with some tempting information, since he'd already shown he was willing to bend principles for gain.

"I'll do it."

Amy's gaze snapped back to Walker. "What?"

"You have to admit, I can play slime much better than you ever could."

"Play?"

Walker winced. "Been holding that back for a while, have you?"

"Yes," she admitted.

Walker let out a long breath before saying, "I appreciate the honesty. But it's exactly why I'm right. You could never be convincingly corrupt."

"I can pretend," she insisted.

Walker shook his head, and when he spoke there was nothing of teasing or criticism in it. "You're honest to the bone, Amy Clark. And it shows. Hell, it glows."

Amy looked at the others. Quinn looked like he agreed with Walker. Hayley was looking from Walker to her and back again, a thoughtful expression on her face.

"He is right about that," Hayley said after a moment.

Amy let out a disgusted breath. And then she nearly laughed at herself. This was something she should be glad about, wasn't it? Hadn't she spent her life being scrupulously honest to counter the influence of the man who tossed off any story that would get him out of trouble or earn him another drink?

"But how could he lure my boss into this?" Amy asked, finally accepting. "How would he even get close enough to him?"

"Easy," Walker said. "I just become exactly who your receptionist thought I was."

Amy stared at him. "But she thought you were…"

"I know."

Something in the look he gave her then sent her insides into free fall. Because Kim had assumed they were together. In intimate ways. She'd only dropped back to the friend with benefits when Amy had denied it.

Because she believed her. Because Walker was right; she just didn't—and probably couldn't—give off the vibe of deceitfulness that it would take to carry this off herself.

"Come on," he said, almost coaxingly, "you can pretend you don't hate me. You've done it. Maybe you can even pretend you like me. A stretch, I know," he added wryly. "But it's a lot more believable that you'd fall for a scumbag than that you are one."

Amy felt the sudden urge to retreat, to go somewhere, anywhere, alone, away from him, so she could sort out the chaotic feelings that were rocketing through her. She wasn't sure what was affecting her more, that he thought so highly of her, or that he was actually willing to play this part, given how she'd treated him.

Not that it would be difficult to act like she was infatuated with him. She had spent over ten years of her life that way, hadn't she?

She'd also spent a considerable and painful amount of time getting over that infatuation.

But that didn't mean she didn't remember what it had felt like. Could she reenact that? Pretend she was head over heels for Walker Cole and his incredible eyes and knock-your-socks-off grin?

Oh, I can do that all right, she thought. *Too easily.*

She remembered the expression on Kim's face, realized half the job would be already done for her, because any breathing woman would be halfway there herself after her first look at him. They'd probably be wondering what a man like him saw in her, but it's doubtful anyone would question her side.

"Amy?"

She looked at him. Her mouth quirked downward at one corner. "I think," she said, "the bigger acting job is going to be yours."

For a moment he just looked at her, but then, slowly, he shook his head. "No. Not to any guy, anyway."

"At the risk of interrupting whatever's going on between you two," Quinn said, "we still have some strategy to work out."

Walker broke the eye contact that had lingered long enough to speed up her pulse all over again.

"I'll need an approach that doesn't undermine Amy," he said. "Just in case we're wrong."

Hayley lifted an eyebrow and after a moment gave him a slight nod. Amy had the impression she was studying her brother carefully when she said, "So that lets out her letting something slip in pillow talk."

Amy thought there was a second of lag time before Walker nodded in turn. She herself felt as if she'd been sideswiped. Pillow talk. And again she was all tangled up. Walker wanted to protect her job, so he had rejected the scenario where she let something slip in an intimate moment. She suppressed a shiver at the very thought of intimate moments with him. It took an effort; she was out of practice. She was sure that was all it was; she just hadn't had to do it for a long time.

And yet...

"I may have a way around that," Quinn said. "Let me make a call."

He took out his phone and walked toward the door. He made a slight motion with his hand, barely perceptible, but Cutter was on his feet in an instant and at his heels.

"Cutter certainly obeys him," Amy said as they stepped outside, and Quinn closed the door behind him. She somehow doubted he'd ever been a door slammer, even as a kid.

"He has since the first moment they met. Or rather, since the first moment Cutter dragged me into his life."

Amy laughed, glad of the change to something more comfortable to talk about. "He does seem to have a nose for trouble."

"And love," Hayley said softly.

"His matchmaking success rate is pretty impressive," Amy said, thinking of the couples she'd met at the wedding.

"Yes," Hayley agreed. "Us, the Burdettes, Teague and Laney, the Kileys, now Brett and Sloan."

Walker looked from his sister to her, and Amy nearly laughed at his expression. "You say that like he meant it all to happen."

"I'm just saying he brought them all together, wouldn't let them leave until they worked their problems out," Hayley said.

"And," Amy added, enjoying his discomfiture, "they're all deliriously happy."

"I thought you said he found you cases, people with problems."

"He does. I'm not sure which he thinks is his main job, though."

"This is a dog we're talking about," Walker pointed out.

"So they say," Hayley said cheerfully.

Walker looked at the both of them as if they'd slipped slightly out of their orbit. But before he could speak, Quinn was coming back through the door. Cutter trotted ahead and, to Amy's surprise, went to Walker, turned and sat at his feet, all the while looking up at her. Almost expectantly. Considering the conversation they'd just been having, it was a little unnerving.

"All right," Quinn said briskly, slipping his phone back into his pocket as he strode toward them, "I think we—or rather you," he said with a look at Walker, "are all set."

"I am? How?"

Quinn looked steadily at his ne'er-do-well brother-in-law. "I got you a job," he said.

But he knew better now. Nothing could ever make this heal. Nothing.

Not even saving a few thousand lives and maybe the damned world.

Chapter 27

This charade, Amy thought, was going to be awful.

"Everything needs to look as normal as possible," Quinn had said. "So as far as anyone is concerned, you were spending time with friends visiting down here for a week. Now it's back to business as usual."

She understood why it had to be this way to work, but it was still going to be awful. She wouldn't miss the long commute. Just a week of it, even with someone else driving and for company—well, except for the times when it had been Walker, and she'd been too wired to relax—had reminded her why she had reluctantly moved into the city. She wouldn't even have to miss seeing Hayley, since they had followed along, taking up residence in a local long-term-stay hotel that was about midway between her condo and the office. And since they didn't welcome pets, she had Cutter with her in the back of her compact hatchback.

Which, she thought as she headed home for the first time in days, might just save her sanity, having the dog to focus on. And he would be, Hayley had promised, an extra layer of protection.

"Trust him," she'd said. "He knows what he's doing, I promise."

Amy was driving because this was her turf, as Walker had put it. And, she'd realized quickly, it freed him to be looking around, watching. Odd, it almost seemed as if he'd done this before, this constant surveillance, the awareness on all sides.

Her self-appointed, Quinn-approved bodyguard masquerading as boyfriend.

And that was what was going to be awful.

"It has to look like you're head over heels," Quinn had said. "You've got to make it seem like he's charmed your socks off."

Even Quinn had looked a bit uncomfortable at the subtext of that. Amy wished he would have chosen a different turn of phrase.

"Charming," she muttered now as she negotiated a turn behind a large delivery van.

"I can be charming," Walker said drily. "All you have to do is pretend to believe it."

"Do you really have to move in with me? That's hardly my style."

"Hard to bodyguard when you're not with the body," Walker said.

"If that's your idea of charming, it needs some work."

"If that's your idea of pretending, I could say the same."

Cutter whuffed softly from the back of the vehicle. Apparently, he wasn't happy with their snippy exchange, either. Hayley had always told her the dog had definite opinions, which she'd thought merely an amusing anthropomorphization. But now that she'd been around the animal more, she wasn't so sure.

She glanced at Walker. He'd changed, she thought. Something had definitely changed since Saturday night, when Hayley had utterly destroyed him with that simple truth of a dying mother's unfailing love in the face of desertion.

She'd been stunned at his reaction. She hadn't thought he cared enough to be so devastated, but there had been no doubt. He'd gone stark white and practically stumbled as he retreated to be violently, physically ill. She'd felt an unwanted qualm, a rush of pity; she didn't like to see anyone so destroyed right in front of her, not even Walker. She wasn't angry anymore; she couldn't be, not after that.

He'd barely said a word all day Sunday, and then only to Quinn, to affirm he would go along with whatever his brother-in-law had planned. But by this morning a bit of the old Walker was back. Yet something was different. It was as if he didn't care any longer what she, or even Hayley, thought of him.

Or as if he'd given up trying to change what they thought of him.

Just when she was realizing her thoughts had changed.

"Let's set some basics, all right?" Walker said. "I'm not expecting you to even speak to me outside of operational necessity. But nobody's going to believe us as a couple if you're this tense."

Operational necessity?

And before, he'd used the words *trained operative*. He must have picked up the phrases from Quinn, who did revert to such jargon now and then.

"It's all an act, okay? A play. Except you need to stay in character from the moment we step outside this door until we're back. Believe me, it's easier than trying to go back and forth and risk somebody seeing or hearing something to give you away."

And just how, she wondered, did he know that?

She gave him a sideways glance before making the turn onto her narrow street. "Do you really think we can pull this off?"

He gave a half shrug. "I hope the fact that we have one kind of history will make the other kind believable."

She hadn't thought about it that way. "You mean because you know things about me from when I was a kid?"

"Something like that. Isn't that the kind of thing lovers learn about each other?"

He said it so simply, in such an ordinary tone, that it

shouldn't have taken her breath away. But it did. She was starting to think that constantly reminding herself of what he'd done was a defensive reaction. Could it be that she was using that to keep a safe distance between them? Did she even want that safe distance?

She wasn't even sure there was such a thing, not anymore. Not with Walker.

"I don't know," she said, not even sure if she was answering his question or her own thought.

Either way, it was pretty unnerving.

"What do you need?"

Since Rafe couldn't see him, Quinn smiled. It was one of the best things about talking to his oldest friend; many steps could be skipped.

"A couple of things actually. Tangible and not so."

"Go."

"First, we're going to need at least one rifle down here, for this office. We're sidearms-only right now. Thought you'd have the best ideas on that."

"You got it. Office going to work out?"

"Charlie found it."

"Yeah. Well."

Quinn knew this wasn't the time so he let it slide. He wasn't sure there would ever be a time, not with Rafe.

"Next?" Rafe asked, proving his thought correct.

"I need you to do something that could get me in a whole lot of trouble."

"Shoot," Rafe said. Not even a split second's hesitation.

"It's kind of about Hayley," he said.

Now came the hesitation. "It's going to get you in trouble with her?"

"Maybe."

"Then I have to ask what I never ask. Are you sure?"

The words told him volumes about Rafe's estimation of his wife.

"It may never go beyond me." He didn't add that it couldn't go beyond Rafe, either; he knew he didn't have to. "I just want to have it, in case I need it."

"All right."

"I need you to get hold of your buddy from Hoover." He knew Rafe would get the reference to FBI Headquarters in DC.

"And?"

"Give him a name to check out. And I'm sending you a rough sketch of a tattoo. Looks familiar, and just that it's a tat should narrow things down, since they're forbidden in some quarters. I need whatever he can find on both."

"Is this a name I know?"

"Yes. Newly arrived."

"Male or female?"

"Male."

"Got it."

Quinn knew he had. Only one person fit, and Rafe wouldn't miss it. For a long moment after he'd ended the call, he stared at the phone. He didn't know what Rafe might find out. Didn't know if he'd ever use it. But every gut instinct he had was firing that there was more, much more, than they knew.

He just had to hope Hayley wouldn't get too angry at him for going where she'd never wanted him to go.

Walker had been curious—okay, maybe a little more than curious—to see her place. Wondering what aspects of her personality would show, if she was still a "place for everything and everything in its place" kind of person. Hayley had always said her drive for order stemmed from the lack of it as a child, which made sense. He'd never been in her childhood home, but his sister had, and she'd said it was the worst kind of mess. Her father was apparently usually too drunk to care, and her mother had stopped giving a damn long ago even then.

It was amazing, he thought as she parked the car in the single garage allotted to her unit, that she'd accomplished what she had. It was a sign of her grit and intelligence and determination.

And, he realized belatedly, his own family had contributed to her success, as well. Not him, of course, but Hayley, and their parents. They'd taken Amy in until he'd started to think of her as a sister. It had even annoyed him much like sisters would have, when he'd been at that difficult transition into early teenage years, and the two girls got their heads together and started giggling as girls did at that age.

Amy opened the back hatch for Cutter, and when he jumped out and promptly sat at her feet, looking up expectantly, she laughed and bent to plant a kiss atop the dog's dark head. Walker felt an odd tug inside. Because it was such a sweet, loving gesture, he told himself. Nothing to do with the way it emphasized the length of her legs, or the slight glimpse of luscious curves he got thanks to the V-neck of her knit top.

Nothing to do with the unbidden wish that she show half as much affection to him.

This, he thought, could turn into a very special kind of hell, if he let it.

He should have run when he had the chance. They probably expected him to run. To take off, as he always had. It was all useless anyway.

But he wasn't going to run. He'd toughened up. A lot.

He'd thought these past five years of living in true hell were the hardest thing he would ever do.

He'd been wrong.

Remember why you're here, he ordered himself. He was here because Amy had run afoul of what could be a dangerous mess. Because a man as ruthless as the man he'd seen in that courtroom video, using every trick in the book and writing a few new ones to win a case, wouldn't hesitate to sacrifice her if he had to.

Because anytime there was lots of dirty money involved, things got ugly.

Because one of the main characters in this little drama was a stone-cold killer.

And Amy was on his radar.

Chapter 28

This party, Amy thought, was going to be hellish.

It was already bad enough that Walker was essentially living with her. Bad enough that she kept thinking of the benefits part of Kim's teasing about him being a friend with benefits. Bad enough showing up with him all week at local gathering spots, meeting him for lunch in the bistro she and Becca had gone to, for coffee at the kiosk downstairs in her building, anyplace where they would be seen by others.

And they were seen. She was teased. She'd been prepared for that; she'd known it would come and had even practiced some breezy, happy answers, sounding like she imagined a woman head over heels would sound. When asked about him, she'd given the answers they'd prepared last weekend, answers that would match what anyone inquiring about him would be told. They had even, with Ty's help, planted a series of back-and-forth emails that, to anyone with less skill than the Foxworth tech expert, would appear to have been going on for a while. And so far it had all gone well; no one seemed in the slightest suspicious.

Kim had been delighted, not just for Amy but for being proven right. So Amy was fairly confident they'd succeeded in putting on the facade they'd intended.

But tonight, masquerading as a newly in love couple in front of nearly fifty people, playing the part of a woman utterly infatuated with Walker's easy charm and eye-catching looks, in front of everyone she worked with, that was going to be a special kind of torture. Not that she thought anyone wouldn't believe it. They'd take one look at Walker and understand completely.

She wondered what they'd say if she told them she'd known Walker since she was a child, the stereotypical book nerd, and he'd never teased or been cruel to her; in fact, had defended her rather heroically, for a teenager.

She sighed as she finished with her makeup. For Walker had indeed been that quiet, shy girl's hero. She remembered the day he'd pulled out of their driveway in the old pickup, which he had spent much of that two years restoring lovingly. She'd understood that; it had been his father's. She'd just never expected him to leave in it and never come back. Well, he had come back, but not to stay. Never to stay.

And you have become a rambling idiot.

She took a step back, smoothed down the simple knit dress. No fancy, flashy style for her; this dress was all about the fabric and the color. The color was a rich teal that somehow turned her eyes the same shade, while the fabric clung here, skimmed there and ended up being, as Becca had told her when she'd picked it out for her last year, incredibly sexy and yet so subtle any guy would be reeling before he even realized why.

She wasn't sure that was an effect she wanted, hadn't even had the nerve to wear it before now. It was a regular battle, to remind herself she was no longer the nerdy girl, that her first gut reaction didn't always have to be protective, defensive. But the dress was perfect for tonight. It needed to be believable that a man who looked like Walker would want her, and this dress just might do it.

Want her.

She bit her lip at the stab of longing that went through her. Then made herself stop, before she messed up the lipstick she'd so carefully applied.

It had only been two weeks since Walker had strolled back into her life, and she was already mooning over him as if she were still that bedazzled little girl.

So bedazzled she sometimes caught herself thinking he was looking at her as if he did want her.

Even if that were true, she thought, it certainly shouldn't give her a thrill. He could be sweet, indeed charming, and those eyes and that smile could still utterly disarm her. But he was still the guy who'd deserted her best friend when she needed him most. Who hadn't been there for the mother she herself had loved, in many ways, more than her own. But she couldn't find that gut-deep anger at him anymore. Not in the face of his anguish.

She took a deep breath, told herself to focus on why she was doing this. It wasn't any more soothing, given she could well be out of a job no matter how this turned out, but at least she knew it was the right thing to do. And they'd prepared as much as was possible; she'd given him a rundown on everyone likely to be there, even warned him about a couple. Mrs. Caden, for instance, who was going to take one look at him and zero in like a starving carnivore.

"Fresh meat, huh?" he'd said, making her laugh unexpectedly.

"The word *cougar* applies in more ways than one," she'd agreed.

She picked up her glasses from the bathroom counter. She'd ordered them specifically to match this dress, but she had yet to wear them together. When she slipped them on, finally able to see the entire effect, she knew she'd done the best she could. And putting it off wasn't going to improve things any. With a final sigh, she picked up the small—miniscule, for her—clutch bag from the bathroom counter, then slid her feet into the heels she would likely regret before the night was over.

Now or never. She turned out the light and headed for the living room.

Walker, who had shaved and dressed using the small powder room, was sitting on the couch, seemingly engrossed in the book he was holding. The legal thriller Becca had given her, saying it was refreshingly accurate, and that she had left on the side table.

He looked up then. His eyes widened. His gaze flicked over her. The book dropped, apparently unnoticed, sliding off his knee and onto the cushion beside him.

"Holy…"

It came out under his breath, in a tone of such awe she couldn't help but be warmed by it.

"Hardly," she retorted, but she couldn't deny how his response had made her feel. There had been no artifice about it, no practiced smoothness, just stunned reaction, and it made her heart race.

Slowly, he got to his feet, still staring.

"You look…amazing."

"Thank you," she said, meaning it.

"I'm going to be fighting guys off all night."

She studied him for a moment. He was wearing that suit again; it fit him as if it had been custom-tailored for his lean, broad-shouldered frame. The tie this time was a light green that made his eyes look even more green. Odd, she thought, how they both had eyes that did that, took on certain colors around them.

"I doubt that, but thank you again," she said. "I thought of wearing contacts. I can do it for a few hours."

"No," he said instantly with a shake of his head and a slight, almost-shy smile.

And that warmed her all over again. She gave herself an inward shake. It wouldn't do to go thinking any of this was real.

"Just for tonight, can we pretend it's real?" he asked softly, and the words so close to her thoughts startled her.

"We have to, don't we?" she said, determined to keep the ultimate goal fixed firmly in her silly head.

She thought she saw a flicker of disappointment flash across his face, but then it was gone. She realized then that Cutter was standing there, looking from her to Walker and back. He backed up, then suddenly sat, oddly as if he'd wanted to be able to look at both of them at once. And odder still, after a moment, he moved his head in what looked amazingly like a nod.

"Glad you approve, Cutter," she said with a laugh.

"How could he not?" Walker said, gesturing at her.

"He was looking at you just as much."

Walker drew back slightly. "Was that a compliment?"

"Did you need one?"

"With you? Yes."

She wasn't quite sure how to take that, but she figured she probably deserved it after the way she'd greeted him that first night. "You'll fit in," she said, and left it at that, although secretly she knew every woman in the place, and a few of the men, were going to take note of this newcomer.

And she was going to do her level best to keep her mind on the task at hand. Despite the fact that he was a major distraction. Which was her own fault. She hadn't had her guard fully up, hadn't thought it necessary since she was so angry at him.

Cutter sighed. It was such an expressive sound it drew both their gazes.

"I can't tell if he's upset we're leaving him, or if we did something wrong in his eyes," Walker said, sounding like he was only half joking.

"Hayley says whatever the most humanlike thing you suspect is probably the right one with him."

"He's…different, I'll give her that."

"Maybe he needs to go out."

He shook his head. "Just took him out. Checked his food and water. He should be fine."

"Thank you," she said, surprised he'd been so diligent.

"My sister's dog."

"My house."

"You were busy." He shifted his gaze from the dog back to her. "Productively. You really do look great."

"As opposed to how I usually look," she suggested.

Walker winced as she resorted to old habits, deflecting. Cutter sighed again, louder this time. If he hadn't been a dog, she'd swear there was a note of disgust in it. Oddly, it was enough to make her feel guilty.

"I'm sorry," she said, irritated at her own knee-jerk reaction. "You were trying to be nice. I should have just said thank-you."

"I wasn't trying to be nice, Amy. It's the truth."

Somehow that disconcerted her more than that she'd let herself be chided by what she imagined a dog was feeling.

"Thank you," she said, meaning it this time.

Cutter got up then and walked over to the door and sat down again.

"If you're looking to sneak out when we open it, you picked the wrong spot, dog," Walker said.

Amy smiled at that. The dog had indeed sat down where he would be behind the door when they opened it. Walker did so, checked to make sure the lock was turned, then held it for her politely. She glanced at Cutter, who stayed where he was, half-hidden by the door. He didn't seem inclined to dart for freedom.

She stepped outside. Walker followed. Turned to pull the door closed.

Cutter head-butted it closed from inside, so hard it almost slammed.

They both stared at the door, then at each other.

"So that's what he wanted," Walker said. "The place to himself."

Amy chuckled; she couldn't help it. "He throws a party in there, Hayley's cleaning it up."

Walker laughed. It was a good laugh. He'd always had a great one, and she only realized in this moment that this was the first genuine, nonironic laugh she'd heard from him. Not that he had much reason to be laughing; his homecoming had been pretty grim, from his point of view.

She needed to set it all aside, for real now, at least for tonight. Tonight she was an adult woman falling in love with a new man in her life. Not a woman longing for a long-gone childhood crush, or an adolescent in love with an image that wasn't even real. She had a part to play, so did he, and how well they did it mattered. It could all fall apart if they messed this up. They, and Foxworth, would have wasted a lot of time and energy and resources. She wouldn't let that happen.

She would, for this night, pretend.

He turned to her then, gave her a rather courtly bow and held out his arm. "Shall we begin, Ms. Clark?"

"Very well, Mr. Cole," she said with mock formality. "Or rather, Mr. Campbell."

She slipped her hand through his bent arm, and the charade began.

Chapter 29

"Leverage at its finest, that's me," Walker said cheerfully.

He watched Marcus Rockwell carefully out of the corner of his eye. The man had been assessing him from the moment Amy had introduced them, through the handshake—perfectly measured in strength and length—and the first moments of conversation. He wondered if the man assessed everyone in that manner, even at a social gathering like his own office party.

He found it interesting that Caden and Rockwell did this, throwing a party for their entire staff every year, not on the anniversary of the founding of the firm, but the anniversary of their first headline-making win. To him it spoke of a mindset, and one that didn't really fit with the vibe he was getting from Amy's boss.

The head of the firm, Robert Caden, who had shaken his hand with a much more challenging grip, then lost interest when he discovered who he was, now there he could see it. The need for fame as well as fortune. He'd once defended a big musical name in a street shooting, and had used it to help put his name in the headlines almost as often as his famous client.

So Caden had no interest in a low-level peon at a rival firm, but Rockwell did, at least enough to bother to assess. The question was why? Because that was his nature? Because he cared about Amy? Or because he had something to hide?

Or worst case, because he suspected Amy…

Walker was having to focus very hard on what he was supposed to be doing here. Because Amy was playing her part with more effectiveness than he ever would have expected she could. She clung to his arm, looked up at him often with a shy sort of excitement, colored prettily when anyone teased her about him and looked pleased in a very feminine kind of way when people reacted with some surprise that she'd brought someone to the annual gala.

He'd withstood the sometimes-genuine-seeming—that was Kim, Amy told him—and sometimes-arch—that was Alan—comments with a smile and the most civilized manner he could manage. And when Caden's wife, Willa, the admittedly gorgeous cougar Amy had warned him about, did indeed zero in on him, he deflected carefully, making it clear Amy had his full interest, while letting enough regret show to flatter the woman's ego.

He'd found Mrs. Rockwell more interesting. A very gracious woman, she'd struck him as the sort who was rock-solid. She wasn't flashy, made no effort to look younger than she was and joked that she'd earned every line and gray hair. Walker didn't see many of either, and thought her much more charming in her own way than the predatory Willa.

And throughout he kept a discreet eye on Rockwell. The man greeted everyone, and worked a room well, he thought. It was probably going to be a while before he had a chance to make a move.

He waved off a waiter, gesturing with his still half-full glass of champagne. Amy, he noticed, was still nursing her glass of soda water, a slice of lime impaled on the rim.

"No champagne to celebrate?" he asked.

"I don't drink."

"There go my plans to get you drunk and take advantage." *Damn. That was stupid.*

And then he realized he was reacting again as if this weren't an act, a show put on for others. But Amy stayed cool. If she was irritated by his words, it didn't show. She just gave a one-shouldered shrug. In that knockout dress, the gesture was beyond elegant.

"It can be genetic," she said. "Why take the chance?"

A memory of her father shot through his mind, and he felt even worse. "Sorry. I should have guessed."

And then rescue—and the opening—appeared, in the form of Amy's friend Becca. The tall blonde with the great smile and a knockout figure seemed to cause a wave in the room as she arrived, clad in a dramatic, elegant suit with a perfectly fitted red jacket and a slim black skirt that bared a bit but not too much leg.

Amy had told him Becca was the nicest of the lawyers, although you'd never know it in a courtroom. She'd always been kind to Amy, who as a paralegal sometimes straddled the line between lawyer and support personnel, and treated her as a friend, not just an employee. For that reason alone, Walker was inclined to like her.

"Well!" she exclaimed as she looked him up and down after Amy had introduced him. "So this is the smart one who saw the gem we have in Amy!" She leaned in and touched him briefly on the shoulder, casually, unsuggestively. "You are a very lucky man, Mr. Campbell."

Well, that was a word he hadn't applied to himself in a while. But then again, he was standing here, breathing, so maybe he should rethink that.

"Yes, I am," he said, making it sound as he was sure it would, if it were real, if Amy really was falling for him. Just the thought made him ache inside, and he was glad for more reasons than one when Rockwell joined them to greet the new arrival.

Chapter 30

s she'd dreamed of for years wasn't what she'd
of.

much, much more.

hock that he'd done it was burned away in the
ment, leaving nothing but the sudden, fierce re-
hat swamped her. It was stunning in its heat and
g in its power. None of her muscles seemed to
ymore, and that tiny, sensible part of her brain
still working couldn't seem to command them,
her from leaning into him.

rms came around her, and she felt the heat of him,
gth of him, as she sagged against his chest. He
d the kiss, gently probing, and when she felt the
his tongue, slow, hesitant, as if he were tasting
ng inexpressibly sweet, she lost what little sense
left.

sn't merely everything her girlish heart had
d. It was so very much more that she'd lacked
wledge then to imagine. She'd never known you
l just a kiss in so many places. Her toes were curl-
fingers tingling, and the sensation of heat pool-
and deep inside her was creating an ache unlike
she'd ever experienced.

ead began to spin, and she wasn't sure if it was
or simply that she'd forgotten to breathe. Wasn't
needed to, because it felt like she could live on

After exchanging niceties, Becca turned back to him.
"So how do you like working for Alex Armistead?"

And there it was. The opening he'd been hoping for.

"Let's just say he's not quite the saint he's made out
to be."

He'd made sure Rockwell was in his peripheral vision
when he'd said it, and he saw the instant reaction. The
man's eyes narrowed, and his focus sharpened.

"Really?" Becca's tone of surprise seemed genuine.

He shrugged. "I'm tight with his family, and family
knows secrets others don't, you know? He's pulled some
things, I could tell you…"

"But you won't," Rockwell said, sounding almost stern,
"because it would be highly inappropriate."

Interesting, Walker thought. Rockwell sounded almost
like he was warning him. So was his initial reaction a sign
of interest or something else? Was he rising to the bait,
hoping whatever Walker knew was something he could
get from him privately and use? Did he want to make sure
no one else did?

"Oh, Marcus, you old stick-in-the-mud," Becca said
with a laugh, "we could have learned something juicy!"

"Well, maybe something illicitly tempting," Walker
said with a smile at her, still keeping Rockwell at the edge
of his vision. "If you like lots of money, that is."

The man's expression narrowed again. Instincts honed
in five years of hell fired suddenly, and he left it at that.
Just Rockwell's reaction told him the man was as quick
and sharp as Amy had warned him. And he'd surely cap-
tured his attention.

The bait had been dangled. Now came the slow dance
of luring the mark into the net.

For as well as the night had gone, goal-wise, Amy didn't
seem happy as, much later, they headed back to her place.

"I liked your friend Becca," he said.

She gave him a sideways glance. "Of course you do. Y chromosome."

She sounded merely amused, not upset, but he felt compelled to go on. "I meant how she so clearly put me off-limits."

"Becca's not a poacher. She obviously doesn't need to be."

"I would imagine not."

"And fair warning, she's very, very smart. Mr. Rockwell always said the Soren case wouldn't have gone their way if Becca hadn't been second chair."

Her tone was still amused, her liking for the woman apparent. So that wasn't what was bothering her. Although why he'd thought for a moment it should, he didn't know, since their relationship was pure fantasy.

Yeah. Your fantasy. If she wanted it to be real, why is she warning you about Becca, like she expected you to go after her?

When they reached her condo and were walking from the garage to the door, he tried again. "Kim seemed nice."

"She is. She's very sweet."

He sighed at the short answer. "So what's bothering you? I thought it went well, for our purpose."

She glanced at him. "I was just thinking about Mrs. Rockwell. And their sons."

"I liked her. A lot." That seemed to surprise her. "She seemed like the kind of woman you could really talk to, who would give you advice worth taking."

She was truly surprised now. "That's exactly who she is."

They reached her front porch, a relatively small space that forced them to stand within inches of each other. He tried to ignore that. Just as he had tried to ignore all evening how spectacular she looked, even as he had to play the part of besotted new lover. The dichotomy had set

him so on edge there had been tim
going to fly into a million pieces.

Determined to keep that foolish
to keep the routine conversation g
intimacy of the tiny porch and the
making the darkness around them
the feeling that they were alone, t

"So you're worried how this is
turns out her husband is dirty?" T
should do it.

"Yes," she said as she slid the k
deserves better."

"Not everyone gets what they
the walking proof of that, aren't I?

He said it wryly, fully expectin
He'd take it, if it stirred her out of
kept his mind where it belonged.

But instead, she lifted her gaze t
etly, "I'm not sure what you are an

In an instant all his good inten
had a moment to think, he might
But she was too close—he'd been
evening and he was moving before
His hands grasped her shoulders
down on hers.

And at the first touch of her lips
he'd ever known or thought he'd kr
about want and need, was blasted

this energy that had sparked between them. The world was tilting, and she didn't care. Didn't care about anything except the feel of him, the heat of him, the wonder of finally understanding what all the fuss was about.

When he at last broke the kiss, she felt bereft. Felt the urge to renew it, to begin it herself, just to feel those amazing sensations again. She would, she thought hazily. Surely if Walker had kissed her first, he wouldn't mind if she…

Walker.

Just the name was ice water on the fire he'd started.

She'd not just let him kiss her, she'd liked it, and wanted to kiss him again, this man she'd spent years hating. Years wishing she could see him again simply so she could tell him what a heartless ass he was. Years wondering helplessly what had turned the boy she'd adored into a man she despised.

She struggled for something to say, could only come up with, "Why did you do that?"

"I had to," he said, sounding almost as bewildered as she was feeling.

She opened her mouth to say, "Don't ever do it again." The words wouldn't come. She turned away instead, finished opening the door.

Cutter was sitting just inside, looking up at them with great interest. She had the strangest feeling the dog knew what had transpired on the other side of the door, and was assessing what it meant. She nearly laughed aloud at herself.

"I'll take care of him," Walker said, as if he was glad to have something to do. The thought that he was as rattled as she was should have been reassuring, but instead it only seemed to unsettle her even more.

By the time she heard the door open and man and dog return, she was calmer, curled up under the covers, and if a little voice in her head accused her of hiding here in the bedroom, so be it.

She had a right to hide, she told herself. Every aspect of her world had been upset. Her boss might be crooked; she'd been caught up in an apparent web of deceit and quite possibly criminal activity, and been nearly cornered by a murderous drug lord. She was rattled and off balance, she who so valued a balanced life.

And now Walker Cole.

She told herself that she'd just always wondered what it would be like to kiss him, so her imagination had played it up into enormous proportions once it had finally happened. Except that heat hadn't been her imagination. Nor had the tingling, or the way her fingers and toes had curled, against her own will. It had all happened, along with other sensations she didn't even have words for.

So she was left with the undeniable fact that all the anger she'd carried around all these years hadn't been enough to stop her from turning into a spineless wonder at the first kiss from him.

First kiss.

She'd thought it like there would be more.

There couldn't be more. Because she apparently was a bigger fool than she'd ever thought herself.

It was a long and restless night.

"Can I see you for a moment in my office, Amy?"

Great, Amy thought. Just what she needed after a sleepless night. Even the hour later start time everyone was allowed the morning after the party hadn't helped.

The sight of the tangled blanket and the pillow on the floor next to the couch, speaking of an equally restless night for Walker, hadn't really helped much, either. And that uncomfortable ride into work, with neither she nor he saying anything beyond what was necessary: "Here's the coffee," "Where are the car keys," "I'll take care of the dog."

And the dog. That darn Cutter, sitting there staring at

them, looking from one to the other and then away, as if he was unhappy with them.

"Right away," she answered, shaking off the memories, trying to force her weary mind to alertness. She needed that, to be alert, because this could be very important. He might even be going to quiz her on if she'd seen those files; maybe he was even going to approach her about the bait Walker had cleverly tossed out last night. She had to be on her toes, no matter that she was so distracted that she'd nearly put the wrong shoes over those toes this morning.

The high drama in her mind vanished when she discovered Mr. Rockwell merely wanted to go over changes in the Douglas trust.

"Nothing wrong with what you did, just a change requested this morning by the client."

She managed a smile as she sat down to take notes. "Don't tell me his son's back out again?"

Mr. Rockwell smiled back. "No. Actually, we just need to delete references to the Sonoma property. It's been sold."

"Well, that's easy enough," she said, but the simple answer sparked her curiosity. Why call her in here for that, when a simple mention in passing or an inner office message would have served?

"I wanted to talk to you about something else," he said then. Something about the way he said it made all those thoughts about high drama come flooding back.

"Sir?"

"You may think it none of my business, and perhaps you'd be right, but…are you serious about that young man you brought last night?"

Well, this was an approach she hadn't expected. "I could be," she said hesitantly, hoping her tone would be put down to nervousness about discussing such personal territory with her boss. "Why?"

"I'm a little concerned, Amy. The way he spoke of

Alex Armistead…that was inappropriate for the setting and the company."

She blinked. This was the last thing she'd expected. "Oh," she said, feeling she had to react somehow.

"The fact that he's Armistead's employee makes it even worse. Careless at best, slanderous at worst."

Her mind was racing. He was warning her off Walker because of what he'd said? Not jumping on it, wanting to know more?

Or was he just being subtle, testing, hoping that she would let something more slip. She tried to sound merely wondering.

"It did sound like Mr. Armistead was up to no good, didn't it? Do you suppose it was true?"

"I find it distasteful either way."

"I mean, it almost sounded like something he could get disbarred for, didn't it? That might be worth something to someone."

Her boss's gaze narrowed sharply. "I suggest you think about that, and consider if you want to be involved with someone who would spread that kind of information about his employer."

His tone was beyond stern, and Amy couldn't help wincing, reacting as if he were who she'd always thought him to be. His voice was gentler when he spoke again.

"I'm just concerned about you."

"Thank you."

"Send me the amended trust papers when you're finished," he said, clearly indicating the discussion was ended. She got to her feet and headed for the door. She had her hand on the knob when he spoke again.

"That young man, Walker, was it?"

She half turned back, holding her breath, wondering if in this last second it was going to pay off. "Yes?"

"What is his last name?"

Was that a bite? she wondered. Did he want the name so he could approach Walker about what he knew?

"Campbell," she said. "He knows Mr. Armistead's son."

She wondered if she should have added that, if she was explaining too much. But Mr. Rockwell looked suddenly thoughtful, and she wondered if he was aware of the younger Armistead's prior troubles. Troubles that Foxworth had helped get him out of, setting him on a clearer path for which his father had been deeply grateful. Grateful enough to play his part in this scheme without hesitation.

But he said only, "All right."

It ended there, and she had no idea if it meant anything. But she hoped it did. Or maybe she hoped it didn't. If he'd wanted Walker's last name to make contact, then he'd taken the bait. Or at least, she thought as she went back to her desk, he wanted to investigate him.

Quinn had assured her Walker's background had been thoroughly set up by Ty, that any checks would find exactly what they wanted to be found. Which was that the reason Armistead had been Walker's only hope for a job was that he had an arrest record. For blackmail.

And that was the real bait. Once a blackmailer and all that. And blackmail material on a man like Armistead could be, as she'd said, worth a great deal to someone. Especially a rival law firm.

And to someone already involved in money laundering, what was a little blackmail?

Chapter 31

"So where on earth did you find that simply scrumptious man? Spill, girlfriend!"

Sometimes, Amy thought as she looked at her friend across the café table, Becca talked like someone on a female-centric sitcom. But this was the first chance they'd had for a one-on-one since this whole charade with Walker had started, so it was only natural she'd be curious. It was just that it was rarely Amy's turn to share, since compared to Becca's active social life her own was a drab experience, so it was usually Becca doing the sharing.

"I met him downstairs in the Coffee Clan shop," she said. "We started emailing first, and then…things just happened." Quinn had echoed Walker's statement that it was best to stay in character, not just so you didn't have to keep track, but because you never knew who might say something to who. But she still hated lying to her friend.

The thought brought a flash of memory into her mind. Quinn saying, "If they're a friend they'll understand later, when you can explain. And if they don't understand, then they're not much of a friend." But it was Walker's reaction to those words that had caught her attention. He'd gone very, very still, almost rigidly still. As if he'd had a very strong reaction to what Quinn had said.

Or a very personal one.

She could no longer believe he didn't care. She knew he did. Which had opened the door to much more.

"Girl, you are truly lost. I'd ask where you just went, but I can guess!"

Amy gave herself an inner shake as Becca's laugh brought her back to the present with a snap.

"So, he's that good, huh?" Becca said with a suggestive leer. "About time. You've had a long dry spell."

Amy felt a rush of heat at the suggestion, followed by the question that had been poking at her constantly. What if they hadn't stopped? Just how far would she have let it go, simply because she'd never felt anything like it before?

But Becca wasn't quite through teasing her. "Although I have to say, if I'd seen him first…"

Amy felt a twinge, a physical protest of Becca's words. Because when it came to men, who Becca wanted she generally got. Amy didn't think she'd go after Walker, not when she thought he was Amy's, but she couldn't deny the twinge.

Jealous? Over Walker Cole? Had she truly fallen so far with one kiss? Admittedly it had been an explosive kiss, but still…

"So, how did your boy talk Mr. Ethics Armistead into a do-nothing job?"

For a moment all she heard was the "your boy." She shook it off, focused on the "do-nothing" part. Because that put Walker safely out of Becca's interest zone. Job-wise, that wasn't high power enough. Nothing less than the corner office would satisfy Becca. Amy had never had any illusions about her friend that way, but Becca was so open and honest about her ambition she didn't really mind.

With an effort, she pulled her mind back to what she should be doing. And reminded herself that Becca had her boss's ear, and anything she said might well get back to him.

"Walker said he made him an offer he couldn't refuse."

Becca's head tilted inquisitively. "From what I know

of Armistead, it's hard to believe there's anything he wouldn't refuse to do if he really wanted to."

Amy lifted her eyebrows in a creditable effort at mystification. "Walker said knowledge is power, and he knows things."

"About Armistead?"

"Maybe," she said vaguely. "He knows the son, and he's been in some trouble, I think."

"I heard something about that. It must be tough on the old man and that pillar-of-honesty reputation of his."

Becca said it with a touch of admiration, but just as much amazement, and Amy wasn't sure what had triggered that. She pushed on with practicing the setup.

"Walker knows something. He said the man wasn't happy, but he didn't have much choice but to hire him."

"Well, that's interesting."

Amy realized Becca was looking at her speculatively. And that the picture she'd painted of Walker was in stark opposition to what Becca knew her taste in men was.

"I didn't even want to go out with him at first," she said, then put on her best imitation of a love-struck female, "but he was so persistent, and he's so charming."

"And cute."

"That, too," she said with the best giggle she could manage. "And like you said, it's been a long dry spell."

"Well, you enjoy, girl. You picked a tasty one, might as well live it up. Don't worry about tomorrow. Some things—and men—should be just for fun."

Becca stood up, saying she had the weekly staff meeting to get to. She paid the tab and left a generous tip. They alternated, although Becca had tried to get Amy to let her always pay, since she made so much more. But Amy wasn't comfortable with that, and although Becca had laughed at her principles, she hadn't pushed the issue. Amy did notice she ordered less expensive coffees on Amy's days to pay, though, and she thought that that kind of quiet consideration made her like the woman even more. Becca might be driven and ambitious, but she was also kind and thoughtful when she wanted to be.

On their way out the door at Becca's usual brisk pace, they nearly ran over Walker.

"I thought I might catch you here," he said to Amy with a brilliant smile. It was a different suit today, power black, with a black-and-white diagonally striped tie. And once more the color made his eyes—this time, the dark edge around the iris—all the more vivid.

And she had to admit he struck the perfect balance, placing his arm around her, yet looking at Becca with frank, male appreciation.

"Ms. Olson, isn't it? We met briefly at the party last night."

"Becca, please," she said with a smile. "And of course I remember you. I keep an eye on my girlfriend here. You'd better be good to her."

"And I wouldn't want to cross you," Walker said with a grin. "I've heard you're more than formidable."

Becca raised a brow at him. "Researching the competition, are you?"

Walker shrugged. "I figure it's always good to know as much as you can. Who knows when it might pay off."

"Information is power?" Becca asked.

"Something like that." Walker grinned suddenly, charmingly. "But I'm not after power. Money will do."

Becca studied him for a moment before smiling widely. "In most cases it will do nicely." She looked at Amy. "You take your time coming back. You know how long those meetings go. Marcus will never know."

And then she was gone, walking down the street in those heels Amy always marveled at. How she did it, Amy had no idea. Walker was watching her stride off, no doubt entranced as men often were, by the subtly feminine sway.

"She turns it on a bit, doesn't she?"

"Look who's talking," Amy said drily.

"Just playing my part," Walker said. They were in the way of the door to the popular lunch spot so they began walking, more slowly than Becca's confident pace.

"So why are you here?" she asked.

"Looking to see my best girl, of course," he said as lovingly as if it were true. He leaned closer, until she could feel his heat radiating over her. His arm slipped around her waist, pulling her to him, hip to hip. His head tilted, as if he wanted to be sure he didn't miss the slightest thing she might say.

It took her breath away, and her heart leaped in the moment before she saw Kim walking toward them, headed for the café. So that was why, she thought, her heart calming. He'd seen her coming, recognized her, known the masquerade had to continue. In fact, she was realizing the masquerade really did have to be nonstop, unless they were home alone.

Home alone. Right. Thinking like that will help.

Besides, they weren't alone at her place. They had Cutter, and she'd never thought she would be so glad of the distraction. Although she had to admit the dog had begun an irksome habit of plopping himself down on her one comfortable chair, leaving the couch as the only place for her and Walker to sit. Together. Those had been the awkward times, moments when the memory of that kiss seemed to burn between them, and only the knowledge that they had no choice because they couldn't rush this had made it bearable.

Kim gave them a broad wink as she passed, but kept going, clearly on her lunch hour. And Amy sternly told herself she was not disappointed. She was not standing here wishing that it had been real, those words and the way he'd said them.

"Can your Becca do that?" Walker asked, snapping her back to reality.

"What?"

"Give you a longer break."

"She's not my boss, but she is a partner. So technically, yes."

"Then let's take a walk."

"What do you want, Walker?"

He let out a compressed breath. "So many things," he muttered. Then, in a normal tone, he went on. "I have news. Quinn called."

Her brows furrowed. "He called you?"

He lifted a brow at her in return. "Jealous?"

Just the word brought back those tangled feelings from her discussion with Becca, and she had to fight to keep her mind where it should be. "Of course not. So what did he…?" She broke off as she realized what the call had probably been. "The video?"

He nodded. "It's ready. And I have to say, Quinn—and Mr. Armistead—did a great job. It's quite believable. So now we just have to arrange for your boss to see it."

"You could email it to me."

He shook his head. "Quinn and I agreed we should keep you a step removed, if possible. You've already gotten me in front of him, that's enough. We'll figure the rest out this weekend. By the way, we're heading down south to Foxworth as soon as you're done this evening."

She didn't know which bothered her more, that they were conspiring to keep her out of this, or that Walker and Quinn were conspiring—and apparently agreeing—at all.

"I started all this, if you recall."

"Yes. You did. Doesn't mean you have to stay in the middle of it. Soren or Theo, whoever he is, he's a bad guy. Ty dug back and he's been connected at some level to over twenty murders."

Amy drew in a steadying breath. The man she'd seen in the parking garage seemed quite capable of that. The man outside the mailbox drop, not so much.

"Having doubts?"

She shook her head slowly. "Not really. It's just…he seemed so normal, that second time. Just a guy out for coffee."

She heard an electronic beeping. Walker pulled a cell phone out of an inner pocket. It was the one that matched hers, the one Quinn had given her. She followed as he walked to a more sheltered spot next to a concrete wall, away from the stream of passing pedestrians who might overhear. Then she waited while he answered.

"Hey, sis."

Hayley. So they had progressed to at least speaking normally. But then, this was different; they'd all agreed on that. For the duration of this op, as Quinn had said, everything else had to be on hold.

She watched as Walker frowned. His gaze flicked to her and the frown deepened, although it was clearly in response to what Hayley was saying, not she herself.

"Got it," he said. "Yes, she's right here. I'll tell her." A pause before he grimaced. "I know that." Another pause before he said, "All right," and ended the call.

"You don't look happy about whatever she said."

"Which part?" he asked with another grimace and in a very glum tone. "The part where she said Dunbar's friend talked to the narcotics guy and found out they're scrambling because three of Soren's lieutenants have been found dead in the past month? Or the part where she said the murder I should really be thinking about was mine, if I hurt you again?"

Any blinked. Then smiled.

"Like that, do you?" Walker asked, his mouth quirking. "You'll like this even more. She said she and Quinn would probably argue over who would do it."

"It's good to have good friends."

"Yes. I'm glad you have them."

Any teasing tone had vanished. He'd meant those words.

"Even when they're threatening your life?"

"If I hurt you again, I'll have it coming."

And suddenly it was there, alive and flexing, for the moment pushing the other thing they'd learned aside. The memory of those heated moments, that unexpectedly fierce and devastating kiss, fairly crackled between them. Amy felt an echo of the rippling sensation that had seized her then, down to the faint weakness in her knees. And in his eyes she could see he was remembering, too, and when he swallowed tightly she dared to hope it was as powerful to him as it was to her.

Something flared in those changeable eyes and she knew. She knew, and she did nothing to stop it as he leaned over to kiss her again. She did nothing to stop it because she wanted to know, she had to know, if it had been real. If a simple kiss had truly been what she remembered, or if it had just been the shock of it tangled up with a thousand childhood fantasies.

In the first instant of contact all other awareness fled, the world could have fallen away and she wouldn't have known it. His mouth was warm, firm, yet gentle, so gentle it seemed impossible for it to cause such a tumultuous reaction.

Real, her blood sang as he flicked his tongue over her lower lip. It was real, all of it. Despite everything—the years, the disappointment, the absence, the anger—Walker was the only man who had ever made her feel like this.

He pulled back, and she almost let out a whimper of loss. But then reality hit with a shock as a small cheer went up from two people passing by. Color rushed to her face as she remembered abruptly that they were out not only in public but on a street rarely without lots of pedestrians. Including those two, who were, she realized with even more embarrassment, from her office. And Alan, in particular, had a distinct tendency toward gossip. And she was sure he'd just found his material for the rest of the day.

"Well, that ought to do it," Walker muttered under his breath.

It was an effort to keep her voice steady. "Do what?"

"They work with you, right?"

"Yes," she said, surprised he'd recognized them, although they had been at the party, as were all employees down to the woman who brought in sandwiches and snacks for them.

"Then this'll be the talk of the office, won't it?"

Shy, quiet Amy Clark kissing a man in public, on the street? Oh, yes, it would be.

It hit her then. She stared at him. "Is that why you did it?"

He blinked. "What?"

"Is that why you kissed me? To make sure the whole office knows about us?"

He drew back. Stared at her. "I kissed you because I couldn't not. I never even saw those guys until…after. That was just luck."

She wanted to believe him. At least, she thought she did. But the minute she thought that, her common sense chimed in to tell her she'd be better off if he'd only meant it as a ruse, as a way to spread the idea that they were in an intimate, sharing relationship.

She didn't know which to hope for.

And then she called herself seventeen kinds of a fool for hoping at all, for wanting anything to do with Walker Cole.

And it wasn't until much later, remembering what Walker had said about twenty murders, that it occurred to her to that had they been somewhere other than that parking garage that day, Dante Soren might well have murdered that man right in front of her.

And she would have been a witness.

tesy of Ty—that of Armistead telling the man he called James to head straight to the airport and get out of the country before the trial.

The video was clear, good resolution, and Walker knew if someone zoomed in they'd see the bundle of bills Quinn had checked were large denomination, making the possible total of everything in the case rather awe-inspiring. And when Quinn had picked up the case and walked toward the driver's door of the car, the video zoomed in, giving a quick look at the license number of the car.

Which happened to come back to a man listed—by the name Armistead had used out loud—as the main prosecution witness in an upcoming spousal murder trial in which Armistead was acting for the defense.

And they had a video that portrayed the premiere criminal attorney in the city bribing a witness to leave the country.

That the witness really wasn't one, and that the vehicle belonged to Foxworth and the registration had been, thanks to Ty's genius, temporarily altered, didn't matter. The name was on the court's witness list, courtesy of Alex Armistead's connections, and a registration check would match.

Ty had also made a teaser cut, seventeen seconds of the whole, showing the crucial part but lacking the identifying license plate. It was this they would use as the final bait.

Would it be enough? Would Rockwell bite? Jump at the chance to take down one of the biggest names in his profession, with his own firm next in line for the top? Or since money was apparently his goal, would he perhaps bite at the chance to blackmail the man? Armistead had very, very deep pockets, and Ty's report had indicated Rockwell's wallet had suffered since he'd abandoned the high-profile cases. Plus he had two kids in expensive colleges, and the bills must be staggering.

"It's the only way," Amy said quietly when he looked

away from the phone. "I'll just go to him, pretend to be very upset and show him the clip. He'll think you're going to use that video. I can talk about how desperate Mr. Armistead would be to keep this secret. And that will plant the idea that maybe he could use it first. And then…he'll do what he's going to do."

He asked the big motivation question that was bothering him about the idea. "Why would I send it to you?"

"Because you love me and can't resist sharing everything with me."

His jaw tightened. "If I love you, then why the hell would I put you in the middle of something like this?"

He realized in the moment he said it that he was, indeed, resisting putting her in the middle of it. What that meant he wasn't going to dwell on, he told himself sternly.

"Maybe I picked up your phone by mistake and found it." She spoke as if she'd completely missed that moment. "They are exactly alike."

"He's seen your regular phone, hasn't he?" Walker asked, his voice steadier now.

"Yes." She smiled at him, that slightly too-sweet smile that was a warning in itself. "But we got new ones together, a sharing plan, because it was a great deal. And I'm happy about that, because my silly imagination thinks that means you're thinking permanent."

He blinked. She was clearly bantering, but he was guessing the insight into the thinking was probably real. Which boggled him. "A good deal on a pair of phones translates into a permanent relationship?"

"Don't you just love the female mind?" she asked breezily. She looked at Quinn. "So, are we set?"

Obviously, the final decision was not up to him. He didn't blame her for that; he'd trust Quinn's assessment over his own anyway.

"This gives you the out that you didn't have anything

to do with the video itself," Quinn said with a nod. "But you'll have to wait for the right moment."

"Tomorrow," Amy said. "It has to be. He's leaving Tuesday for Dallas for three days."

And that easily it was settled. Walker felt the urge to protest again, but realized it wouldn't make any difference. Amy was determined, Quinn approved, it was done.

"All right," Quinn added, "we'll all be close by. I'll be in the building, just outside your office. I can fake waiting for a meeting."

"And since no one will recognize me," Hayley said, "I'll come to your office and ask to see whoever's available at the time. Which will likely be no one, but I'll be in the waiting room, actually inside."

Quinn grimaced slightly at that, but he said nothing. For a moment Walker wondered again at the amazing relationship they had, his sister and her man. He guessed Quinn's first instinct was to protect, but he smothered it so that he didn't smother her. And Walker was more certain than ever, by this ceding of control from a man he doubted did it often, just how much Quinn Foxworth loved his sister.

"I'll be in the building, too, then, whenever it goes down," he said.

"They'll recognize you," Amy pointed out.

"So I'm getting coffee, waiting for you. Or on my way to get my phone back. Either way, I'll be there."

"Once you know we're all in place, you can go for it," Quinn said. "And if anything, and I mean anything, feels off to you, you hit that alarm. Twice, so we know it's you and not just Rockwell by accident if he's handling the phone."

Amy nodded. She seemed so calm it was a bit unnerving, while his mind caromed around like a berserk billiard ball, bouncing from thought to idea to wish in a way he'd thought himself long past. He thought he'd given up railing at unfairness. But then, he'd underestimated what it would feel like to try and pick up some of the fragments of his life.

And he hadn't counted on Amy.

Chapter 33

Amy ran the video clip through one more time. Her boss was on the phone, and she was waiting until he hung up. She'd already had to delay everyone when she found out Mr. Rockwell was at a last-minute, unscheduled meeting with a client. But he was back now, and since it was nearly the end of her workday, she was out of time. Everyone was in place, so it had to be now, before her boss also left for the day.

She tried for calm, but she was too nervous. But then she decided nervous could easily be interpreted as upset, which would be a good thing in this case. Because if this were real, she would be beyond upset. She would be—

"Sexting?"

Becca's voice from right behind her made her jump. "Oh!"

"Should I buy you more condoms?"

She sounded hopeful; Amy blushed despite herself. "No, thanks."

Then the nervousness flooded back as the light on her phone console went out. He had hung up.

Becca frowned. "There's something else, isn't there? I mean, I know everybody's glued to that terror cell news, but you seem extra edgy."

She'd been only vaguely aware of the buzz about the news story. She had no room in her mind just now for anything else. Her mind raced as she tried to think of what to say.

Tell the same story to everyone. Quinn's warning echoed in her mind.

"I picked up Walker's phone by mistake, and I found something that's...bothersome," she said. "I'm afraid he might do something foolish with it."

Somehow saying the words to her friend calmed her, like a dress rehearsal. She could do this, she told herself. Even as she admitted Walker would never do anything like this in reality.

"You be careful," Becca said. "He's sexy as hell, but don't let that blind you."

"I know." She managed a grimace now, but decided a troubled expression would work better with Mr. Rockwell. "He's got some questionable ethics," she said, practicing.

"At least you realize it," Becca said soothingly.

That would do it with Mr. Rockwell, Amy thought.

Moments later she was beside her boss's desk, watching him as he watched the video. When it was done, he glanced up at her. He said nothing, instead watched the short video again, this time freezing it in the moment when Mr. Armistead's face was revealed.

"Walker told me he had proof of a bribe to a major witness. He only showed me this edited clip. But he joked about selling it to the highest bidder," Amy said, putting on that troubled expression. "I'm afraid you were right about him."

He looked at her steadily now. "I'm sorry, Amy."

"Me, too," she said.

"Unless he has an innocent explanation, that video is evidence of a crime."

"What do you think I should do?" She tried her best to sound distraught.

"Alex's reputation is—I thought—unassailable," he

said thoughtfully. "Let me consider tonight about the best way to approach this."

Amy nodded. She was still a little shaky, but relieved all the precautions for her safety had been unnecessary. She sent an all clear to the Foxworth phones as she headed back to her office. When she arrived, she was startled to see Becca still there.

"I forgot," she said with a laugh, "what I came over to give you in the first place." She handed her a file folder. "Think you can get to this tomorrow?"

Amy nodded, thankful for the interruption of the complaint papers Becca had wanted her to go over. The embezzlement situation was fairly complex and would be a good distraction tomorrow. "I should be able to."

"Thanks, girlfriend. You're a lifesaver."

"You need your own paralegal. You work so hard."

"Why, when I can borrow you? See what happens when you're so efficient?"

Amy laughed, feeling much calmer now. When Becca had gone she locked the folder in her desk, gathered her purse and the sweater she doubtless wouldn't need in the early-evening LA heat and headed downstairs.

When they connected outside the coffee shop, Walker seemed to need reassurance that she was okay. She insisted she was fine. In fact, she felt pretty darn good that she'd gotten through it so easily. So good that she was looking forward to a romp with Cutter when they arrived back at her place.

"So now we wait," Walker said as they got into the car.

"Yes." She fastened her seat belt, then sat tapping her fingers on the armrest. "To see what he does."

"Quinn's got Ty monitoring my email address at Armistead's office, and the personal address that was attached to the video. Do you think he noticed that one?"

She shifted in her seat, then shifted back. "It was showing when I handed the phone to him. I made sure of that."

"Good." He glanced at her. "You did good."

"Better than I thought," she admitted. She pulled out the phone, looked at it, then put it back in her bag. No point in looking at it again.

"Adrenaline still up?"

She looked at him. "What do you mean?"

"You're fussing. You don't fuss."

"Oh."

"Only to be expected," he said. "Just don't get addicted. It'll wear you out."

He sounded like he knew what that felt like. Baseball, when he'd thought he was going to make the big leagues? Or something else?

She was still wondering when they got to her place. Cutter's delighted greeting made her smile, and she wondered why she had never gotten a dog. There was a lot to be said for having someone so happy to see you.

Later, her mood shifted. The three of them playing with the baseball Walker had bought for the dog was so…domestic seeming, it made her edgy. Not because she didn't like it, but because she did. Added to that was her observation that Walker was wearing a long-sleeved T-shirt despite the warmth, and she couldn't help wondering if it was to hide the tattoo she'd seen. And she wondered again what it stood for, which compounded her nerves.

Still, she ended up laughing at the dog's antics, and admiring Walker's skill with the ball, throwing it the length of the long courtyard between the units of her building, at least twice as far as she could throw it. But Cutter still brought the ball back to her part of the time, and she laughed aloud, wondering at the dog's decision-making process.

They kept it up until the light started to fade, then finally retreated back inside. Cutter didn't seem reluctant to give up, although amazingly he didn't appear tired, either. Once inside, Cutter danced up to them. Dropped the ball dead center between them this time. It bounced loudly on the wood floor. They both bent to pick it up at the same moment. Bumped heads. Jerked back. Stared at each other.

And then Walker was kissing her, so swiftly she barely had time to take a breath. And then his mouth on hers took all thought of breathing away.

Kissing her had been a bad idea, Walker thought. It had been a bad idea the first time, and the second, out on the street, had been just as bad. And kidding himself that it was part of the act made no difference.

Kissing her again had been insanity.

He stood there, staring at her, thinking once more of the transformation. Even as a child he'd recognized the intelligence, had even appreciated that his sister didn't have the cadre of popular girls she could have had clustered around her. She preferred Amy—her brain, her heart, her absolute loyalty.

Good taste, sis.

And just thinking the word *taste* had been a very bad idea, Walker thought. Because taste was what he wanted to do. Every sleek, lovely inch of her. But that was only the start of what he wanted.

He stumbled. Lost in the fog of need he was startled, since he hadn't even been moving. Then he realized what had happened.

Cutter.

The dog had come up behind him. And caught him just behind the knees, sending him forward. As if he were pushing him, crazy as that sounded. Pushing him toward Amy.

"Dog," he said warningly.

Cutter moved away. For a moment he thought the dog had heeded the warning. But then he went to Amy. And did the same thing. More gently, only nudging her forward, but the same result.

The dog was pushing them together.

She looked so impossibly…kissed. Her eyes were wide, her mouth soft, inviting more. Irresistible.

Cutter forgotten, he gave in. Could do nothing else. He took her mouth again, not a swift, urgent kiss this time, but slower, savoring every sensation, every sweet response, urging, coaxing, every response more fuel to the bonfire he was kindling. His body surged, convinced it was going to get what it had wanted, ached for, at last. He deepened the kiss, probed with his tongue, fire racing along his nerves when she opened for him.

When he felt her tongue teasing along the ridge of his teeth in turn, the fire exploded. Took his breath away, making his head spin.

He had to breathe. He hadn't been, he realized. It was the pause he needed, and he grabbed at what remnants of control he could.

He backed away from her. For the first time became aware of his own heightened breathing. Damn, he was actually panting after her.

Amy looked at him, the faintest of creases furrowing her brow, as if she were puzzled. By what he'd done?

Or that he'd stopped?

God knows he hadn't wanted to stop.

"Walker?" she said softly.

"It's the adrenaline," he said almost desperately. "You pulled this off beautifully and you're high on it. You're not thinking straight."

"I'm thinking straight for the first time in a long time."

He took another step back. Put up his hands. "Go, Amy."

"Why?"

He nearly groaned aloud. "Because if you don't, I'll kiss you again. But this time it won't stop there."

"What if I didn't want it to stop?"

"Don't," he said hoarsely, "play with me. Not now. Not you."

At his last words something changed in her face, her eyes. The puzzlement vanished, replaced by a slow smile that kicked heat through him all over again. Because it wasn't just a smile of warmth and acceptance—things he now treasured more than he ever would have thought possible—but a sexy, tempting smile.

He'd thought, maybe even hoped, that someday, somewhere, he'd find a woman who made him feel this way, a woman who perhaps didn't know how he'd let down everyone he cared about.

He'd never thought when he found that woman, it would be at home and she would know everything.

And now he was drowning in that smile, barely able to draw breath. Had she not been sure? How could she not have known how he reacted to her?

It hit him then. This was Amy. With Amy's past. Amy, who had grown up as she had. The awkward little girl, the more awkward adolescent, scorned, not wanted. She would never assume any man wanted her. And he'd been one of the ones to do that to her, however unintentionally.

So he would make it clear. And then the decision would be hers.

"I want you," he said bluntly. "More than I've ever wanted anything or anyone. So if your answer is 'Go to hell,' say it now."

Her expression changed again. Became even softer somehow. And she reached out to cup his cheek.

"But you're already in hell," she said quietly, almost sadly.

What was this? She felt sorry for him? That was the last, the very last, thing he wanted from her. Especially now.

"Pity, Amy?"

"No. A hundred times, no." She drew in a deep breath,

then looked up at him steadily. "Just need. Want. And impatience."

Then she slid her hand down along his arm, took his hand. Her fingers, warm, slender and strong, curled around his. She turned, clearly headed for the bedroom. Fool that he was, he resisted.

"Be sure, Amy. Because I can't promise to be polite or even gentle."

"I don't want polite or need gentle. I want you," she said, her voice so low and husky now he thought it alone was going to send him over the edge. "I've always, always wanted you, Walker Cole. Even when I thought I hated you."

It had been a shock to Amy herself when she realized it was true. Even at the height of her anger at him, she'd still been drawn to him. The proverbial moth to the flame. And Hayley had been right, she couldn't have hated him—or thought she did—as much as she had if she hadn't loved him first.

Only now she realized that pull, that love, had never really gone away. The coin had merely turned, showing its other side when she thought the worst of him. And she realized the truth of something she'd once heard, that the opposite of love wasn't hate, it was indifference.

And she had never, ever been indifferent to Walker.

Even once they were in her bedroom he seemed to hesitate.

"Changing your mind?" she asked.

"God, no," he said, his voice nearly hoarse. "Just afraid you'll change yours. Or regret this later. I couldn't take that, Amy."

"I won't. I live with my decisions. And I've waited my whole life for this one."

She reached up, ran a fingertip over his mouth, that mouth that did such incredible things to every nerve in her body. She saw a shiver go through him, and this proof of his response to her touch sent her heart pounding all over again.

He had been in hell. She knew it, because she knew him. She'd doubted, before, but it had been her faith in her own judgment that had been shaken. It was all so clear once she accepted that he was still Walker, who didn't lie.

"Let me show you the way out," she said softly.

He moved then, quickly. Decisively. He kissed her again, so deep and hot and urgent this time that it seemed to turn her bones to liquid. She sagged against him. One arm caught her, held her against his chest. He kissed her again, his other arm sliding down her back, pressing her against him. She felt the ridge of flesh against her lower belly, felt a deep, low cramp of need as she imagined it filling that aching, empty place in her.

"You...have something?" he asked, his voice thick.

It took her a second, through the haze, to realize what he meant. And thought thankfully of Becca's teasing gift.

"Yes, thanks to a friend," she said, registering as she answered that apparently he wasn't a man to carry a condom around with him on the off chance. That warmed her somehow, foolish though it might have been.

He had her shirt unbuttoned faster than she could have done it herself. She watched, spellbound, her heart pounding. And for some reason she thought of his baseball days, when the slightest adjustment of his fingers would change the trajectory and action of the pitch.

And then those fingers were on her, those strong, beautiful fingers. He brushed them over her cheek, down her jaw, then her throat. He left impossible wakes of tingling fire as he went, until she was shivering herself, wanting his touch everywhere so the neglected places wouldn't be cold.

He cupped her breast through the pale blue bra. She nearly shuddered. Then he let his thumb swipe over her already-taut nipple, and she did shudder. A moan escaped her. He lifted her breast free of the cloth and followed with his mouth, stroking, teasing, flicking her nipple until she cried out, a sharp exclamation she couldn't help, and didn't want to. Just that seemed to fire him higher, and any pretense at proceeding slowly vanished.

She found herself pulling at his clothes even as he divested her of hers. She saw his gaze flick down over her, but the heat that flared in his eyes seared away any shyness or embarrassment. Besides, how could she blame him when she'd done the same, taking in the broad strength of his shoulders and chest, the flat belly, narrow hips and the jutting male flesh that made her fingers curl.

He grabbed her then, and they went down to the bed, arms and legs tangled. She was stunned by her own eagerness. Even her wildest imaginings about him had been nothing compared to this.

And then he was all over her—touching, kissing, tasting—and sanity fled. She could only react, respond, her body fairly rippling under his hands and mouth. She was glad he remembered the little foil packet, because she wasn't thinking at all, only feeling.

She thought that moment before he slid into her would last forever. She felt as if she were balanced on a precipice, hovering, waiting, knowing she could fly, but trapped in that split second before taking off.

And then he was there, his passage eased by her fierce arousal. Slick, wet, she was more than ready for him, and yet it still shocked her, the sudden wonderful invasion. She felt stretched, filled. Whole. For the first time she felt whole, as if the world had finally come right.

She heard him groan, low and harsh. He lifted his head to look at her, and his eyes, those incredible eyes, were so intense and hot she nearly had to look away. As if he'd read her thought, he whispered, "No. Look at me, Amy."

She complied. She could do nothing else. And then

he began to move, long, deep strokes, driving her breath from her on another cry, this time of his name. Her hands slid down his back, marveling at the sleekness of his skin. She cupped the taut, flexing muscles of his backside, urging him on.

He drove deeper, harder, faster. Again and again she cried out, unable to stop it, and not caring.

"Yes," he said, again and again, with every sound she made.

And then he lowered his head to her other breast, caught the nipple and drew it into his mouth, tugging, suckling, sending darts of hot, rolling sensation to the flesh that now surrounded him. She cried out his name as she felt it begin, the deep clenching, and wave after wave of nearly unbearable pleasure rolled through her.

She heard her name, groaned out in a voice taut with an echo of the same wonder she was feeling. Felt his body go rigid as one last time he drove deep and home.

For once, reality had far surpassed the fantasy.

Chapter 34

All the miles, all the places, all the years...he'd finally found home.

Walker stirred, still more asleep than awake, the remnants of the dream still wrapped around him. It was an amazing feeling, in that dream, being filled with the knowledge that he'd finally found the place he never wanted to leave, and the certainty that he never would. He'd never expected to feel that way, yet on some level he knew it was what he'd been looking for, what would make all the wandering not just unnecessary, but unwanted.

He felt as if he were swimming up from warm, cozy depths, and the instant he came fully awake he wanted to go back.

And the instant he came fully awake, he knew there was no going back.

It wasn't the dream wrapped around him. It was Amy.

Memories of last night flooded him, stealing his breath and hardening his body. Time after time they'd come together, and every time it was better, as they learned, tested and learned more. And he realized that he truly had found the place he never wanted to leave. Only it wasn't a place, it was a person.

It was Amy.

He was afraid to move. He'd had a few morning-afters, some pleasant, some awkward. But he'd never had one he dreaded.

What if she had second thoughts? What if despite her words she regretted it? Although how anyone could regret what they'd found together last night was beyond him. But then again, knowing how angry she'd been at him, he was still amazed she'd wanted him at all.

"Hey."

Her sleepy voice whispered in his ear, and her deliciously naked body shifted closer, until she was spooned up against his back so closely he could feel every inch of her silken skin. Her arm slipped around him, and he drew in a deep breath in reaction. It suddenly became an ache as strong as the fierce hardness of a body ready for her again, this want, this need to just stay like this. But he knew the moment the inevitable morning-after started, it could all be shattered.

"I can tell you're awake," she murmured. "How..."

"Please, don't."

"Don't what?"

"Whatever you want to say, please, not yet."

She went silent, but he thought he felt a slight tension from her, a lessening of the relaxed, easy warmth of her body.

It was no use. It was already gone, that sweet, easy warmth. He let out a breath he hadn't really been aware of holding. He moved, rolling over to look at her. She shifted herself, to give him room. But she didn't go far, and when he settled on his back she came back to him. That was good, wasn't it?

"Never mind," he muttered. "Let's have at it."

"Have at what?"

"The morning-after."

She propped herself up on one elbow, looking at him. She was so beautiful like this, her hair a glorious tangle, her makeup a bit smudged around her eyes, those gorgeous blue eyes now sans the glasses he was so used to.

"What is it you think I want to say? That I expect a

declaration now? That I expect a future? That I expect you to—gasp—*stay*?"

Now it was he who was tense. She said it almost mockingly, as if all of those expectations were ridiculous.

And yet he'd been ready to give her all of them. Something he'd never, ever done. And for the first time he wondered why. Why she'd wanted this, allowed this.

"I used to dream about this," she said quietly.

His breath caught in his throat. Maybe he'd been right to dread this. Maybe she hadn't really wanted him last night—at least, who he was now. Maybe this had been more in the nature of getting him—the old him, the boy she'd had the crush on—out of her system. Did women do that, try to rid themselves of past infatuations so they could move on?

He was not used to this, this need for understanding a woman's motives, for trying, and no doubt failing, to understand the way her brain worked.

"Don't you just love the female mind?"

Her words, tossed off so lightly, echoed in his head. Well, he was afraid he loved this one. But this was throwing him. Wasn't it women who always analyzed things to death in a relationship?

But then apparently this wasn't a relationship in her eyes.

"Is that what this was about?" he asked, not wanting the answer but knowing he had to hear it.

"Is that what you think?"

"What I think is that if it wasn't, you wouldn't have answered a question with a question. And now that I am thinking, unlike last night, I realize you didn't want me—you hate me. You wanted that guy I was a long time ago."

She sat up sharply before he even finished. "Walker Cole, if you think I would go to bed with a man I hate, no matter what I used to feel for him, then you don't know me at all."

He felt suddenly tired. He'd managed to move her from sleepily relaxed and warm to tense and angry in a matter of minutes. But then something hit him.

"You don't…hate me?"

"Oh, please," she said, shoving her hair back where it had slipped forward, masking one eye. It immediately fell forward again, which almost made him smile, since he liked both the look and the fact that it had been his hands that had tangled the burnished mass. But somehow he didn't think smiling was wise at this moment.

"You don't want a declaration, a future or for me to stay. So what do you want?"

She stared at him. "I never said I didn't *want* all those things. I just said I didn't expect them."

He was more confused now than ever. And had no idea what to say to avoid making this worse. He should have taken the coward's way out and left before she'd awakened.

"Do you want to know what I was going to ask?"

"Do I?" he asked warily.

She ignored that. "I was simply going to ask how you slept. If you had more nightmares."

"Oh." Well, that sounded completely stupid, he thought. "No." He remembered the dream he had had. And smiled, closing his eyes for a moment as that warm certainty flooded him again. "Not at all."

"Good," she said softly. "About time."

The tone of her voice seemed to make that warmth stay. He told himself he was a fool to risk destroying the mood, but he had to know. "What made you decide you don't hate me?"

To his surprise—and gratification—her tone didn't change. As if she understood why he wanted, had to know. "Simple," she said. "I believe you."

"Believe me?"

"You don't lie. That means you really did have a very good reason. And that you can't share it."

The simple acceptance would have brought him to his knees if he'd been standing. He'd never expected, never dared hope for it.

"Besides," she said, "you're also smart. I meant what I told Hayley. If you were going to lie, you would have made up a better one."

"I thought about it," he admitted. "Amnesia, maybe. Decided it was too much."

"And when it came down to it, you couldn't lie to your sister."

"Or you."

She smiled. "And therefore, you didn't."

He should have known. It was true; she never would have gone to bed with him if she'd still hated him or thought him a liar. So she had to be sure he wasn't. She knew him better than perhaps she even realized.

In fact, she probably knew him better than he would ever know her. And he realized with a jolt that if he was going to learn everything he wanted to about her, it would take forever.

A buzzing alert yanked him out of his reverie. He shook his head sharply, then rolled out of the bed to grab the phone from his hastily discarded and tangled clothes.

He listened to Quinn.

"All right," he said. "I'll tell her."

He dropped the phone on the bed. Amy was clutching the sheet to her, as if he hadn't already seen every delectable inch of her. He hated having to say it, having to confirm their suspicions, but there was no way around it.

"The account on the video got an email. He bit."

It was so quiet it made Amy even more nervous. They'd picked this place, an underground parking garage for a now-vacant office building, outside the city limits into county territory—there were, Hayley had explained, limits to how far Quinn was willing to push Brett's contact

knew the plan was to force the meeting there, in the light, so Hayley's camera could get it all.

It also put Walker on full view. And her stomach knotted painfully. This part of the plan was based on her judgment, her assessment that her boss didn't keep a gun handy. He had, back in his criminal defense days, she knew, but he'd once mentioned after the switch to the civil side he was glad when he hadn't needed it anymore. He'd transferred it to someone else on the criminal side, but that didn't mean he couldn't borrow it back. Not like anyone would refuse one of the two founders of the firm.

Or he could own a different weapon, and what if he'd brought it tonight? Walker was lit up like a doomed duck in a shooting gallery. She thought that even she, who'd never fired a weapon in her life, could probably hit him. Little waves of cold rippled through her, and if she'd had any doubts about her feelings for Walker, they were vanquished now.

"Come on into the light," Walker called out. "I don't deal with shadows."

God, he sounded as cool and calm as he was acting, Amy thought. She was the one who was a nervous wreck.

The driver didn't move.

"All right, then," Walker said with a shrug, and turned as if to walk back the way he'd come.

"Wait."

Amy sucked in a harsh, shocked breath. Walker turned back. Smoothly, as if he hadn't heard what she'd heard. But she knew he had.

"Well, well," Walker drawled.

The dark figure moved into the light. Confirmed what Amy had known from that single uttered syllable.

It wasn't her boss who had come to buy blackmail material on his firm's biggest adversary.

It was Becca.

Chapter 35

"I confess, I didn't expect you," Walker drawled. He watched Becca Olson walk toward him. She was carrying a large messenger bag—full of cash as agreed?—and dressed all in black, slim slacks, turtleneck sweater, a brimmed fedora-style hat with her telltale blond hair tucked inside and fancy knee-high boots. Attire for the fashionable blackmailer, he supposed. More importantly, very high-heeled boots, he noted.

And underneath all the information he was taking in was a slow, brewing anger.

This was Amy's friend. Her best friend at work, next to Kim. And she was over there, in the shadows, watching, seeing this. He could only imagine how she must be feeling. The sense of betrayal that filled him was stunning and spoke volumes about how he felt about Amy. He was so far down that rabbit hole he doubted he would ever get out.

He didn't want to get out. Ever.

"Disappointed?" Becca said.

It was all he could do not to glance toward where Amy was, to try and give her some sign that this was an act. She knew that, he told himself. She had to know it.

He made himself focus. Drew on the hard lessons learned in the past five years. Nothing mattered but making this work, taking down the target.

"Now what man on earth would be disappointed to have you show up?"

"One that's in love with somebody else?"

Yes, he thought. But he kept his tone light. "I would have pegged you for a woman who knows love is a fool's game."

"And Amy?"

"Nice enough. A bit naive, don't you think?"

"She is that. An innocent. But that's only a help to people like us, isn't it?"

He nodded. "That's the thing about innocent people. They don't even think of the kind of things we do, so it's easy to get things past them. Is that how you found out about my little moviemaking project?"

"Amy trusts me. Besides, it wasn't hard to get a look over her shoulder at your little teaser. And I have my own technical skills. Do you want the money or not?"

She wasn't going to be one to brag; she was too practical for that.

"How do I know it's not fake, if you're so technically competent?"

She spat out a word about a personal bodily function. "Do you really think I'd go to the trouble of faking used, nonsequential bills for a freaking two-minute video?"

"Depends on what you want it for."

"So I can do what you did," she snapped.

He got it then. She was going to try and leverage this video into a better position, maybe a senior partnership, at Armistead's firm. Amy had said she was ambitious, but he guessed she'd underestimated how much. And how far she was willing to go.

"Not rising far enough fast enough at Caden and Rockwell, huh?" he asked, giving her a grin he hoped she'd read as understanding.

"They're fools," she said. "And that stiff-spined Rockwell is the worst. Man has no flexibility at all."

For the first time Walker felt a bit of cheer. He hoped Amy had heard that. Perhaps knowing she'd been right in the first place about her boss might ease the betrayal of this woman she'd called friend.

"How's Mr. Soren these days?" He didn't use the new name they'd discovered, for fear it would alert her that he knew more than an average scoundrel would.

"What?" She snapped it out, clearly startled.

"I assume you had him sic his minion in the van on Amy? Nice little scam you had going there. Running his dirty money through Rockwell's accounts so he'd take the fall if it got found out. Wish I'd thought of it."

"How did you…?" She broke off, shook her head. A couple of strands of long, blond hair escaped the felt hat. It didn't matter, Walker had Amy's answer. That alone made this worth it. "You have the video?" she demanded. "The whole video, undoctored?"

"I do."

"The entire transaction?"

"Yes. That little clip was just a highlight reel."

"I want to see it. All of it."

"That's going to cost you. As agreed, half for the view, half for the video itself."

"And for you not using it yourself. Which I guarantee would be a huge mistake."

I'd as soon cross a rabid skunk.

Becca's right hand moved toward the large, expensive leather bag. She had to look down to unlatch and lift the flap, and he thought he could take her down at that instant, but Quinn had said to get as much information as he could, and he thought he could push her just a bit more.

She came out with a large packet wrapped in paper.

And a small, semiautomatic handgun.

He swallowed. A .380, he thought. Kind of wimpy, but that didn't mean he wanted to test it.

"Is that necessary?" he said, eyeing the weapon with what he hoped was civilian-style wariness.

"I'm carrying fifty grand around," Becca snapped. "Of course it's necessary."

She tossed the packet at him. He kept his eyes on her—and the gun, which she thankfully slipped back into the bag—letting his peripheral vision and old baseball skills tell him where the object was. He caught it easily. Opened it, riffled the edges to make sure it was all money, then went to stuff it into his jacket pocket. He frowned when it wouldn't go, then chuckled audibly as he reached in and pulled out a tooth-marked and grass-stained baseball.

"Friend's dog," he said as if she'd asked for an explanation.

He switched the ball to his right hand and reached into his left pocket and pulled out the Foxworth phone. The video was cued up and ready. He tapped the arrow, held it out and let it play. When the video ended, there was a look in her eyes that reminded him of a viper ready to strike. The mask she showed everyone was very, very good, he thought, but this was the real Becca Olson.

"Worth every penny, right?" he said cheerfully. "You'll own him."

"Yes," she said. "Give me the phone."

Power, Walker thought, not money, power. Somehow he preferred the good old greed for money over the kind of avarice that was glowing in her face right now. "I'll send you the video."

"I want the phone it's on. And it better be the only full copy."

"I need my damn phone. I'll delete the thing once it's sent. While I may not be the most upstanding citizen in town, I'll stick to our deal."

"No." The handgun reappeared, aimed at him.

Walker scrambled back a few steps as if terrified before she ordered him to stop. He only slowed, protesting with every small step while his mind was racing. His hand tightened around the baseball, his fingertips finding the seams in an old, familiar way. Her weapon had a short barrel—might not be as easy to hit him as she expected, unless she was an expert with it. The more distance, the better.

Quinn, I hope you've got her in your sights. And that you don't decide to just let her kill me first, solving two problems.

The moment he thought it he knew it wouldn't happen. Quinn was a man of honor, and he would never let that happen if he could stop it. For Hayley, if nothing else. No matter how mad she was at him—and even that had lessened of late, although Walker suspected that was Amy's doing—Quinn would never want to be the one who let her brother die, especially right in front of her.

But would he shoot a woman? One that Amy had considered a friend?

He had ten feet between them now, but it was still too close. And the small pistol looked no less deadly.

"Just put that away," he said, gesturing toward the weapon with the hand that held Cutter's ball.

"Give me the damned phone."

"Sure, sure, just put that…"

A loud, ringing bark echoed from the shadows to his right. Becca jerked around, toward the unexpected noise. Cutter burst out of the shadows. Headed toward them at a dead run. Head down and meaning business.

Becca lifted the weapon. Pointed it toward the dog.

Walker's arm snapped back and flew forward in a quick, fluid motion.

The baseball caught Becca's right wrist. She screamed. The pistol flew sideways. She wobbled on the high-heeled boots. Went down on one knee, clutching her wrist.

Walker sprinted forward. Becca yelled something, a name, just as he bent to pick up her pistol. In the same instant he heard a crack. Concrete chips spit up around him. Then again. For an instant, he thought Quinn really was trying to take him out. Then he realized the shots were coming from the opposite side of the garage. Cutter pelted past them.

Toward the shooter. The dog had known. Becca had brought backup. And he was a sitting duck. He grabbed the more powerful weapon from the small of his back. Turned toward the shadows where Cutter had disappeared. But he couldn't see the dog, and he wasn't sure anymore where Quinn was. He held his fire.

Another crack. Something tugged at the right side of his shirt. Something that stung. The sting suddenly exploded into a sunburst of pain, staggering him. He grabbed his ribs, felt the wet warmth.

"Walker!"

Amy. He turned to tell her to stay back, safe. But the movement ripped something in his side and he went down. And then Amy was there, in the line of fire. Another shot echoed. And Amy, impossibly, threw herself over him, shielding his body with her own.

Walker tried to roll, to reverse their positions so Amy would be protected. She resisted. "Stay down," she hissed. "You're hurt."

Then he heard a fierce growl. A sharp yell echoed through the garage. Cutter had found his prey. Did the dog know enough to go for the hand that held the weapon, to avoid being shot himself? Somehow he thought Quinn would have handled that.

He had to trust Quinn would deal. Because he was out of it.

Hayley was there. She shouldn't be. Too dangerous. But the shooting had stopped. And oddly, she, too, held a handgun. Looking more than competent. And she had it aimed at Becca.

"Clear!"

Quinn's shout came from the shadows, followed by

a sharp, triumphant-sounding bark. He breathed again. Amy was safe.

"Sit down. Legs crossed. Hands on your head." His sister gave Becca the orders in a tone he'd never heard from her. He felt a burst of satisfaction when the woman who had endangered Amy let out a cry of pain as her wrist protested the movement.

"Cutter to you," Quinn's voice echoed from the shadows. Walker realized it must mean he had the situation over there under control. How he'd made it down there so fast he didn't know. Then again, knowing a bit about the man, he'd probably jumped down from the upper level.

Amy eased off him. There was blood all over her shirt and jacket. He struggled to sit up. "Were you hit?" he asked sharply, fear spiking through him, giving him strength, making the pain ebb just a little.

"No. It's yours." She was staring at him, wide-eyed with obvious worry. She pulled off her jacket and rolled it up, then pressed it to his side. The pain jolted him, but he looked away so she wouldn't see it. Just beyond her he could see Becca staring at Amy in shock. No doubt wondering how she had managed to misjudge her so badly.

"She's tougher than you'll ever be," he said to the woman who had betrayed her. "And in the best possible ways."

Becca, lawyer that she was, stayed quiet.

And then Cutter was there. And to Walker's surprise, the dog came straight to him, nudged his cheek with a damp nose. And whined.

"He'll be all right," Amy said rather fiercely to the dog as she increased the pressure. He must still be bleeding, he thought. He was starting to feel light-headed. Odd how calm he was. Nothing seemed to matter except that Amy was here and unhurt.

"Guard," Hayley ordered Cutter, gesturing at Becca. The dog spun around, his entire demeanor changed.

With a warning growl, he crossed the short distance between them and stood perilously close. Well within throat-ripping distance, Walker thought. That dog was…well, something.

Hayley vanished then, but seconds later she was back, a small case in her hands. She knelt beside Amy and opened it. First aid kit, he realized.

He heard Quinn's voice as he approached.

"Locals and medics are on the way. Our shooter's out for the count and trussed up like a holiday turkey. I think it's Soren's guy, matches Amy's description." He came into view, and looked down at Walker. "How is he?"

Approval, Walker realized. That was what was in Quinn's expression. And it was aimed at him.

"Grateful," Walker answered for himself, although his head was starting to spin now.

"Hurt," Amy said.

"Good call, holding your fire," Quinn said. "I was on him after the second shot."

Walker nodded, surprised at how much strength it took. "Thought…so. Couldn't see…you…or Cutter."

He heard Amy make a tight, choking little sound. Looked at her. Something in her face scared him.

"I love you," he said urgently, suddenly afraid he might never get the chance to say it again.

She made that sound again. Her lips were trembling, her eyes glistening with tears. But beneath it all was the one shining emotion he clung to, even before she voiced it. "And I love you. So don't you dare die on me, Walker Cole."

He tried to smile at her. He couldn't die now. Not now, not when he had hope for the future for the first time in five years. He couldn't have survived all that only to die here like this.

"I love you," she said again. And he clung to the sound of it as darkness closed in.

Chapter 36

Amy paused to steady herself before stepping through the hospital doors. The sun already had warmed the small patio outside the hospital side doors, and at the moment Quinn and Hayley had it to themselves.

Amy was thankful for how Quinn had taken charge, not even able to imagine all the chaos that was now theirs to deal with, not the least of which was explaining a gun battle and a shooter with an arm chewed up by an impressive set of teeth, and most amazingly, a wrist shattered by a baseball.

It had taken most of the rest of the night. He'd come to the hospital just before dawn, telling them in short, sharp sentences what had happened. Including that the LA police thought Soren, who they now had in custody, had been cleaning house in an effort to go legit, and that night she'd seen him with her boss he'd been asking him to get the cops off his back. The image of the normal-looking guy with the coffee cup had run through her head at that, and she wondered how people got so twisted that murdering their associates seemed the way to go straight.

It had been a long night here, too. She remembered the moment when they'd handed Hayley a bright orange bag with Walker's things, including his wallet. Curious and needing distraction Hayley had peeked inside. And seen that in the very front, where normally an ID would go, was an old photograph. A picture of two smiling children, a little girl and an older boy. The girl was on the boy's lap, and his arms were holding her carefully. Walker and Hayley.

Hayley had burst into tears, and Amy had joined her. And then there had been the waiting. Waiting to hear Walker had survived, that he was in surgery, that he was going to be all right.

She had just now gone to check on him as the hospital's shift changed at 7:00 a.m. He had been declared in fair condition a couple of hours ago, still sedated. The off-going nurse had smilingly told her he'd be upgraded to good condition as soon as he woke up. It still tore at her to look at him lying there with tubes and wires attached. She tried not to let the endless loop of that horrible moment when she'd realized he'd been shot play in her head. She'd had to touch him to reassure herself, to feel that he was warm and breathing and alive.

And now she was headed out to tell his sister the good news. She pushed the door open, stepped out into the morning sun. She stopped suddenly as voices carried over to her. She knew she shouldn't eavesdrop, but supposed it was only human nature when you found yourself being discussed. So she stayed where she was, concealed by a bush full of new spring leaves, as Quinn spoke to his wife.

"First, tell me how serious it is. Amy and your brother, I mean."

"She looks at him like I look at you."

Amy could almost see him smile; it echoed in his voice. "That good, huh?"

"I think—and hope—my best friend is going to end up being my sister." Amy's last bit of tension released at Hayley's clearly heartfelt words. And she knew she couldn't—and didn't need to—eavesdrop any longer. She walked around the corner that had concealed her just as Hayley said, "What does that have to do with it?"

"Just thinking she should probably hear this."

"Hear what? And why are you being so cryptic?"

"Yes, why are you?" Amy asked as she approached.

"We shouldn't have been so hard on him," Quinn said.

Amy blinked, a little taken aback, knowing what a hard sell Quinn was. Hayley looked at her husband in surprise. "I'd already gotten there, but I thought I'd have to convince you. What brought this on? What he did last night?"

"He did a great job," Quinn admitted. "Better than I expected, at the time. As good as any of us could have done."

"At the time?" Hayley asked.

He seemed uncomfortable, Amy realized. She'd never seen that, wondered what it would take to make a man like Quinn uncomfortable. He glanced at her, as if he'd sensed her speculation.

"You were right," he said. "If he was going to lie, he'd have made up something better than 'I can't tell you.'"

"Yes." And the moment she'd realized that was the moment she'd also realized she'd fallen for him all over again.

Hayley looked intently at the husband she knew so well, then said sternly, "Quinn Foxworth, you're dodging. Why?"

"Because I did something you told me not to do."

"News flash. Not the first time."

He smiled, looking as if it were in spite of himself. But it faded when he said, "But this was personal. To you."

Hayley's gaze narrowed. Then widened in obvious realization. "You started digging, didn't you?"

"I wanted to know, to find out what I could. And to have it, in case you changed your mind."

Amy knew Hayley had told him not to, the first time he'd asked. But she also knew she couldn't deny how many times she herself had come very close to asking Hayley to change her mind and tell him to go ahead in these past couple of weeks.

And she had sensed that her friend had felt the same way. Quinn, being Quinn, could well have picked up on that.

"And did you find out anything?" Amy asked, trying not to sound apprehensive.

"Yes. No real details but enough, I think."

Amy took a deep breath. If it was enough to soothe Quinn's anger toward Walker, then it must be something convincing.

"Talk," Hayley said.

He shook his head. "Someone else needs to explain. Turn on your tablet and the video chat, will you? I need to make a call."

A few minutes later the three of them were huddled together to look at the small screen. It was on, a video window open, but blank until Quinn hit a couple of buttons on his phone and sent the feed to the bigger screen for all of them.

A man's image appeared, square-jawed, dark-eyed, with skin the color of a rich, dark tea. He was wearing a suit and tie, and behind him was a plain wall, only a clock visible. Amy wondered if that was purposeful. Then she noticed the time on that clock. Three hours later. East Coast, she thought. And it wasn't a big jump from that to DC.

"Tobias Cabrero," Quinn said, then gestured toward Hayley and Amy. "My wife, Hayley, sister of the subject in question. And her friend Amy, who…has reason to need to hear this."

"You come with the highest of recommendations from a man I revere, Mr. Foxworth," Cabrero said, his voice matching the strength of his appearance. "Otherwise, I wouldn't be trusting you with even this much."

"I revere him, too, Mr. Cabrero," Quinn said. "Rafer Crawford is the finest man I know."

Cabrero nodded. "Let's dispense with the formalities. I don't have a lot of time, so I'll give you what I can, and say up front I probably won't be able to answer many questions, nor will I confirm any names. I can only say this much because the operation has now concluded with the last arrests made yesterday."

"That's all we ask," Hayley said.

Cabrero nodded again. "Very well. About eight years ago the Bureau became aware of a terrorist sleeper cell." FBI, Amy guessed then. She'd been right about DC. "We had reason to believe it had spread to multiple cities and was behind two bombings in suburban Chicago and in Philadelphia. Rather than taking it down, we monitored and tried to infiltrate. For three years we tried without success. Then one day a man walked into a field office to report something he'd stumbled onto. It was quickly apparent we had found our back door. He was completely unsuspected by the cell, and had a way in."

Amy's breath caught. She heard Hayley's gasp, but neither of them dared look away from the screen.

"I can't say much more, since I can't disclose operational procedures, but I will say that that man, that civilian who had only what training we were able to give him in a very short period, did an incredible job. For five years he risked his life every day. In the process we saved hundreds, perhaps thousands of lives by foiling three different bomb plots."

"Oh, my God," Hayley breathed.

"It had to be. For Walker, it had to be something that big," Amy whispered.

"Twice we offered to pull him out when they began to suspect him, but he refused, because he knew they were readying more attacks. He stuck it out, once barely managing to stay alive. He gave us what we needed, we pulled him out and this week we finally moved to take down the cell in six different places. You may have heard about that."

Quinn swore under his breath.

"Yes," Cabrero agreed.

Amy sucked in an audible breath. She remembered

people, even Becca, buzzing about that story at the office. Walker had done this? Pride rose in her like sunrise, bright, brilliant and forever warm. She glanced at Hayley, saw an echo of her own welling emotions in her friend's face. She'd already accepted—at first without even realizing it—that whatever the reason was, it had to be good enough. Because it was Walker. He'd had to do what he did. At eighteen, and five years ago.

She'd just never expected anything like this.

She'd known she would forgive him. But she'd never expected that *she* would owe *him* an apology.

And she would give it. Gladly. She suspected Hayley would, too.

"This civilian paid a high price for his courage. He witnessed some things...some awful things, that we couldn't let him do anything about without blowing everything."

The nightmares, Amy thought. Her stomach knotted at the thought of what he'd been through.

"And we did some things to keep his identity hidden that we weren't happy about. Including swearing him to complete secrecy. I gather from your inquiry he's kept that oath."

"Yes," Quinn said again.

"I'm not surprised." For the first time, the man smiled. "We tried to recruit this civilian afterward. He said no, he had fences to try and mend at home. He doubted there was much hope, but he had to try."

Amy felt tears sting her eyes, then overflow. She glanced at Hayley, and saw her blinking rapidly against the same onslaught.

"One more thing you should know. It was our doing that he was out of touch. We kept him isolated, severing all communication except through us. It was, I'm afraid, necessary."

"You sent those occasional texts?" Hayley asked.

Amy glanced at her friend again; she hadn't thought of that.

Cabrero nodded. "And we—*I* am sorry, given the circumstances, that they were so…detached. He never knew what was happening with you. We were afraid it would distract him and jeopardize both the operation and his life." He grimaced, waggled his jaw. "I'm still sore where he punched me when he found out."

Amy looked at Quinn, remembering the way he had greeted Walker in that first moment. Quinn looked suitably rueful.

"Again, I apologize on behalf of the entire Bureau. We all regret that aspect, because we all came to admire and respect him, but this truly was a much-bigger-picture kind of situation."

"Thousands of lives," Amy said softly.

"Yes. Without doubt." He glanced over his shoulder at something or someone, and Hayley sensed they'd gotten all they were going to get. He looked back. "He's a remarkable man, Mrs. Foxworth. His country owes him a debt of gratitude, and he deserves all the forgiveness you can manage, and then some."

"He has it," Hayley promised. Then, with a glance at Amy, she added, "And much more."

When the screen had gone dark, Hayley looked at her husband. He was watching her, the slightest touch of wariness in his gaze.

"Worth it?" he asked.

She looked at Amy with a lifted brow.

"Oh, yes," Amy said fervently.

"Thank you," Hayley said softly to her husband.

"Double from me," Amy said. "Now, if you'll excuse me, I feel the sudden need to go kiss someone, even if he's not awake yet."

Epilogue

"I feel so bad for having suspected Mr. Rockwell for even a moment," Amy said.

"You know, his extra attention was really because he noticed you were on edge. He was concerned about you," Quinn said.

"That makes me feel both better and worse." Walker reached over and squeezed her hand. That was definitely better.

"Alex and I made sure he knew you were the only one of us who just couldn't believe he was crooked," Quinn said. "He appreciated it. I'm sure he'll tell you himself."

Amy felt a rush of relief.

"That reminds me," Quinn added. "I meant to tell you—he called Alex, after you showed him the video."

Amy's brows rose. "He did?"

"He wanted a meeting. He was going to confront him about it, and the witness tampering. Give him a chance to come clean. Said he always looked at him as a colleague, not competition. He seemed pretty relieved that it had all been a setup."

Amy smiled. Her boss was everything she'd thought he was and more, and she was going to make it up to him for even imagining he could be involved. "I'm glad. After Becca, he could use some good news."

She'd managed to say calmly the name of the woman she'd once called friend, the woman who had used her and everyone else to build a network not of friends but of people she might be able to use on her pathway to power. Who had had no qualms about setting up an innocent man. And who, Amy had belatedly realized, she had inadvertently tipped off with her question about Dante Soren.

And for that calm she thanked Walker. He was the one who had urged her to let it out, validated her every feeling about the betrayal and then held her as she had sighed over her poor judgment in one case, and her validation in the other.

He'd been out of the hospital a week now, and had promised Amy he was feeling decent most of the time. He'd proved it true last night, the first time since he'd been shot that she'd allowed herself to give in to her fierce need for him. Mindful of his still-healing injury, she'd taken the lead, until the final wild moments when neither of them could think of care or caution.

He'd slept for ten hours, nightmare free. And told her just before his sister and her husband arrived to check on him that, all things considered, he'd never felt better.

That thought took her back to the day he'd awakened in the hospital, when she'd told him what they'd learned from Agent Cabrero. And been surprised at how quietly he took it.

"That you know as much of the truth as you can," he'd said, "doesn't mean nearly as much to me as the fact that you trusted it existed before. Trusted me."

"You're a hero, Walker Cole. Some part of me knew that all along, I think."

He'd talked to her then, of the days spent living on the edge, the times he thought he'd been found out, the times he wanted out so badly he considered just running. Of the days he'd spent sickened by what drove these people, yet having to live among them. Of days of having to constantly remind himself of why he was doing it, of the innocent lives that might be—and eventually were—saved.

"It got better after they stopped the first bombing," he'd told her, "and I knew I'd done some good. But it was never easy."

He was no hero, he insisted. He was just a guy who had tried to do the right thing for his country.

"Did the right thing," Amy had corrected softly.

She glanced at him now. He looked so much better, but it was still going to take some time for her to get that image of him in that hospital bed out of her mind.

"You were right, by the way," she said. "About Leda Limited."

His brow furrowed. "I was?"

"The swan part. Becca lived in the Cygnus Towers. And their logo is a swan." She could see him working it out. "Leda and Zeus," he said.

"Yes. I should have seen that. I had it right in front of me, that day we saw Alan outside the bistro and I noticed his parking sticker was the same as Becca's. But I didn't make the connection."

"She was your friend—how could you?" Walker said quietly.

Warmed, Amy squeezed his hand in thanks.

Quinn looked at Walker then. "You feeling up to talking?"

Walker looked back at his brother-in-law for a silent moment. Amy knew he'd come to admire Quinn—even more so when he'd finally seen the wedding video, seen how he had looked at Hayley as she had come down the aisle toward him—but he hadn't quite adjusted to the shift in Quinn's opinion, or that Amy assured him it had begun well before they'd talked to Cabrero.

"About what?" he asked, still somewhat warily.

"Are you done wandering?"

Walker looked at her. Held her gaze steadily. "Yes." Then he looked back at Quinn. "I was done when…"

Quinn nodded in understanding. "Good. I need some-one I trust to get Foxworth up and running here."

Walker blinked. Amy smiled; she'd known this was coming. Hayley had told her.

"And?" Walker asked, clearly not assuming anything.

"I don't mind keeping it in the family, if they're quali-fied."

It took him a couple of tries to actually speak. "You think I am qualified?"

"You're tough, you're smart and you can learn. That and belief in what we do is all I ask. Well, that and loy-alty, and you've already proven that. On a large scale."

"I don't want charity," Walker said, his tone a bit sour.

"When you get to know him better," Hayley said, "you'll realize Quinn doesn't give anyone anything. They earn it. You earned it long before that night."

Still, Walker hesitated. Then Cutter, who had been lounging on the thick blanket Amy had folded up for him near the sliding door so he could look out, got up and walked over to him. The dog sat at his feet, rested his chin on his knee. Walker looked down at him, and even as Amy watched, his expression smoothed out. She smiled again—she'd been smiling a lot lately—because she knew exactly what he was feeling. The Cutter Effect, she and Hayley had dubbed it.

He lifted his gaze to his brother-in-law. "I do like what you do."

"We'll get you up to speed on everything you need."

"Why do I feel as if I'm about to step onto the biggest roller coaster in the world?"

Hayley laughed. "You'll love it, bro, I promise."

Amy saw what flared in his eyes when his sister used the old nickname, saw the love, the hope, the relief. And now that she knew what he'd gone through, not only dur-ing the past five years but the past five weeks, knowing they'd despised him based on what they knew, and unable to tell them the only thing that could change their minds, she was even more amazed.

But he'd kept his word. No matter the cost, he'd kept to the oath they'd sworn him to.

Walker always would.

After Hayley and Quinn had packed up Cutter to head back to the new office—they were going to stay awhile and help Walker get started, and to give Hayley and Walker time to heal their relationship—Amy went to curl up beside him on the couch.

"Do you know why I really always moved on? Even after I finished Dad's list?" Walker asked.

She shifted her gaze from the bouquet of daffodils he'd brought her. She'd been delighted, as much that he'd remembered they were her favorite as for the flowers themselves. "You got bored?"

"No. It was because I'd learned all I wanted to know about it. That's when I knew it was time to move on." He reached out, cupped her face in his hands. "I will never, in a hundred lifetimes, know all I want to know about you, Amy Clark."

She didn't miss the inference. "I'm going to hold you to that."

"You won't have to."

There was rock-solid certainty in his voice, in his expression, in his eyes. He meant it. Every word, every emotion, every promise.

And then he kissed her, putting everything that had been in his words, his look, his voice, into it. It was as hot and alluring as ever, but it was also that promise, and he made sure her body and heart knew it. He was home at last, with forgiveness, understanding and the future he'd never dared hope for. And for the first time he began to feel it had all been worth it.

Much later, as they lay sated and lazy in her bed, he reached out and caught a lock of her hair between his fingers. The tattoo was at the edge of his vision. He wondered if it could be altered to say her name. He'd have to look into that.

"I think we should go shopping," he said.

She blinked. "For what?"

He grinned. "That's one of the things I love about you. You need a reason to go shopping."

She smiled back. He was finding it easier every time, to say things like that. And it went deeper every time.

"For phones," he said. "I need a new one, and I hear you can get a good deal if you share a plan."

He knew she'd remember his words. *"A good deal on a pair of phones translates into a permanent relationship..."*

Her smile widened. "You're sure about that?"

Instead of answering, he went on. "And after that, I think we should go to the animal shelter. I'm going to miss that rascal Cutter. So we need a dog of our own."

He heard her breath catch. She knew what that meant. It wasn't quite having a kid, but it was close. "Yes," she said quickly, because she was afraid in another second she wouldn't be able to speak at all. "Yes, we do."

"And later," he said. "we'll talk about the rest of our lives."

"Yes," she said. "To everything."

"You're sure?" he asked in turn, knowing she was answering what he hadn't yet asked.

"I am."

"I love you," he said.

Instead of returning the vow as he'd thought, she just looked at him for a long moment. And then she said, softly, words he'd once thought he would never hear.

"Welcome home."

* * * * *

REQUEST YOUR FREE BOOKS!

2 FREE NOVELS PLUS 2 FREE GIFTS!

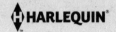

ROMANTIC suspense

Sparked by danger, fueled by passion

YES! Please send me 2 FREE Harlequin® Romantic Suspense novels and my 2 FREE gifts (gifts are worth about $10). After receiving them, if I don't wish to receive any more books, I can return the shipping statement marked "cancel." If I don't cancel, I will receive 4 brand-new novels every month and be billed just $4.74 per book in the U.S. or $5.49 per book in Canada. That's a savings of at least 12% off the cover price! It's quite a bargain! Shipping and handling is just 50¢ per book in the U.S. and 75¢ per book in Canada.* I understand that accepting the 2 free books and gifts places me under no obligation to buy anything. I can always return a shipment and cancel at any time. Even if I never buy another book, the two free books and gifts are mine to keep forever.

240/340 HDN GH3P

Name	(PLEASE PRINT)	
Address		Apt. #
City	State/Prov.	Zip/Postal Code

Signature (if under 18, a parent or guardian must sign)

Mail to the **Reader Service:**

IN U.S.A.: P.O. Box 1867, Buffalo, NY 14240-1867
IN CANADA: P.O. Box 609, Fort Erie, Ontario L2A 5X3

Want to try two free books from another line?
Call 1-800-873-8635 or visit www.ReaderService.com.

* Terms and prices subject to change without notice. Prices do not include applicable taxes. Sales tax applicable in N.Y. Canadian residents will be charged applicable taxes. Offer not valid in Quebec. This offer is limited to one order per household. Not valid for current subscribers to Harlequin Romantic Suspense books. All orders subject to credit approval. Credit or debit balances in a customer's account(s) may be offset by any other outstanding balance owed by or to the customer. Please allow 4 to 6 weeks for delivery. Offer available while quantities last.

Your Privacy—The Reader Service is committed to protecting your privacy. Our Privacy Policy is available online at www.ReaderService.com or upon request from the Reader Service.

We make a portion of our mailing list available to reputable third parties that offer products we believe may interest you. If you prefer that we not exchange your name with third parties, or if you wish to clarify or modify your communication preferences, please visit us at www.ReaderService.com/consumerchoice or write to us at Reader Service Preference Service, P.O. Box 9062, Buffalo, NY 14240-9062. Include your complete name and address.

HRS15

SPECIAL EXCERPT FROM

H HARLEQUIN®

ROMANTIC suspense

*Can this Colton cowboy save his wife—and his
beloved ranch—when a killer threatens everything
they hold dear?*

*Read on for a sneak preview of
PROTECTING THE COLTON BRIDE
by New York Times bestselling author* **Elle James**,
*the fourth book in the 2015
COLTONS OF WYOMING continuity.*

"Why don't we get married?"

Even though she'd known it was coming, it still hit
her square in the chest. The air rushed from her lungs
and a tsunami of feelings washed over her. A surge of joy
made her heart beat so fast she felt faint. She crested that
wave and slid into the undertow of reality. "A marriage of
convenience?"

"Exactly." Daniel reached for her hands.

When she hid them behind her back, he dropped his
arms. "It wouldn't have to be forever. Just long enough
to satisfy the stipulations of your grandmother's will and
save your horses, and that would help me get past the
Kennedy gauntlet. We could leave tomorrow, spend a
night in Vegas, find a chapel and it would be over in less
than five minutes."

With her heart smarting, Megan forced a shaky smile.
"Way to sweep a girl off her feet."

He waved his hand and Halo tossed her head. "If you want, I can make an official announcement in front of my family."

Megan shook her head. "No."

"No, you won't marry me?"

"No." She pushed past him to pace down the center of the barn. "Your plan is insane."

"Do you have a better one?" he asked. "I'm all ears."

The plan was the same as the one she'd been thinking of before Daniel had woken up. Only when she'd dreamed it up, it didn't sound as cold and impersonal as Daniel's proposal. Somewhere in the back of her mind she'd hoped that marriage to Daniel would be something more than one of convenience.

After yesterday's kiss, she wasn't sure she could be around Daniel for long periods of time without wanting another. And another.

Don't miss
PROTECTING THE COLTON BRIDE
by New York Times *bestselling author Elle James.*
Available September 2015

www.Harlequin.com